D1235384

DECEPTION
Colleen K. Snyder

Fiction and Literature: Inspirational
Christian Romantic Suspense

ISBN: 978-1-956654-39-4

DEDICATION

Because everything I do is devoted to God, I dedicate this book to all the "good dogs" we've known, loved, and been part of their lives.

Working backward: My "niece dogs": Tilly. Zoey. Teddy (yes, Mom). Sophie. Georgie. Blue Dog. Harley. Jett. Sydney. Goldie. I know there were many others, but I can't remember to name them all.

My "gran-dogs": Brutus. Ares. Hurley. Allie. Madden.

The "family" dogs: Cookie. Alfie. Duke. Roxie.

Finally, my companions: Isaac (who is living my life at the beach. Talk about a "lucky dog"). Maggie. Daisy. Brandy (my "Gretchen"). Sarah. Jesse.

You are all loved. And will forever be part of my heart, my life. We will meet again I know.

MONDAY

The temperature dropped ten degrees in the office when the visitor opened the door. Jeff Farrell looked up from Erin Winger's desk. Erin had gone out of town, and Jeff wanted to try to keep his brother-in-law's inbox from resembling the leaning tower of Pisa. A vain effort, but he could say he tried. "Can I help you?" *First impression: I don't like you. Why?*

The younger man smiled and extended his hand. "Ryan Woolfort. Is your boss, Erol, in?"

Jeff shook the man's hand. The grip felt like an iron vice. And lasted one…two…three ticks longer than it should have. *Second impression: I really don't like you. And his name is Erin. Not Erol.* "How can I help you, Mr. Woolfort?"

Mr. Woolfort spun a chair around and sat facing Jeff. "I represent Lyon Ebertson. He is running for Chair of the Agency on Housing Inspections. I talked with Erol the other day. He said he'd be happy to support Lyon's candidacy. He promised he'd leave a generous donation for me to pick up today. I'd appreciate it if you would get the check for me."

Jeff tapped his finger on the wooden desk. "Hmm. There might be a problem. Since Trinity Builders bids on contracts with the city, supporting any candidate for the office would appear to be a conflict of interest, wouldn't you agree?" He raised his eyebrows as he looked Woolfort in the face.

Woolfort shrugged. "Your boss knows how these things work. If you want to get your bid noticed, you need a friend in the office." He smiled. With teeth. "The right donation could secure such notice."

"Uh-huh. And how much is the 'right donation'?"

"I don't think that concerns you. Give me the check, and I'll be on my way."

"I need to know how much the check is to make certain you get the proper one."

"Well, your boss mentioned something in the range of six figures."

"Were those before or after the decimal point?" Jeff saw the snarl in Woolfort's eyes. It didn't make it to the man's face. Close, but not quite.

"Very funny."

Jeff straightened the pile of invoices in front of him. "Out of curiosity, how did you plan to get this past the Builder's Commission? I know quite a few builders who would object to this 'donation.'"

Woolfort's brows raised. "Again, not your concern. If your boss left a check, you deliver it to me and say, 'Yes, sir.'"

"I'd love to. But as his secretary, I'm responsible for the distribution of all monies. I need to know what accounts 'Erol' planned to run these through. I'm certain he wouldn't want them taken out of the general operating budget."

"Take it up with him after you give me the check."

Jeff shook his head. "I'm sorry, but the distribution must be entered before a check can be cut. Since he hasn't cut it yet, I can't cut it, either. Not without knowing the accounts. I'm guessing this activity is meant to be untraceable, correct? Surely, he told you how he intended to move it."

Woolfort's eyes burned holes in the desk. He gritted his teeth. "Erol indicated he could pass the money through several small holding companies he owns. Off-shore interests. He indicated you do this all the time. Can I have the check now? Or do I have to call your boss and tell him his secretary is holding up affairs?"

Erin's only off-shore interest is the eight-seater boat he wants to buy.

Jeff leaned his chair back. "I don't think it's going to help you much. You see, Erol..." he stressed the name, "...knows large checks require two signatures. One could be his. But the other has to be from another of the senior management officers. And I know for a fact none of them have signed off on this."

Woolfort's eyes narrowed. The challenge burned. "And how do you know?"

Jeff held up his index finger. "One, his name is Erin, not Erol. He's my brother-in-law." He held up a second finger. "Two, Erin's been in Indiana on family business since last Monday. And neither Erin nor I are interested in bribing any city official, no matter what their capacity." Jeff stood. "I'm sure you can find your way out of the office."

Woolfort stared at Jeff. Jeff read amusement. He didn't like it. But Woolfort ducked his head. "Of course. You have a good day, Mr…" Woolfort trailed off in question.

"Farrell. Jeff Farrell. Co-owner of Trinity Builders."

"Mr. Farrell, then. Tell your brother-in-law I'll speak with him later."

Jeff didn't bother getting in the last word. The less verbiage wasted, the better. He made a note to speak to Erin about the matter, then promptly put it out of mind. Scam artists. Always hustling. He had better things to think about. Like, going home. It might be only three-thirty, but the boss said he could. So he did.

Mr. Woolfort leaned against the wall talking on the phone as Jeff exited the office. Jeff nodded to the man; Woolfort nodded back. Saluted Jeff. The temperature dropped another ten degrees. Clouds shadowed the sun. Jeff shook his head. Paranoia. Too much paranoia. Home waited.

FRIDAY

The minefield directly ahead taunted Collin. One misstep and she'd lose her basket and its contents, contents she'd spent the better part of the day toiling over. Step left around the multi-colored popcorn-popper-sweeper. Two steps forward. Right around the two-foot-long plastic firetruck ("with authentic siren sounds"—if you put in the batteries, which they didn't). Another step right to clear the swirly yellow-colored ball. Three steps forward. *Almost there. Almost there...*

The finish line came into view. Only one more obstacle...high step over the cardboard building blocks...

Made it! Collin set the basket and its load of "sorted and folded" articles on the table. She took a breath...

A scream of anger, frustration, pain, and fear, amplified through the baby monitor, echoed from the playroom. Another equally amplified scream of, "Mama!" followed. Collin dropped her head, closed her eyes, and muttered, "I'm coming. I'm coming." She checked her watch. Ten minutes. A new record.

Collin walked to the scene of the murder, judging by the sound of the caterwauling. As she suspected, not-yet-three-year-old triplet Joshua lay on his back on the floor. He kicked his feet, flailed his arms, and generally expressed his dissatisfaction with the world.

Joshua's brother, Caleb, stood behind a rocking chair, grasping the spindles and repeating, "Joshua fawd down."

Their sister, Talitha, sat on the floor beside her brother. She ducked his wayward limbs, patted his chest, and repeated, "You 'kay, bubby? You 'kay?"

Collin picked up her hyperventilating son, hugged him to her

4

shoulder, and rocked back and forth. She held his head and soothed, "You're fine, buddy." She felt the back of his skull for lumps. *Not possible. This carpet has Olympic-grade padding under it. Safest room in the house.*

She waited until he stopped crying, held him back to look him in the eyes. "What happened, Joshua?"

"I cwimb a mountain. Mountain move. I faw down."

Collin closed one eye and stared at Caleb. "Did you make the mountain move?"

Caleb shook his head very emphatically. "No, Mommy."

Collin gazed at Joshua. "How did the mountain move?"

"I set foot ona mountain. I say, 'Cayeb, hol han'. Cayeb hol han'. I set udder foot ona mountain. Mountain move. I fawd down."

"Uh-huh." Collin kept from smiling. Her fearless pack leader. "Joshua, I love you want to climb mountains. But this chair is not a mountain. It's a chair. It is for sitting in, not climbing on. Right?"

Joshua hung his head. "Yes, Mommy."

Talitha's sweetness poured into the conversation. "Bubby be 'kay, Mommy? He 'kay?"

Now Collin smiled. "Yes, Talitha. Joshua is okay." She set the still-a-toddler down, brushed his strawberry blond curls back. "No more climbing, Joshua." She looked at Caleb, her linebacker. "Thank you for calling me to tell me Joshua had fallen." *Thank you, you weren't the one who shook the chair. I'm not ready for fratricide yet.* She pointed to the beanbag chair in the corner. "Talitha, would you read your brothers a story while Mommy finishes putting away the laundry?"

Talitha's eyes ignited like a million-candle-watt light. "Yes, Mommy!" She ran to the book pile, pulled out the only book she could "read," and ran back to the child's school chair. She sat in front of her brothers, who got comfortable lying back in the beanbag. Talitha opened the first page. "Sam. I am Sam."

Collin smiled, turned up the volume on the monitor, and went to the kitchen. Of course, Talitha couldn't read the book. But she'd memorized enough of the story that she could entertain her brothers with the pictures. Enough for one or two read-throughs, anyhow.

Jeff sat at the coffee bar, reading a piece of paper, a puzzled look on his face. Collin kissed her husband as she passed him. It amused her to see him still in suit and tie. He'd had "business" in the morning and had an image to protect. However, being home before four in the afternoon didn't serve the image. "What are you doing here?"

"Hiding so I can get some work done." He held up the page. "What is this? Ice breaker for group? A little strange, even for you."

Collin narrowed her eyes. "What are you talking about?"

"This." He waved the paper at her. "I found it on top of the laundry basket."

Collin held her hand out. "Give me that." She cast him a sideways glance, pursed her lips, and looked at the letter.

Choose one.

Collin's eyes widened. She stared at Jeff. "What? Where did this come from?"

"This isn't yours?"

"No! Where'd you find it?"

"On top the laundry."

"There was nothing on the laundry when I brought it up here."

"Well, that's where I found it."

Collin went catatonic. A voice screamed in her head. *NO! Talitha! No! Not my baby! She's gone! No!* Collin's eyes widened but saw nothing. Nothing of the here and now. An empty baby bed. A hole in her heart. Emptiness. Despair.

An animal scream tore from her innermost being. "No!" Terror poured adrenaline into her limbs. She raced to the playroom. Unseeing, she caught all three of her children to her chest. She collapsed to the floor, hugging the triplets tight. *Tighter. Tighter. No one will ever take them away from me again. No one.*

The babies were crying. She could hear them. "Mommy!" "Mommy! Stop, Mommy!" "Mommy, u hur-ted me. Stop!"

Someone is hurting my babies! I have to hold them! I can't let them go… I have to hold them tighter…

"Mommy!" "Mommy!"

Jeff's voice. Strong. Calm. "Collin. Lady, it's okay. It's okay. No one is trying to get the babies. Collin. Hear me."

His hands massaging her arms. "Come back, Collin. Listen to me."

The babies were still crying. *Why are they crying? Jeff is right here. Why are they crying?*

"Let go of the babies, Collin. Let your arms relax. Just a little."

Stronger massaging. "Let go, Collin. Let go. I've got them. I've got the babies."

Collin obeyed. Jeff would never let anyone hurt the babies. If he said let go, she could let go.

Her arms emptied. Her sight returned. Jeff sat in front of her, all three children in his arms. All still snuffling. All heads buried in his chest and shoulders. None of them looking at her.

Jeff caught Collin's eyes, held them. "Are you with me, lady? Are you here?"

Collin leaned back. Awareness seeped over the edges, then slammed into her consciousness. She'd been the one scaring the babies. She'd hurt them.

Collin lifted her chin and closed her eyes. Tears cascaded down her cheeks, poured off her chin, puddled on her shirt. "I'm sorry. Oh, Lord, forgive me. I'm sorry. I'm so sorry."

She didn't try to touch any of the triplets. She waited until she mastered her own tears, wiped her face with her shirt. She bit her lip, nodded to Jeff.

Jeff didn't release the toddlers but turned them to face her while still maintaining his protective hold. Collin read the fear in their eyes, and it sliced to the core of her being. She kept her voice soft and even. "Babies, Mommy is very, very sorry she scared you and hurt you. Mommy went to a bad, dark place."

Collin had to swallow hard. "I never want to hurt you, and I'm sorry I did. I love each of you. Caleb and Joshua and Talitha. Mommy is very, very sorry. She would like you to forgive her, but she understands if you can't right now." Her soul shattered, the pieces remaining linked by a whisper. "I love you."

Jeff did not pressure the toddlers. He sat and held them. Collin sat in front of them. Jeff looked at Caleb. "Do you think you can forgive Mommy?" Caleb held Collin's eyes. He nodded very slowly. "Will you give Mommy a hug?"

Collin assured him, "I won't hug you unless you want me to. I'll put my hands behind my back." She did, sitting on her hands. *Lord Jesus, this is killing me. My babies. I hurt my babies. Help me, Lord.*

Caleb stepped away from his father's protection, crossed over, and hugged Collin. She whispered, "I love you, buddy."

He kissed her on the cheek. "I wub you, Mommy."

Her soul would make one attempt. If it failed, she would splinter irreparably. "May I hug you? I won't squeeze you. I'll only put my arms out this wide."

She showed him the size of a circle larger than he was around. Caleb eyed her arms, then nodded. Collin kept her arms the specified circumference. Caleb walked inside her arms, turned around, closed them himself, and sat in her lap. He reached up, looped his arms around her neck, and smiled. "I wub you, Mommy."

"I love you, Caleb. I love you so much, buddy."

Joshua came over to join his brother. He wiggled his bottom next to Caleb until he could sit in Collin's lap, too. He reached up, kissed her as Caleb had, and smiled. "I wub you, Mommy."

"I love you, Joshua. I'm sorry I held you so tight."

"It 'kay. I o-kay."

Collin looked at Talitha. The little girl's eyes were deep and round and solemn. She did not move from her father's sheltering arms. She looked down, then back at Collin. "Mommy go bad place?"

"Mommy went to a bad place in my head. I'm sorry."

"Why, Mommy?"

"Mommy remembered when"—*Careful. Very, very careful—*"when someone took…a baby from me. My mind played a trick on me and made me remember and be afraid."

Talitha's eyes deepened. "Someone take you baby?"

"Yes. It made me very sad and very scared."

Caleb cocked his head. "You have 'nuther baby?"

"I had a very, very tiny baby. Much littler than you are. Teeny tiny baby."

Jeff watched her eyes. She knew his thought. *Almost six years of marriage. We should know what each other is thinking.* Collin kept her voice quiet. "The people who took the baby brought her back. She's very safe and very loved."

Talitha stood, crossed over to Collin, and kissed her cheek. She did not sit in her mother's lap, however. She stood beside

Collin. Collin bit her lip. "May I put my arm around you?"

Talitha stood for a heartache of moments, then nodded. "Yes, Mommy."

Tears fountained down Collin's cheeks, baptizing the triplets. "I love you. I love all of you."

Jeff stood and joined the group hug. Collin lay her head on his shoulder and whispered, "I am so sorry. I am. I'm so sorry."

"It's going to be okay, Collin. We're here, we're together, and we'll make it through."

* * *

Braydon, Collin's half-brother, came out with a security team, swept the house and the yard, but found nothing. Jeff waited until the crew left to talk to Collin. "Braydon promised we could have as many security cameras as we wanted if we so choose. Any ideas on who would leave something like that? Or why?"

Collin turned her gaze internal. She scanned her memories for anyone who might hate her, harbor a grudge against her, or covet her children. No one came to the center stage. No one hovered in the wings. No one even peeked from behind the curtains. Collin shook her head. "I can't think of anyone. You?"

"No. Maybe it's someone we don't know."

"I'm not sure that's better."

Jeff leaned over and kissed Collin. "We will get through this."

Collin wrapped her arms around Jeff's neck and kissed him intently. "I love you, Jeff Farrell."

Any dreams of passion disappeared in a child's giggle and the call of "Daddy kiss Mommy!"

Jeff pulled back and shouted, "Yes! I'm kissing Mommy. And I will kiss her again…" He performed his promise… "and again and again and again…" kissing her every time.

All three littles ran in and jumped on the couch to join the game. The free-for-all ended in a group hug, and Mommy's declaration of, "Enough. The three of you…bath. Clothes in the hamper."

Six feet pounded down the hall toward the bathroom. Jeff kissed Collin one final time. "Your turn or mine?"

"Yours. Monday, Wednesday, Friday, remember?"

"No. If I remembered, I wouldn't have to ask you." *Good point. I'll remember that.*

Wanna bet?

She smiled. "Okay, then how about we share the duty tonight?"

Jeff slid off the couch. "Sounds good." He followed his offspring down the hall, Collin a step behind.

Collin watched the children play in the tub for their allotted "until the water turns cold" time. Then Jeff took charge. He pointed to his offspring and smiled. "Okay, bubbies, enough. Everyone out. One at a time. Talitha." The littlest Farrell climbed out of the tub. Jeff wrapped her in a large towel, dried her, rubbed part of the towel over her hair, hugged her. "Pajamas." Talitha clutched the towel and ran for the nursery as fast as her legs could carry her.

Jeff pulled up a second towel. "Joshua." Joshua climbed out, grabbed the towel, and tried to dry himself. Jeff battled his son for a moment, long enough to dry most of the boy, then laughed. "PJs." Joshua dropped the towel and ran down the hall, nekkid. Collin sighed. *That's my boy.*

Caleb climbed out and stood at attention. Jeff wrapped him up, dried him off. "You know what to do." Caleb clutched his towel around his middle and followed Joshua and Talitha up the hall.

Jeff let the water out of the tub and set the rubber ducks (which only float upside down), the plastic doughnuts, and the toy boats on the side to dry. "What do you think about the cameras?"

"Can we stay up and watch the babies?"

Jeff's shoulders drooped. "We can't, Collin. We have to sleep sometime. You know we can't both function without sleep. And being on alternate watches, we'll never have a life together. Or a family." He put his hands on her shoulders. "We have to trust God on this one."

"How?" It came out in an anguished whisper. "How? Every night I close the door to their room, my heart rips open. I want to trust. I do. I know He's God. I know He loves us. I know He is in control. I still hurt."

Jeff pulled her into his chest and held her. He dropped his head on hers. "I know, milady. I know. I fight it every night. Every time I pull the door shut, I pray He protects them. Pray He will leave them with us another night. Another day. Then I walk away. And I leave them in His hands."

Collin closed her eyes. "Because they're His children, not ours. I know. I know. It's so hard. Even now, after all this time." She motioned her head towards the kitchen. "This only makes it harder. It brings it all back."

The tightening of Jeff's arm matched the tightness in his voice. "Which is what they're trying to do. To tear us up again. I don't know who, and I don't know why. But we will not let them win." He moved Collin away from his chest to focus on her eyes. "You hear me, milady? They will not win."

She nodded. "Right."

Cries of "Mommy!" "Daddy!" "Help!" came from the nursery. But the cries weren't frantic or fearful. Just normal cries. Jeff hugged Collin again. They walked arm in arm to the bedroom to discover the cause of the distress.

Caleb had both feet in one leg of his PJs and hopped around trying to find the other leg. Joshua had his head through a sleeve hole. And Talitha had her nightgown on inside out and backward. Collin grinned. "Okay, babies. One at a time." Jeff rescued Caleb, Collin rescued Joshua, then turned Talitha right side out and forward. Once everyone had been dressed properly, they retrieved their respective stuffy (Caleb got his bear, Joshua, his lion, and Talitha, her penguin.) The children crawled into their respective beds and settled down.

Collin and Jeff sat in the rockers, and Jeff brought out the children's Bible. He thumbed through until he found a page he wanted. "Here's a story about a boy who became a king. His name was David..."

Jeff read from the book. Collin listened, watching while six eyes closed. Two thumbs went into mouths. One blanket pulled tight into a fist. And three babies fell asleep. Jeff closed the book, stood, and held his hand out for Collin.

She hesitated. The urge to curl up on the floor and sleep in the nursery clawed at her heart, her mind. She swallowed hard, stood. *Help me, Lord. Give me strength to do Your will. And to trust You. One more night. I love You.* Collin took Jeff's hand, rose, and walked with him out of the room. She lay her other hand on his, and together they closed the door.

Jeff prayed, "Lord, thank You for giving us our babies. Please leave them with us another night, another day. You know my heart, Lord. You know my fear. Take it from me. Take it from both of us. Help us to trust Your will, whatever it is. In Jesus's Name."

Collin added the "Amen." She kissed Jeff. "Thank you." Together they walked back to the living room. Jeff rechecked the doors to be sure they were locked. Collin resisted the compulsion to check all the windows. She would not yield to paranoia. Not again. She curled up on the couch. Adult time waited.

SUNDAY

Collin walked the trio into their classroom for Sunday school. Ms. Luis met them at the Dutch door. "Hi, babies! How are you today?" All three headed straight for the toys. Collin handed Ms. Luis the diaper bags. "Talitha is in training pants. The boys are in pull-ups. Reminders are good."

Ms. Luis smiled. "You got it. How's the training going at home?"

Collin shrugged. "It's going. We have our good days. And our not-so-good days. But we're a work in progress."

"As are we all, Collin. They here for both services?"

"Yes. I'm in the four-year-old preschool this month. Jeff is greeting."

Ms. Luis nodded. "I saw him as I came in. It's not a problem with your three. They play so well together."

Collin smiled. "They're a work in progress, too. But they do well. Thanks, Ms. Luis."

Collin left the nursery and headed for her assignment in the preschool. She paired with Kells to manage the ten or so four-year-olds who came to the early service. Kells was already in the room, setting up for the lesson. She looked up as Collin entered. "Wondered when you were going to show up."

Collin side-eyed her friend. "What's the problem? I had to drop off the trio."

Kells shook her head. "Never mind. I'm having a bad day. Can you handle the lesson?"

"Sure. We're covering forgiveness, right?"

"Right. And I don't need the reminders." Kells moved away from Collin to greet the first students being dropped off.

Collin watched her friend slide into "happy teacher" mode. She laughed and carried on with each parent, then directed the children to hang their bags. Once done, they were to go sit on their colored mats. With only ten students, Collin decided to only use two color mats. Blue and red. Everyone pick one.

Once picked, Collin split up the troublemakers, the "can't keep their hands to themselves" or "can't stop talking" students. Putting them with different groups usually helped keep the attention focused on the teachers, not on each other. But they were a good group. Collin breezed through the lesson on "forgiving each other because we've been forgiven." She looked at the clock and decided they had time for each child to tell a story of when they had to forgive someone and when they had to ask for forgiveness. The stories did not disappoint.

"I hit my brother and had to say I'm sorry. He said he forgave me."

Collin nodded. That's going to be a common theme.

"I bit my baby sister on the hand. I didn't mean to. I had to tell Mommy I'm sorry. And I had to go sit in my room."

Do not ask why she bit her sister. The baby is only six-months-old.

Maybe the baby had her fingers in Fiona's mouth.

Maybe.

"My brother broke my favorite truck, and he didn't say sorry."

"It made you feel sad, didn't it?"

"Uh-huh."

"Can you forgive him even if he doesn't say sorry?"

"Huh-uh."

"If you don't forgive him, will you want to play with him again?"

Long silence. "I want to play with him."

"Sometimes we have to forgive someone who isn't sorry so we can still have them as friends. They may not realize they did something to hurt us, and forgiving them is a way to keep the friendship going."

Long silence. "I want to forgive him."

"Great idea. I'm sure he will say he's sorry."

Kells walked by. In an aside, she whispered, "I wouldn't bet on it. Tally doesn't have a brother. He's an only child."

Colling kept a straight face. "Thank you, Tally, for sharing." She looked around. "Does anyone else have a story they want to tell?"

Misa raised her hand. Kells asked, "Does anyone else want to talk before Misa starts?"

No one moved. Kells sighed. "Okay, Misa. You can tell your story."

"The other day, when we went to the park, it was raining. And Mommy wanted to get to the park fast, so she made us run all the way there. And then when we got there, the sharks were out, and they were eating people. I didn't want to get eaten, so I ran and hid. Mommy yelled at me to come back, but I didn't want the shark to eat me. So I stayed where I was. And then a seal came behind me and told me he would keep the shark from eating me. He would tell the shark he shouldn't eat people because the people don't like being eaten…"

The story continued until Kells held up her hand. "Misa, thank you for the wonderful story. I don't know what the point is or how it connects to forgiving someone, but it was a nice story. Let's all get ready for snack, okay?"

The children moved to the wall. Collin got out the hand wipes, washed everyone's hands. Kells came behind with a small paper cup filled with animal crackers. Collin got out the small carpet cleaner to whisk up the crumbs. The children were released one at a time to get a drink from the fountain (wiped down and sprayed after each child) then return to their mat to wait for Mommy and/or Daddy. Collin put on music to say goodbye with. Before the alligator could chomp the last time, all the children were gone. The second crew came in. Collin and Kells walked out.

Collin stopped her friend. "We've got time. You want to talk about what's bugging you?"

"No. Not right now. I'll call later in the week. And I'll see you on Thursday for group."

Collin smiled. "Winona is bringing a guest. First-time visitor. Eliza. She's not bringing her children until she's comfortable with who we are and what we do. I told Nonnie that would be fair."

Kells snorted. "I don't like being 'checked out' like we've got some agenda to hide."

"It's not about an agenda, Kells. It's about someone wanting to protect their children."

"If they knew the Lord, they'd have all the protection they would need."

Collin's stomach dropped. A black hole opened in the past. Memories of pain, of despair, of incredible loss assailed her. Collin swallowed hard. "I hear you." *I hear you every week. When are you going to get it? It's not that simple. Never. Ever.*

And You know I love You, Lord. And I know You love me. How do I explain it to her so she'll understand?

Peace, child.

Right. Not my job. Okay. I get it.

Kells blew past Collin without seeing the turmoil she left in her wake. Collin pounded the door in her mind closed. The memories could stay buried. Gone. Dealt with. Over. Move on.

Collin joined Jeff at the preschool door. They went in together to see the trio and find out how first service had gone.

Ms. Luis smiled. "No accidents. Everyone's still in their original outfits."

Collin gave her a thumbs-up. "Score one for the home team."

Ms. Luis hesitated, and her face lost the smile. "I saw a bruise on Caleb's arm." She moved closer to Collin and lowered her voice. "He said Mommy hurt him."

Collin closed her eyes and hung her head. "I did. I had a flashback and hugged them too tight. I imagine all three of them have bruises."

Ms. Luis nodded. "Yes, they all had to show me. They don't seem the worse for having them. All three of them are the same as they always are."

Jeff's eyes narrowed. "You'd think otherwise? Why?"

She shook her head rapidly. "No, no. I meant them seeing you go through a flashback might have affected them. But they haven't said a word about it."

Collin sighed. "They forgave me. We talked about it, they understood as much as a toddler could, and we moved on."

Ms. Luis put her hand on Collin's arm. "As you should. You have beautiful children. You're rearing them in the Lord. They'll do fine."

Collin smiled, her lips pursed. Jeff took her arm and led her away from the door. "Let it go, Collin. It's fine. They're fine.

You're fine. If you want to call Dr. Sujit and talk to him, you might. I don't think one flashback in almost three years is a major setback. But it's up to you."

She shrugged. "I'll think about it. It's not something I need to do right this minute." She smiled. "Let's go find who's sitting in 'our' seats today."

Jeff grinned. "Oh, but of course. And we will be highly outraged, correct?"

"Of course. You know we paid good money for those seats. We're entitled."

They went in, found two unoccupied seats, and sat. Collin noticed a few new people and smiled to let them know they were seen and welcome. A younger man in a deep blue three-piece suit smiled back at her. Dipped his head. Saluted her. Collin didn't return the gesture but nodded to him. A little strange, but then, who wasn't these days? She turned her attention to the platform.

MONDAY

Jeff slid the proposal across his desk to his brother-in-law. "Here. See if you can find the flaw in the presentation."

"Flaw? What flaw? I put it together, and it's perfect."

"You think so?"

"I know so. I don't do shoddy work."

Jeff grinned. "And you don't lack in self-confidence either, do you, Erin?"

Erin Winger rolled his wheelchair closer to the desk. "Not the last time I looked. Why? Did you see something in there?"

"No, but I'm afraid the city council might. They're cracking down on specifics in the plans now."

Erin snorted. "A little late, isn't it? South Hall collapsed, and everyone knows who approved the blueprints. Fudged figures and all."

"They're only lucky no one was hurt on the site when the house of putty came crashing down around their ears. Literally."

Erin nodded. "Okay, so someone is finally looking at the fine print and running the numbers. Trinity Builders has always played by the rules. We answer to a Higher Authority."

"Right. We know that. We say that. Now we have to prove it to the city planners."

Erin pounded the table crisply. "If they give us the project, this will be the cleanest, safest, best-built recreation center in town. One that will last fifty years and never go out of date."

Jeff chuckled. "I know, Erin. I know. Your sister is equally passionate about this one."

Erin nodded. "We're twins. We get excited about the same things sometimes. Not always, but sometimes."

Erin's phone beeped. He answered it. "Yes, my love, my wife. What did the doctor say?"

Jeff held his breath. Erin's wife, Vy, had been experiencing bouts of vomiting, back pains, and generally feeling like death warmed over the past couple of weeks. She'd gone to have it checked out in the morning. Jeff studied Erin's eyes closely. *Not the eyes. The fingers. If he's flexing his fingers, it's good news.*

Erin stared at the desk without moving. He laughed. "Yeah, Jeff's here. He's trying to read my fingers to see if I'm happy or not."

Jeff tossed a paper wad at him. "Low life."

Erin tossed it back. "I'll tell him." He leaned over toward Jeff. "She says we can discuss all of it at our regular Monday night meeting. She's bringing lasagna."

Jeff groaned. "Which means tomato stains and a bath after dinner."

"She says if you learned to use a fork, you wouldn't have the problem."

Jeff pulled the phone away from Erin. "Thanks, Vy. I'll keep it in mind. The kids will love lasagna. With or without the forks. I'll dress them in their raincoats. Then I can take them outside and spray them down with the hose."

He smiled. "Right. I'll send him home on time, and we'll see you at the house about six. Love you, Vy."

He handed the phone back to Erin. The man took it with a pout. "You stole my line." He spoke to his phone. "I love you, Vy. See you in a bit." He pocketed his phone and turned serious. "There's nothing in there they can object to. It's all to the letter, by the book, straight up the best deal they are going to get from anyone. I don't know what they could object to."

"I don't either. Let's hope they see it our way."

"How about we pray they see it our way and let the Lord decide?"

Jeff chuckled. "I'm supposed to be the spiritual mentor, remember? I trained you."

Erin grinned. "And you've done a fine job of it, sir. Exceptional. Now can we pray?"

Jeff nodded. "Yes, Erin. We can."

They laid all their plans before the Lord, asking His guidance,

His wisdom, His insight, and above all, His will be done. Then they left it there. Erin returned to his office to clean up for the night. Jeff stayed to "sign off" on some projects still nagging him. Camp Grace needed oversight. He wasn't putting in the hours he had worked there before he married Collin. And even less since the triplets were born. But the camp remained dear to his heart and soul. He needed to find that "one good man" to take the reins.

Then there were the three other projects still on his desk. But they, like Camp Grace, needed more attention than he could give at the end of a long day. He pushed everything aside, picked up his briefcase, grabbed his jacket, and headed out the door. Collin and the babies were waiting.

A ring on his phone stopped him. He looked at the number. Cocked his head. "Pastor Thomas. What can I do for you?"

Thomas's voice sounded smooth. "Are you free for lunch tomorrow? I have something I need to discuss with you, and I prefer to do it face-to-face."

Jeff's stomach tightened. "Sure. I'll meet you where?"

"How about the Salad Bowl? My wife wants me to eat healthy."

Jeff chuckled. "I hear you." *Except Collin doesn't bug me about my eating habits.* "What time works best for you?"

"What does your schedule look like?"

Jeff looked at his desk. The three projects looked back. They could wait a few more hours. "I'm free anytime."

"If we meet at eleven-thirty, we can avoid the rush. Sound good?"

"I'll see you there and then. Any hint what this is about?"

Thomas cleared his throat. "I'll fill you in then. Bye, Jeff."

Jeff stared hard at his phone before putting it back on the desk. While Pastor Thomas and Jeff occasionally had lunch together, they usually talked about finances for the church, nominations for the elder board, or something related to a new project. But none of those kinds of undertakings were going on at present. And wanting to talk face-to-face? Hmm. Sounded personal. Jeff lowered his head. "Lord, whatever this is, guard my attitude. And my tongue. Keep me in Your will and not my own. Please." God knew. It would have to be enough.

* * *

Collin kissed Jeff as he came in the door, put down his briefcase, and hung his jacket on the coat rack. He embraced her warmly. "I missed you today."

Collin swatted at him. "No, you didn't. You were working with Erin. He doesn't give you time to miss anything."

Jeff looked up the hall. "Time for a quick update?"

Before he could get an answer, the answer came pounding up the hall. "Daddy home! Daddy home! Daddy! Daddy!"

The triplets dove on him from all sides. He swung Talitha up first to keep her from being crushed by her more solid brothers. He kissed her, set her down, repeated the action with Caleb and Joshua. He kneeled to be at their level. "How was your day?"

Caleb raised his hands above his head. "We see big bear!"

Joshua added to the story. "Bear chase us. We run run run."

Talitha hugged Jeff's neck and whispered in his ear, "Bear eat Cayeb. Bear not eat 'litha. Too yiddle."

Jeff wrapped the trio in a gentle hug. "I love you. Auntie Vy and Uncle Erin are coming over tonight. You can tell them all about the bear, too."

The news set off a celebration marked by jumping and cheering. Jeff grinned. "They do love their Auntie and Uncle." He looked at Collin. "Erin used his wheelchair today. No comments, but he's hurting again."

Collin's face drew down. She closed her eyes and whispered, "Lord, please. Your will, but if there's room, heal him."

Jeff added the "amen." He hugged Collin. "I'm going to change into something grubby. Vy is bringing lasagna."

Collin shook her head. "I'll get out the raincoats."

"That's what I said."

Jeff started down the hall, his progress impeded by a son clinging to each leg. Talitha stayed with her mother, at least. Jeff slipped out of his suit and tie and into blue jeans. He had to chase his tennis shoes around the room as they each grew chubby legs and ran in circles. He finally corralled his shoes long enough to get them on and pointed the boys down the hall to the family room. "Let's get ready for Vy and Erin, okay? Erin is using his wheels, so we need to make sure everything is picked up."

The Farrell men raced down the hall and careened into the family room. Jeff looked over to the kitchen and saw Collin sitting on the floor in a corner. She had curled into a tight ball, rocking back and forth. Talitha stood beside her, patting her head. "You 'kay, Mommy? Mommy, you 'kay?"

Jeff left the boys to throw the toys in the toy box and went into the kitchen. He kneeled beside Collin. "Milady? Are you in there? You with me?"

Collin didn't lift her head. She didn't speak. She rocked. Jeff saw the envelope on the floor beside her. He picked it up by the edges. *One lives.*

Fire lit his gut. He wanted to rip the thing to shreds. To crush it and throw it and stomp it and scream and roar... Instead, he stroked Collin's head and murmured, "Come back, milady. It's all good. We're all here. We're all safe. It's only the shadows. We're together. We're safe. Come back, Collin."

Talitha lifted her face to her daddy. Her eyes were pools of innocence. Her lip trembled. Her voice caught. "Mommy 'kay, Daddy? Mommy 'kay?"

He hugged her. "Yes, darling. Mommy is okay. She's fine." He set his daughter beside her mother. "Give her a kiss, Talitha. Tell her you love her."

Talitha hugged as much of her mother as she could get her arms around. She leaned over and kissed Collin on the ear. The littlest Farrell crooned, "I wuv oo, Mommy. I wuv oo."

Collin's rocking slowed, then stopped. Jeff continued to stroke her head. "Come back, Collin. We're here. Your daughter needs you."

Collin lifted her head. Her eyes were clouded with pain and emptiness and loss. She closed her eyes, lowered her head, then sat up. She put an arm around Talitha and kissed her daughter. "I love you too, little one. Thank you. You helped Mommy. I'm sorry if I scared you." Collin patted the girl's back. "Why don't you go help your brothers pick up the toys? Thank you." Talitha ran to join her brothers.

His wife looked at him. "I'll call Dr. Sujit's office tomorrow."

Jeff motioned to the envelope and its contents. "Where did you find this?"

"Just now. On the countertop."

"I'm calling the police."

Collin shook her head. "Don't. What are they going to do?"

"Find out how someone is breaking into our house and leaving threatening messages. Put a stop to this before it goes any further."

Collin motioned to the trio. "I don't want them scared. I don't want their security broken."

"Someone has already broken it, Collin. Someone is coming into the house and leaving notes for you to find. What else are they planning? We need to catch them and stop them."

Collin nodded. "But we have no proof someone has broken in. My word, and with my history, will they even take it?"

Jeff helped her off the floor. "Your history is not different than anyone else's. You spent time in a hospital after your daughter was kidnapped. You needed help processing it. You got help, and that's all you needed."

Collin kissed him. "Compromise. Call Braydon again. Let's see if he can find anything first. If he does, we'll call the police. If he doesn't, well…we'll figure it out."

Jeff hugged her. "We will figure it out, lady. I'm going to have him put cameras on the outside of the house."

Collin shook her head. "We agreed we weren't going to live that way."

"I understand. I agree we walk by faith and not in fear. Locking the doors at night isn't a sign we're not trusting God. We're using the brains and resources He gave us. The cameras are no different."

Collin looked at the floor, then looked up and met his gaze. "Okay. Tomorrow."

He nodded. "I'm calling him now. He can come out tomorrow and install everything."

"Can you be here in case he needs to explain something?" Collin stopped. "No, wait. Rob can be here."

The thought of their adult adopted son made Collin smile. "He gets the biggest kick out of being with the trio. Says they help him figure out his thesis."

Jeff grinned. "Yeah, and then he raids the pantry and the fridge to take food back to the dorm."

"You were in college once. You remember how it is."

"Yeah, I do. But Dad restricted my forays into the kitchen. I could graze all I wanted, but I couldn't carry anything out in a bag."

Collin laughed. It sounded good coming from her. "I know your mom better. She had provisions packed for you, didn't she?"

Jeff grinned. "I'll never tell. Not while Dad's alive."

The garage door activated. Collin called, "Auntie Vy and Uncle Erin are here."

Pandemonium broke in the family room. Cheers and shouts and bodies bounced. A toy flew into the air. A stuffed toy, fortunately. The littles' toys were all "age-appropriate" and "Mommy and Daddy approved" for safety.

The back door opened. Erin walked in with his arm crutches. Vy followed close behind, carrying dinner. Collin kissed her brother, then Vy, then took the casserole carrier. "I'll set this in the kitchen. Get in the door."

The littles ran to the kitchen to be the first to dogpile on Uncle Erin but stopped upon seeing his crutches. Erin leaned them against the wall, sat down on the floor, then grinned. "Okay, now come say hi."

The littles mobbed him as they had their father. Talitha ducked under her brothers' tackles and dove into Erin's lap for the first hug. Vy slipped to the floor beside her husband to give the littles equal time.

It took a good five minutes for the welcoming to end. Jeff dispatched the trio to get their paint shirts from the playroom so they could eat dinner. The littles climbed in their booster seats at the "big table," and dinner was served. Surprisingly, the triplets managed to keep most of the food on the table. And in their mouths instead of all over themselves. No one ended up with tomato sauce in their hair...not even the adults. Call it a win.

Vy and Erin participated in the nighttime rituals of reading a book and saying prayers. Then came "night-night" and a final kiss. The adults retired to the family room for conversation.

Jeff looked at Vy. "So what did the doctor say?"

Erin chuckled. "Nothing like getting down to business."

Jeff nodded. "Straight up, bro. Only way to do it."

Vy smiled. She tucked her arm in Erin's and stared at him with such love Jeff knew the answer before she said it. "We're going to have a baby."

Collin jumped up and caught both Erin and Vy in a hug. "I'm so happy for you! Fantastic! When?"

Vy relaxed back on the couch. "I'm only eight weeks. It's too early to determine an exact birthdate yet."

Jeff pointed to Erin. "I want those contracts finished tomorrow."

Erin held his hands high. "Why? They're not due…"

Jeff cut him off. "You're gonna be useless after this. I know you. Once the word gets out, you'll be so preoccupied with managing the pregnancy you won't be worth anything to me. Get those contracts done tomorrow."

Erin launched a stuffed giraffe across the room at Jeff. "Stuff it, Farrell."

Vy cautioned, "We haven't told the folks yet, so you can't say anything."

Collin cocked her head. "Why not?"

"They're up in Akron for a funeral. I didn't feel right about calling them with the news. I want to tell them in person."

"Good plan." Collin beamed. "I'm so happy for you both. I can't believe it." She lifted her chin as tears rolled down her cheeks. She swallowed hard, brushed the salt away. "I'm sorry. I'm a little… I'm a wreck right now."

Jeff curled up on the floor beside his wife. He hugged her. "Someone has broken in the house while Collin and the babies are here alone and left notes for her to find."

Vy's face hardened. Her extensive law-enforcement background roared back into existence. "Notes? Saying what? How do you know they're breaking in while you're home?"

Collin drew in a deep breath. "Because the notes aren't there, and then they are. On the laundry basket. On the kitchen counter. 'Choose one.' 'One lives.' I'm having flashbacks. And I hate it."

Erin's tone turned as dark as his face. "I hate it, too. This can't go on." He looked to Jeff. "Police?"

Collin interrupted for Jeff. "I told him not to call. What are they going to do? It's not like the perp has actually threatened me or the children. They'll only think I'm crazy or forgetful or am doing it on my own for attention…"

Collin trailed off. Jeff kissed her head. "Stop. No one thinks that except you."

Vy's expression softened. "Collin...you had PTSD after Talitha. You got treatment. You're better. No one holds it against you. It's not like a scarlet letter on your chest for all the world to see."

Collin shook her head sharply. "I'm sorry. I'm not thinking straight."

Erin came to his sister's defense. "Anyone in your place would have their thinking scattered. Give yourself some grace, Cane. God does."

Jeff hugged her. "And His is the only opinion that matters in the end. We're going to figure this out. We are."

Erin pulled out his phone. "Have you called Braydon yet?"

Jeff shook his head. "I was about to when you pulled up."

Erin punched in a number, set the phone on speaker, and set it on the arm of the couch.

An automated voice stated, "This is First Watch..."

Erin hung up. Dialed again. Muttered, "Answer the phone, Braydon."

It took a moment, but Braydon's voice came on the line. "Erin! Brother. What's happening? What can I do for you?"

"I'm at Jeff and Collin's. They need some security installed." He looked at Collin and added, "And a dog to see if there's something or someone in the house."

Collin waved him off. Erin ignored her. "A big dog. Gretchen. I like how she works. And she's great with kids. Can you bring her along tomorrow?"

A pause. Another pause. "Yeah, I can make it work. What time?"

Collin called, "Whatever time is good for you. Naps are at noonish."

Braydon chuckled. "We'll be careful not to wake the babies."

"I'm talking about my nap. The babies never sleep."

Braydon chuckled. "I hear you, sis. I'll come out in the morning, about ten? Will that work?"

Collin hesitated. "I think Rob has a class at ten. Let me check on something." Collin looked from Erin to Jeff and back. "Either of you available?" Both men nodded. "It's fine. Someone with brains will be here."

"Which means neither Erin nor Jeff. Will Vy be available?"

Vy joined the call. "I'm sure I can be. We'll see you tomorrow, Braydon."

"Bye, y'all." The connection when dead.

Erin pocketed his phone. "Step one. Gretchen searches the house. Step two, you get cameras on the perimeter. Step three, you get 24/7 monitoring." He stared at Jeff. "Right, brother?"

Jeff nodded. He wanted to take offense at Erin's usurping his authority in Jeff's home...but the steps were the right ones, in the proper order. "We will protect this family." He added, "By God's grace, and in His will."

Collin nodded. "Amen."

Erin leaned back. "Now we've settled that, let me tell you what happened today."

Collin looked from Erin to Jeff. "What? Something good?"

Erin nodded. "Oh, yeah. Very good. We hired a new intern. He's agreed to be my assistant in the planning department. He's got some exceptional ideas about housing and urban development. Excellent mind. Sharp presentations. I am very impressed."

Jeff kept his face straight. "I met him, too. He'll be a good addition to the office."

Collin looked at her brother. "Who is it?"

"Young guy, right out of college. Still working on the master's program but will be finished by the fall. Good man. Good background. He is familiar with the streets, which makes him invaluable if we get the contract for the downtown housing development."

"Who is it?"

Erin's face twisted. His eyes looked far away. "I'm trying to remember his name. Started with an 'R,' didn't it, Jeff? Ron? Rufus?"

Jeff shrugged. "You interviewed him."

"I know. Picked him out of a field of twenty applicants. Head and shoulders above the rest. Can't quite..."

Erin paused for dramatic effect. Collin pitched a stuffed flamingo at him. "Enough! Who is it?"

"Rob. That's it. Rob Farrell. I asked him if you two were related. He said there might be a distant connection." He grinned at Collin.

She sneered at him. "You think you're so funny." She swung

on Jeff. "You hired our son and didn't tell me?"

Jeff pointed defensively to Erin. "Him, not me."

Erin shrugged. "He came in on his own. Wanted to compete like all the others. No gimmies. I measured him against all the other candidates. He seemed the most qualified. Maybe not the most experience with planning, but his knowledge of the streets will more than make up for it. I'm looking forward to working with him."

Collin leaned back. "Fantastic. Why didn't he tell me?"

"Because the announcement hasn't been made at the office yet. Not before tomorrow. Have to get the senior staff to sign off on it, you know."

Collin rolled her eyes. "I agree. I'll sign off on hiring Rob."

Jeff chuckled. "He's got my vote."

Vy smiled. "I'm in."

Erin rubbed his hands together. "So it's unanimous."

Collin muttered, "And probably the first time senior management has agreed on something so quickly."

Crying came over the baby monitor, coming from the nursery. Collin hopped to her feet. "I'll get him."

Jeff shook his head. "Sounds like Caleb."

Collin disappeared into the nursery. Five minutes passed before she came out and closed the door behind her. She returned to the family room. "Caleb." She looked at Jeff. "What book were you reading to them?"

"Uh, 'The Man in the Yellow Hat.' Joshua picked it out."

"Now I understand, then."

"Understand what?"

Collin smiled. "Caleb said George scratched him. I think Caleb scratched himself in his sleep and dreamed George the monkey did it. His imagination is so active all the time."

Vy tapped Erin on the shoulder. "Listen, love of my life. We need to get home. If I'm going to be here in the morning, I need to get some laundry done. Otherwise, the babies will see Auntie Vy in her nighty. And I know the world doesn't want that."

Erin pulled himself to his feet, reached out for his crutches, and stood. "Yes, my love. No one gets to see your nighty but me."

Jeff held up his hand. "Wait. One more item. It happened Friday, but I forgot it until now. We had a visit at the office from a

Ryan Woolfort. Said he'd talked to you, and you promised him a check for Lyon Ebertson's campaign."

Erin looked from Jeff to Vy, then back to Jeff. "What? I'd never…"

Jeff stopped him. "I know you'd never. He didn't even have your name right. Called you Erol." Jeff chuckled. "How much of a scam artist can you be?"

Erin shook his head. "Did you call the police?"

"For something so small? No. I didn't even bother Lyon about it. If it happens again, I will. But for now, I'm passing it off as nothing."

"You sure that's wise?"

"Yeah. It's no big deal."

"Okay, then, I guess we're out of here."

Vy and Erin gave kisses all around, then left. Collin and Jeff watched them drive away. Collin smiled. "My brother is going to be a father."

Jeff muttered, "God help their baby."

Collin shoved him. "He will. You know it. He's been helping you, hasn't He?"

"Every day."

Collin kissed him. "Shall we call it a night, dear?"

"I think that's an excellent idea. I love you, milady."

"I love you, Jeff Farrell."

Arm in arm, they walked down the hall to their room.

TUESDAY

Tuesday almost-afternoon, Jeff met Pastor Thomas at
The Salad Bar. It had plenty of tables to choose from. And despite
its name, the menu offered more than salad. Jeff waited to sit down
until Thomas arrived. The two men hugged briefly, then sat near
the back. The server took their orders. True to his word, Thomas
ordered a salad. But with steak. So call it a compromise. Jeff
ordered a burger but turned down the fries. No sense tempting
Thomas with food he shouldn't have.

Thomas made small talk until the food arrived. Only after he
blessed it and put his napkin in his lap did he look Jeff in the eyes.
"We have a situation at the nursery. A visitor came in to see how
we work and saw bruises on a child. Apparently, they're a
Mandatory Reporting Agent for Child Protective Services. They
seemed to think the bruising indicated abuse. Our volunteer tried to
assure them there had been no abuse. The nursery worker knows
the parents and knows they would never abuse their children. But
the visitor demanded to know the child's name and address. Our
volunteer refused to give it to her, and the person left."

Jeff's eyes narrowed. "We don't give out names to anyone.
Police, maybe, if they have a warrant. But we don't give out
information. What happened next?"

Thomas chewed his salad. "Someone called CPS. An agent
came to the office first thing Monday morning. He wanted
information on the volunteer to talk to her about the incident. Any

time a call is made, CPS has to follow it up. The agent wanted to know if we were aware of any problems. He asked if we have a procedure for reporting if we suspected abuse or domestic violence."

"What did you tell him?" *And why are you telling me? What is this about?*

"I told him as a church, our volunteers are exempt from mandatory reporting. But if something did happen, we would make inquiries of our own. And we would obey the laws of the land and report it. But only after we had checked into the situation."

Jeff nodded. "Didn't satisfy him, did it?" He pushed the plate away. The burger lost its appeal. "What did he say?"

"He disagreed with our stand but admitted it is the law. He suggested we look into the matter ourselves and then decide. He would wait to hear from me about it by the afternoon."

"And?"

Pastor Thomas chewed through a healthy portion of the steak. But moved aside the leafy greens. "And so I spoke to the volunteer. She spoke to the child after the visitor left. He admitted his mommy hurt him, and she caused the bruise."

Jeff's jaw muscles tightened. "Mommies can hurt children in a lot of ways which aren't intentional. I can't see how one bruise reflects abuse."

Thomas nodded. "I agree with you." He smiled. "My Tommy was always covered black and blue. He had to be the clumsiest child of the five. He'd bruise if you looked at him funny."

Jeff ignored the rabbit hole. "Why are you telling me about this?"

Thomas gazed at his salad. "If it had only been one bruise on one child, maybe we would ignore it. But two other siblings had bruises as well. And they echoed the first child their mommy hurt them."

Jeff's gut twisted. "Are you talking about my children, Pastor?"

Thomas met Jeff's eyes. "Yes."

Lord, this is where You guard my mouth. Tell me what to say. Politely. Jeff laid his napkin on the table. "Someone broke into our home. Collin had a flashback and hugged the babies to keep them from being taken away. There were some bruises on their arms from how tight she held them. But in no way was there any abuse, nor will there ever be. You know us. You know Collin. You can't believe we'd hurt our children."

Thomas nodded. "Of course, I don't believe you'd abuse your children. Never. I stand behind you both one hundred percent." He jerked his head to the side. "But I wanted you to know what happened. In case CPS decides to pursue this any further. I'm sure they won't. They have plenty of real cases to pursue. But you know…"

Jeff nodded. "I know. They have a tough job, and it can make you jaded. Which I'm very aware of." *Collin worked as a social worker. She saw both sides of the aisle.* Jeff swallowed half his soda. "Any other reason you wanted to meet with me? You could have told me this over the phone."

The pastor picked through the greens looking for any morsels of meat he might have missed. "It gets…complicated. And I am truly sorry. I don't know who made the call, but someone didn't keep the news of the incident confidential."

A slow burn began in Jeff's gut, followed immediately by his jaws locking and his teeth clenching. "Let me guess. It's all over the congregation Collin abused the babies, right?"

Thomas turned his palms up. "I can't speak for the whole congregation, but some of the Elders heard about it. I took some calls wanting to know what we were doing about it."

Raging conflagrations from his fireman days had nothing on the anger he felt right now. He could only offer, "I see."

Thomas's voice remained level. "I hope you do, Jeff. I'm counting on you, more than anyone else, to handle this the way the Lord would."

What a low… Jeff measured his words. "What do they want you to do?"

"They think it's in everyone's best interest if Collin steps back from working in the nursery until this is all resolved."

"You said you had resolved it. You know Collin would never do anything to hurt her children. End of story."

Thomas nodded. An exaggerated nod. "And I agree. Collin wouldn't. But we have to have some sort of policy if someone else does. We screen our volunteers before we allow them to work in Children's Ministries. We never thought about what to do in this sort of situation, where a complaint has been lodged."

Jeff swallowed more of his drink. "So Collin becomes the fall guy. You work out your policy and let her suffer the consequences until you get it right. Am I hearing you right? And I'm supposed to 'handle this the way the Lord would?'"

Thomas stared at Jeff. "Yes, I am. And yes, you are. You say I know you. I do. And I know you will behave exactly the way the Lord would. I'm counting on it."

Jeff dropped his gaze to the table. He closed his eyes and chose his words with extreme caution. "I understand. But there's one thing you have to do first."

Thomas cocked his head. "What?"

"You have to tell Collin yourself. You and the Elders who are drafting this policy. Because if you and they know—really know—Collin would never hurt a child, then you can explain it to her. You explain how her stepping away from working with children is only an example of what *would happen*. And you and the Elders will gladly announce to the congregation itself how this is a dry run for something we pray we never have to do."

Tears threatened Jeff's eyes. His hands shook. He placed them in his lap to grip his legs instead of the table. His voice trembled, and he didn't try to stop it. "Because you know as well as I do, an accusation is as good as a conviction in some eyes. Collin stepping down will be an admission of guilt. And nothing will ever erase that."

Thomas put his hand on Jeff's shoulder. Jeff squelched the desire to knock the hand—and the owner—across the room. The pastor squeezed the shoulder. "Give yourself some time to calm down. We're not accusing Collin of anything, Jeff. Absolutely not. I know what this may look like, but no one thinks Collin did anything wrong. Not on purpose."

Jeff jumped on it. "But she might be unstable, so she should give up volunteering with the kids, right? No one suggested she step back once she completed counseling after Talitha was kidnapped."

Thomas nodded. "True. Which I also mentioned. The suggestion is a person who is accused can be evaluated by a church-approved psychologist, and those recommendations will determine whether or when the person can return to working with children."

Jeff shook his head. "What's driving this, Pastor? What is this all about? There's one bruise. Each child has one bruise on their arm. The babies aren't traumatized, they aren't afraid of Collin, and they probably don't even remember what happened. Who is trying to blow this out of proportion?"

"I can't share the information, Jeff, and you know it."

"But they sure can share Collin's information all over the congregation." *Lord, I'm sorry for snapping. This is Collin we're talking about! Your child. She loves You. Protect her, please!*

Thomas stood and placed cash on the table. "I'm very sorry, Jeff. I can understand your feelings. I can. If it were my wife, I'd be fighting mad as well." He hesitated. "I'll tell the Elders they have to face Collin. They can tell her why they've chosen to act on an unsubstantiated accusation instead of standing in her defense. Then they can tell her how they're going to find out who broke confidentiality and how they're going to deal with it." Thomas smiled without mirth. "I'm sure they'll be thrilled."

Jeff stood. Thomas's words did little to mollify him. "I'm sure they'll respond the way Jesus would, right?"

Thomas held Jeff's eyes. "I would hope so. I would hope we all reflect our Lord." He paused. "And if we don't, or can't, then we've got other problems to deal with." He squeezed Jeff's shoulder again. "Thanks for hearing me out, Jeff. And not punching me out."

Jeff shrugged. "The Lord does have some control of my life, Pastor. I haven't punched anyone in years." *Or ever. Wanted to but didn't. Does that count?*

They walked out. A line had formed at the front of the restaurant. Patrons stood against the windows, filled the benches, crowded around the host's desk. Jeff's eyes widened, then narrowed. Ryan Woolfort sat on one of the benches. The man smiled at Jeff, nodded to him. Saluted him. Jeff turned away. *I don't need him on top of everything else. I don't.*

He drove back to the office in silence. Only after he could shut his door and hit his knees in private did he speak. "Okay, God, I don't get it. This is wrong. Collin is faithful to you in everything she does. For someone to hint she would abuse our children—or anyone's children—is absurd. It's wrong on so many levels. What do You want me to do with this? How do I face her? Do I tell her? Do I wait and make the Elders tell her?"

He sat back on his haunches and waited. And waited. And waited. *When He suffered, He didn't fight back. Instead, He threw Himself on the mercy of the Only One Who can judge correctly.*

"Is that Your answer? We allow ourselves to be slandered? I'm going down with her, Lord. We're in this together."

Consider all Jesus did, so you don't get discouraged.

Jeff let out a small breath. In a long mental sigh. "I hear You. Your will, Your way. No matter what. Thank You, Lord."

TUESDAY AFTERNOON

Braydon called off Tuesday morning. A family emergency. Child with a raging fever. "Don't want to expose your kids, too. Don't know what bug I might carry. Better safe."

Which Collin heartily agreed with. Cameras seemed far lower on the priority list than multiple children sick. Caution demanded patience.

Three in the afternoon. The babies were up from their naps, Collin had dinner planned out, and everything timed for perfect delivery at the right time. Maybe they could sit at the table with all the food courses being served at the same time? Maybe.

A knock sounded at the front door. *Okay, maybe not.* Collin glanced out the side window. A man and woman in professional attire stood on the porch. The man held a briefcase. The woman had a clipboard with a sheaf of papers. Her face seemed familiar, but Collin didn't wait to recognize her before answering the door.

"Can I help you?"

IDs and badges came out. The woman spoke for both of them. "I'm Agent Tresalyn, and this is Agent Gege. We're with Child Protective Services, and we'd like to ask you some questions."

A check quieted Collin's soul. "Questions regarding...?"

"Regarding a complaint we received. It's nothing. A few questions we need help with."

Collin drew in a deep breath. *Lord? What is this? What do You want me to do?*

Speak Truth. The Truth will make you free. Speak it. All of it.

Do I call for a lawyer first?

Speak Truth. Only Truth.

Collin waved the two agents in the door. "Why don't you

36

come into the kitchen and have a seat? We can talk there."

She led the two through the living room into the kitchen area and offered them seats at the coffee bar. She smiled. "Give me a moment. I need to check on the children."

Giggles and singing came from the playroom. Collin stuck her head in the door. "Okay, you three. Mommy has visitors. You can come meet them in a bit, but Mommy needs to talk to them first. Okay? I'll tell you when you can come meet them."

Three voices called, "Yes, Mommy," as three heads bobbed in agreement. Collin smiled. "Thank you, bubbies. I won't be long."

Collin returned to the kitchen. She offered beverages, poured water for herself, and sat opposite the two. "How can I help you?"

Agent Tresalyn cocked her head slightly to the side. "I think I know you."

Collin nodded. "I think I know you, too. How long have you been in CPS?"

"Ten years."

Collin grinned. "I do know you. Collin Walker, social worker. We used to process cases together when our clients overlapped."

Agent Tresalyn smiled wide. "I thought so. I didn't recognize the name Farrell."

"Married. Six years, now."

Agent Gege frowned. "This could be a problem. There might be a conflict…"

Collin interrupted him. "There won't be. I remember Sierra as a woman of high professionalism. If anyone can keep her personal life out of her work, it's her." *She? Go with it.*

Sierra returned the compliment. "You kept your feelings out of the way of getting the job done." She smiled. "And when you couldn't, you stepped away from it. I remember Rob."

Collin nodded. "When I got too involved, I moved him to another counselor." She laughed. "And then we adopted him. He'll graduate with his master's in Urban Planning in the fall. I couldn't be more proud of him."

Agent Gege cleared his throat. "Maybe we can get to the questions about the case?"

Collin's eyes crinkled. She went to say something… *Don't. Just don't.* Collin took the hint. "What can I help you with?"

Sierra's smile dimmed. "We received an anonymous report

about excessive bruising on your children's arms."

Collin went internal. Her voice remained calm. Remarkable, considering she shook inside. "My children? When was this report filed? And where did this person see my children?"

Sierra continued to direct the investigation. "We can't give you those details. May we see the children?"

Collin kept her cool. "Legally, I don't have to allow it. I'm assuming you don't have a warrant." She raised her eyebrows. "And you are hoping you don't have to get one. Which is why you came out today." She ducked her head towards Sierra.

Sierra nodded. "Correct. You don't have to let us see the children. We can come back with a warrant…"

Agent Gege cut her off. "…but it will look better if we don't have to. Your cooperation…"

Collin cut him off. "…doesn't make any difference in the results of the investigation. Whether I cooperate or not, you will base your report on the physical evidence as you see it." *I know the law. I know the system. Don't try to bull me.* She laid both hands on the table. "However, because this complaint is a total fabrication and a vicious lie, I will happily let you meet the children. And see the bruises for yourself."

Sierra drummed her fingers on the bar top. "Do we have your permission to ask the children questions?"

Collin nodded. Curtly. "You have my permission to ask questions." She chuckled. "Whether you can decipher the answers is another question." She shook her head. "I'll get them." She eyed Sierra. "And you can accompany me, so I don't threaten or coerce or otherwise cause them to give a false answer."

Sierra's eyes softened. "I know you won't."

"But we need to keep it legal. So no one can question whether we did this by the book." She nailed Agent Gege. "And you have permission to examine the family room, living room, children's playroom, spare bedrooms, and the nursery to determine if the living conditions are safe and healthy. The main bedroom and the office are off-limits. The children do not play there and do not go in unaccompanied."

Agent Gege's eyes narrowed, but he nodded. "Thank you." He got up to start his "look-see" while Collin and Sierra walked down the hall.

The voices from the playroom were happy, laughing, playful. *Score one for our side.* Sierra motioned to the room. "How old are the children?"

"You don't have the information?"

"Collin, honestly, this is a preliminary examination. We have one person who called in a situation. The bruises they described were consistent with a pattern of abuse. So the person said. We had nothing else to go on, so we decided to come out and see the children before we did anything else."

Collin nodded. "It's what I would have done. See it for myself before I did anything."

They stepped around the corner into the brightly painted room. The triplets were building towers with soft "age-appropriate" blocks. Caleb looked up from his labors and saw Collin. He chortled. "Mommy! We build tower!"

Collin hugged him. "You sure do build a tower. A very nice tower."

Caleb nodded. Big nod. Definitive nod. "We build tower. Yion roar, knock tower down."

"A lion roars and knocks the tower down?"

Again, the definitive nod. "Right. You see."

The three-sided tower wobbled. Joshua pointed to Talitha. "You be yion."

Talitha formed her hands into claws, snarled, let out a roar, then leveled the tower. Blocks flew everywhere. She stomped through the wreckage, roaring and growling. And her brothers laughed and giggled and wiggled until the tower disappeared. Then the three toddlers gathered the blocks together and started building once again.

Sierra laughed. "I like this game. They play well together."

Collin snorted. "Most of the time. They're not angels. But they are pretty good about playing without fighting." She called. "Okay, enough with the blocks for a moment. Come meet Ms. Sierra. She and Mommy used to work in the same building. She's a friend."

The babies surrounded Collin and Sierra. Sudden shyness filled the little faces. Sierra smiled big. "Hello! It's wonderful to meet you. What's your name?"

She looked to Caleb. He eyed his mother first. Collin nodded to him. He crossed his arms over his chest. "I Cayeb."

Sierra side-eyed Collin. Collin mouthed, "Caleb."

Sierra laughed. "It's good to meet you, Caleb." She turned to Joshua. "And your name is?"

Joshua didn't look for his mother's approval but stepped forward. "I Joa-u-a."

"Nice to meet you, Joshua. " She shook hands with him. "I liked your tower."

Joshua and Caleb jumped and danced with joy. "We make biiiiig tower! We make big tower!"

Collin held up her hands. "Ms. Sierra will watch you build your tower in a moment." She pointed to the littlest triplet. "Talitha hasn't been introduced yet."

Talitha stared into Sierra's eyes. The little face was solemn, and she whispered, "Ta-yith-a. Tayitha. I yittle one."

Collin hugged her. "Yes, you are Mommy's littlest one." She released the girl and turned to Sierra. "Where did the complainant say the bruising occurred?"

"On the outside of their arms. Between the elbow and the shoulder."

Collin pulled up Talitha's sleeve. A faint trace of a bruise crossed the little girl's arm.

Sierra's eyes widened, then narrowed. She stared at the mark. Sierra smiled gently at Talitha. "You have a boo-boo. What happened?"

Not to be left out, Caleb and Joshua pulled up their sleeves as well. Both announced, "We hab boo-boo, too! We aw hab boo-boo."

Sierra sat on the floor to be at eye level with the littles. "Can you tell me how you got the boo-boos?"

Caleb started to speak, but Joshua jumped in first. "Yion bite me! Big yion! It jump an' bite bite bite!" He pretended to bite his brother's arm.

Sierra laughed. "Bad lion! Did it hurt?"

Joshua shook his head in exaggerated toddler fashion. "No. I big boy. Not hurt." He smiled. "Mommy chase yion away."

"I see." Sierra pointed to Caleb. "How did you get your boo-boo?"

Caleb's face fell. He stuck out his lower lip and admitted, "I not know."

Sierra tousled the boy's hair. "It's okay, Caleb. I don't know how I get bruises, either. Sometimes they happen."

Caleb nodded once. He sat on the floor beside Sierra. The woman looked at Talitha. "Do you know how you got your boo-boo?"

Talitha nodded, walked over, and whispered in Sierra's ear. Sierra's face grew solemn. Talitha finished, crossed over to her mother, and sat in Collin's lap. The littlest Farrell put her arms around Collin's neck and kissed her.

Sierra kept her voice soft. "She said Mommy got scared someone wanted to steal the babies. Mommy hugged the babies so they would be safe. That's how she got the bruise. She wanted me to know she loves her mommy."

Collin felt the sting of tears. She closed her eyes. Her voice strangled. "I had a flashback to when..." She stopped, breathed deep, then held Sierra's eyes. "...when another baby, much littler than Talitha, was taken from me. I got very sad about the tiny baby being gone. But the people who took the baby brought her back, and she has grown up and is happy and safe, and no one will ever take her away again."

Collin held Sierra's eyes. And held them. And held them. Until Sierra nodded slowly. The CPS Agent closed her eyes. "That was you? Your family?" Barely above a whisper.

Collin nodded. Barely a whisper. "Yes."

"Flashback?"

"Yes."

"First one?"

"First in two years. Since I finished therapy." Collin smiled at her babies. "Why don't you three show me how you build the tower?"

The three scrambled to their feet, and all began scrabbling after blocks. Collin shrugged. "We had a break-in while the babies and I were in the house. When I realized it, I freaked. I grabbed the babies and held them. Jeff brought me out of it, the babies forgave me, and it was over." She shook her head. "I didn't even see the bruises until Saturday. We didn't go anywhere until Sunday, and then only to church. I don't understand who would have filed a complaint. I told the volunteer what happened. The bruises are barely visible."

Sierra nodded, and her face scrunched into a deep frown. "What they showed me is the right spot. But those marks are nothing like what I saw in the report. The complaint said they were angry, red, yellow, with multiple bruises up and down the entire arm." She tossed her head. "I'm sorry, Collin. There is nothing to go on. Nothing. My report will state these were false charges, with no basis in fact, and we'll end it there."

Collin dropped her gaze to the floor. "Except it won't be. The fact CPS came to the house says something happened... I'm guilty simply for being investigated. You know how it goes."

Sierra sighed. "I'm so sorry, Collin. What can I do?"

Collin looked up. "Say I'm exonerated. Saying you found nothing means you didn't find the proof you needed...not that abuse didn't happen, but you couldn't find the smoking gun to convict. People will read into it. But if you say I've been exonerated, it will mean nothing happened to begin with."

Sierra nodded. "You got it, girlfriend. I hope it makes a difference."

"It's my best hope, anyhow." *Besides You upholding my honor. But if You don't, nothing else will.* "Thanks, Sierra."

Both women stood. Agent Gege walked into the playroom and raised an eyebrow at Sierra. She shook her head. "Nothing. Totally bogus claim. The descriptions of the marks are nothing like what the children have. And they barely have a mark as it is. There's nothing here to investigate."

Agent Gege shrugged. "The house is as baby-proof as I've ever seen. Nothing here to endanger a child or speak of neglect of any kind. If you're satisfied, we'll close it." He extended his hand to Collin. "No hard feelings, ma'am? We are only trying to protect..."

"...the children. I understand. I know what your job is like, Agent, and I appreciate you do it and do it well. Thank you for being professional and unbiased."

Collin shook the man's hand. She hugged Sierra. "Thank you. And it is good to see you again. Now that you know where I live, stop in sometime. I'm usually home." She gestured towards the playroom. "It's less complicated here than out."

Sierra laughed. "I'll bet. Take care, Collin." The two CPS

agents gathered their paraphernalia and exited.

Collin leaned against the door to catch her sanity. She closed her eyes but spoke aloud. "Thank You, Lord, for sending someone who knew me. For sending professionals who didn't come with an agenda. And thank You for my children being safe from me." Collin paused. Paused. Paused. "I forgive whoever made the call, Lord. If they made it out of a good heart but a less-than-all-seeing eye, I understand. It happens."

Her voice hardened. "But if this was malice..." She breathed hard. "...I still forgive. Because You forgave me. Show me what I need to learn from this. Guard my children. Guard my husband. And Lord, above all, Your will be done. I love You."

Collin pushed off the door and headed to the kitchen to see what short-order menu she could arrange. Movement outside caught her eye. Someone moved beside a car. She didn't remember seeing anyone walking on the street... Were they standing outside their car? Waiting to get in? Waiting on what?

Collin tried to get a good look at the driver. She couldn't see his face clearly, but something struck her as familiar. As if she'd seen him before. *Where?*

The suit. The man at church. He had the same suit. Is this the same man?

Collin stared. The man leaned against his car, nonchalant and calm. He pushed off the fender, raised his hand, and saluted toward the house. Then he climbed in his car and drove off.

A chill ran up Collin's spine. Who could he be? More important, what did he want? Collin shuddered. Then snapped the rubber band on her wrist. Just because. She opened the refrigerator. *Dinner. Fast and easy. Like usual.* She sighed.

* * *

Collin determined she would wait until Jeff arrived home, unwound, played with the triplets, and sat down for dinner before telling him about her visit with CPS. No hitting him straight in the door. Bad form. Be patient.

As they ate, she asked, "How was your day?"

Jeff swallowed a mouthful of food. "Tough. I had lunch with Pastor Thomas. There's a situation at church with the nursery."

Collin nodded. "Yeah. CPS visited me this afternoon."

Jeff's eyes flared. "So soon? Collin, I'm sorry. I didn't want to tell you…"

She finished it for him. "…on the phone. And I appreciate it. I'd have done the same. No, it turned out fine. I knew one of the investigators. They saw the babies, saw the bruises, and determined the complaint was totally bogus. Malicious, almost." *Okay, I added the last part. It feels like it.*

Jeff looked at his plate. "There's more, though. Someone broke confidentiality. The word went out you were accused of abusing the trio. And CPS is investigating."

Collin went still inside. Outside, too. She took a moment to gather herself. "Okay. That hurts, but it shouldn't be unexpected."

Jeff thumped the table with his fist. "It should be very unexpected. We're a body of believers. A family. We're supposed to be better than that. We're supposed to fight for each other, not against each other."

Collin could hear the vehemence in Jeff's tone. So he's been battling this all afternoon. Father, we both need to put this in Your hands. Leave it in mine, and I'll find someone to tear apart. Take it from me. Please.

She lay her hand on top of his. "Agreed. Except we're a family of humans who fail. I won't add to the fray. I will commit myself to God and let Him deal with it."

Jeff lowered his head. "I'm trying. But every time I think about it, I get madder and madder. I want to find the culprit and string them up."

Collin chuckled. "I know the feeling. We have to be better."

A knock interrupted the peace. Collin started to rise; Jeff waved her off. "I'll get it."

She listened carefully to the exchange at the front door. She couldn't make out words, but tones conveyed the theme equally. And she didn't like the vibe she got.

Jeff walked into the dining area accompanied by two men Collin vaguely recognized. He introduced them. "Collin, this is Greg, this is Samuel. They're Elders from the church."

Collin nodded. "Sirs."

Jeff continued. "I told them we were finishing dinner."

Greg smiled. "And I told Jeff we would wait."

Collin swallowed a smirk. "Thank you. The children will be finished shortly, and then we can talk." Jeff led the men to the living room. *Not the family room? Okay, this is serious stuff.* She turned her attention to getting the babies to finish the food on their plates. It took half an hour before they had cleaned their plates, carried them to the counter, washed faces and hands, and were brought into the living room to sit and quietly read books. *Yes, we include them in everything. At this age, it's easier.*

Once the triplets were settled, Collin offered the men beverages. Both turned them down. Greg took the lead. "We really won't be long. I'm sure your husband has told you about his discussion with Pastor Thomas regarding the incident at the nursery."

Collin nodded. "He told me there had been a breach in confidentiality if that's what you are referring to. And my name is being associated with child abuse. It will ease your minds to know CPS came out today and exonerated me of any wrongdoing. There is no abuse. Their report will state as much."

Greg dipped his head. "Which is great news, of course. But at the church, we have to deal with people's perceptions as well as the truth. You can understand."

Collin's gut tightened. "What perception? I abused my children when I didn't?"

The elder shifted slightly in his chair. *Uncomfortable in your duty here tonight? Didn't expect CPS to clear me so soon?* He held out his hands. "Rumors fly faster than truth. It will look bad if someone the congregation—or part of them, anyhow—believes has been accused of child abuse is working with children. You can understand how that would seem."

Collin weighed her words carefully. "I can understand how it would seem if someone has been falsely accused, but since church leadership knows she has been exonerated, they would stand behind her and say, 'We won't compromise our values for public opinion.' I know how that would look."

Samuel nodded to Collin. "Of course, we intend that to happen. But for this weekend, and until we can figure out how to get a message to the whole congregation, we'd like you to step down as a volunteer."

Jeff leaned forward. "The simplest way would be from the

pulpit this Sunday. A statement Collin had been accused, the charges were false, CPS exonerated her, and the church stands with and behind her. That will reach the congregation."

Greg held his hands out again. "It might. But we can't count on reaching everyone we need to reach. Even if we did, it wouldn't help us deal with any possible situations should this happen again. We're only asking you to step down until we can get a policy in place."

Collin's insides burned. She kept a lid on the fire. "I know how long it takes to get a policy in place, Brother Greg. You're asking me to step down for several months. Which will give fuel to the lie I'm guilty, and you know that, which is why I've been banned from volunteering."

Greg shrugged. "I'm sorry. But you need to understand how it looks."

Jeff's voice carried some heat. "It looks like leadership is ready to throw Collin under the bus rather than address the breach of confidentiality and the outright lies. Has anything been done about finding the person?"

Samuel shook his head. "We have no way of knowing who it might have been."

Jeff pushed. "Except you could find out who worked in the office and who talked about it. Shouldn't be hard to figure out."

Greg shrugged again. "Finding out won't change the perceptions people have. We want the church to be an inviting place. One where people can come meet the Lord and feel their children are in a safe environment. Having this pall over the children's ministry won't accomplish our goals."

Collin eyed both Elders. "Again, you're talking about people perceiving I'm guilty when you know I'm not. And rather than address the rumors, you tell me to step aside and let them believe you've 'handled' the problem." Collin bit her lip, her tongue, her anger. She lifted her head. "Tell me, is the whole leadership team in one accord with this action?"

Samuel cleared his throat. "Greg and I discussed it, and we wanted to get ahead of the rumors. The full leadership team won't meet until Thursday. A lot of damage can be done before then. Since Greg and I are responsible for Children's Ministries, we felt this would be the best way to put a stop to the rumors."

Greg interrupted him. "We wouldn't reveal who voted for what if the whole leadership had met. Regardless of how split we might be, once a decision is reached, it's final."

Collin nodded. "I see. Brother Greg, Brother Samuel, I will step back because you ask me to." So much she wanted to say choked her. *And it's probably better.* Tears burned in her eyes. "Our Lord was betrayed by those closest to Him. And He chose to forgive." She looked at the two men. "I hope I can be like Him. Someday."

Greg stood. "We're very sorry this has happened. And believe me, we will do everything in our power to get a policy in place so you can return to volunteering."

Jeff's face wore a mask of control. He stood. "But why would she want to?" He caught Samuel's eye. "You should get a replacement for me as well. If Collin can't serve, I won't, either. I will show solidarity with my wife if no one else will."

Samuel cringed. "Jeff, that's not necessary. It isn't. This will all blow over. We need teachers like you in our youth department."

Jeff led the men to the door. Samuel made one last plea. "Pray about it, Jeff. The church needs your leadership. You have a tremendous impact on the junior high students. If you step down, there won't be anyone to replace you."

Jeff lifted his chin. "My first responsibility is to the Lord. He declared my second responsibility is to my wife. You've told her she can't serve. I can't then, either. Good night, gentlemen."

He closed the door without actually slamming it in their faces. Which showed exceptional restraint on his part. Collin took his hand and kissed him. "Thank you. You don't have to quit teaching."

"I do. I absolutely do. This is all bogus." He hugged her, and Collin felt the depth of his hurt in his embrace. He murmured, "I think we deserve medals for not saying what we wanted to say."

Collin chuckled. "Yeah. The angel on my tongue got a workout."

"Mine, too." He kissed her again. "Let's get the babies to bed. I can use a good bedtime story."

Collin nodded. "Agreed. Okay, babies. Time to get ready for bed."

THURSDAY

"Wob!" "Wob!" "Mommy, Wob here!"

Collin reached for Rob as he came in the door. She got her one hug before the babies bull-rushed the young man in the doorway. Over the excited chatter of little voices, Collin asked, "How are the classes going?"

Her son shrugged. "Eh. I'm still working on the thesis. It's slow, but it's getting there."

"I know you. You'll get it done." She pointed to the hall. "Babies to the playroom. Rob will be in to play with you in a few minutes."

Little feet pounded down the hall. Collin handed Rob a cup of coffee and a muffin. She nailed him with a firm look. "Do not let them eat your muffin. I don't care how cute they look. They've had theirs already."

Rob feigned innocence. "Me? Give them my muffin? Are you kidding?"

"Uh-huh." She smiled. "You've got the usual suspects today. Macie, Oscar, and our three. We are getting a new woman today, but she's not bringing her child until she 'tries us out.'"

Rob nodded. "I can handle the crowd. So long as the crackers hold out."

"I restocked this weekend. I think you'll be fine."

Rob sipped his coffee. "What's going on, Mom? I see a look in your eyes I don't like."

Collin snorted and shook her head. "Nothing. Everything. Someone broke in while I was home and left an envelope with a threatening message. I had a flashback, someone reported me to CPS for abuse."

Rob's eyes darkened. Collin continued. "CPS came and exonerated me, but the church is concerned about how it might look if an 'accused abuser' were working in the Children's Ministry, so they told me to step back from volunteering until they figure out a new policy to deal with the possibility of someone actually being guilty..."

She ran out of steam from the run-on emotions. She waved her hands wide. "Other than that, nothing."

Rob wrapped his arm around Collin. "I got you, Mom. No one is going to hurt my family. Not with God watching."

Collin nodded. "I know, bro. I know. It's what I hang on to." *The only thing keeping me sane.*

Which ain't saying much.

Oh, shut up.

Collin pulled out of the fight in her head. "You know how much I appreciate you sitting in with the babies while I have the mother's group here."

Rob shrugged. "I get to raid the fridge after. I think I'm getting the best part of the deal."

Collin heard voices in the front hall. "There's our cue."

Rob set his muffin down. "I'll say hi to the moms, then guard the playroom."

Collin and Rob walked to the front entryway. Tia carried in Samuel. All three months and fourteen pounds of him were having a meltdown. Kells followed directly behind with her Allison, also three months old but tipping the scales at sixteen pounds. A chunky monkey, to be sure. Collin grabbed the diaper bags. Kells kissed Rob on the cheek. "Good to see you, Rob. Missed you last week."

Rob grinned. "Prof. sprang a test on us. Not good to miss the tests."

"Got that right."

Rob chucked Allison under her chins. "Hey, little one. How you been?" Allison waved her hands and cooed. Rob laughed. "I'll take that as a 'fine.' You want me to carry her to the living room?"

"I got her. Thanks, Rob."

Tia breezed past Rob and Kells to get Samuel into the living room and out of his carrier. He settled down as soon as she put him on her shoulder and began bouncing him. She called, "Hi, Rob."

The door opened again. Brianna stepped in, holding toddler Oscar by the hand. The little boy dove into Rob's legs and shook them as hard as his solid frame could manage. Rob bent down and picked up the youngster. "Hey there, little man. How you doing, bud?"

Oscar head-butted Rob, but gently. Rob returned the gesture. Brianna gave Rob a wane smile. "We got a new word. Don't know what it means yet, but he keeps repeating it. Maybe he'll say it for you."

Collin sensed the hurt in Brianna's words. Only a few months younger than the triplets, Oscar didn't talk. A sound here and there, but no real words and no sentences. Reassurances "all babies develop at their own rate" wouldn't make the nagging fear disappear. Collin ached for her friend. She ached more for Oscar.

Grace had parked up the cul-de-sac and made her way carrying ten-month-old Archie. Julie fought with the car seat before freeing her six-month-old daughter, Ayisha, threw her over her shoulder, and headed for the house.

Collin kissed the familiars. No need to direct them to the coffee. They knew the way. Diaper bags and satchels were dropped by the couch. Collin saw Winona and her daughter, two-year-old Macie, coming up the walk. They were accompanied by a woman Collin didn't know. *Must be the new girl. Eliza. Hope she's ready.* Collin hugged Winona quickly and extended her hand to the stranger. "Welcome. You must be Eliza?"

Winona nodded. "Right. Eliza, this is Collin Farrell. It's her house. And this is her son, Rob. He watches the kids while we meet."

Rob stepped forward and held out his hand. "Welcome. Nice to meet you."

Collin saw Eliza's eyes dart from Collin to Rob. *Ah, yes. The cultural difference. Rob takes after his African-American roots, and I am uncolored with my Saxon DNA. She'll get over it.*

Eliza took a moment, then shook Rob's hand. "Thank you."

Collin waved the threesome in. "Coffee is this way. Tea if you don't drink coffee, or juice if you prefer. Water is available at a small price."

Again, Eliza's eyes flared.

Not catching the humor, hmm? Okay, I'll tone it down.

Sure you will.

Oh, shut up.

Macie and Oscar left with Rob for the playroom. Collin turned to Eliza. "Would you like to see the playroom for the children?"

Eliza nodded. "Yes, yes, I would." Her tone registered a great deal of uncertainty. Collin motioned for her to follow down the hall to the brightest, most colorful room in the house. Collin and Jeff had spent hours making it as kid-friendly but adult-approved as possible. The top half of the Dutch door had been removed. No pinched fingers or banged heads, thank you. The walls were painted with flora and fauna of the most colorful and imaginative kind. The ceiling had a sunrise (or set, depending on your orientation) while the remainder sported increasing darkness, stars, and planets. Granted, they weren't astronomically correct, but hey...they were stars.

Three play stations graced the room: a kitchen, a workshop, and a dollhouse. All parts interchangeable, of course. And usually were. A low sink sat near the back wall, outside the bathroom. It made craft cleanup much simpler.

Collin watched Eliza's eyes for a reaction. Again, the woman's eyes flared, then narrowed, then returned to normal before she smiled at Collin. "Very nice. I'm sure you spared no expense with this room."

Sing it. 'Let it go. Let it go.' And do it. "Thank you. We tried. With triplets, they needed a place to run around. I can usually keep the majority of the chaos in this room." *Usually.* They walked back to join the group in the living room.

After everyone had a beverage of choice and had found a comfortable place to sit (Collin took a place on the floor, propped against the couch), Winona introduced Eliza to the group. "This is Eliza Majors. She is new in my neighborhood, and after we met and started talking, I told her about this mother's group. She expressed an interest in coming, so I invited her." She smiled at the woman. "And she came!"

Kells took over the meeting. "We're glad to have you, Eliza. We're a group of mothers trying to support each other through early childhood development."

Trying to survive childhood development, you mean.

Best behavior, right?

You're no fun.

Collin silenced the internal jaybirds. Kells continued, "Collin offered for us to meet here, and we're grateful for the space."

Collin shook her head. "I'm grateful not to have to pack up three toddlers. You're doing me the favor, believe me."

Kells laughed. Collin noted Eliza didn't. *Sigh.* Kells finished giving the pertinent details about the group's formation, how it ran, the snack schedule, and anything else she thought might be needed. She then looked around at the regulars. "Introduce yourself, your child, and anything else you want Eliza to know. Remember, we're trying to get her to want to come back."

Collin noted the others smiling and Eliza not. *Is she always this pleasant? Is it us? Me? This place? I hope she can relax. A little anyhow.*

Tia had Samuel wave hello, told about him being a surprise baby, ten years behind the next oldest sibling. Going from working mom back to child-in-diapers mom had been a shock. And not a welcome one at first. Thus her attendance in the group.

Brianna shared about Oscar. She and her husband foster-to-adopted the boy from when he was three days old. The developmental delay in his speech, some of his mannerisms... None of which they had expected. Now she needed support to cope with all the internal (and sometimes external) accusations of "what did I/we/you do wrong" that followed his not talking. Which she found in the other mothers of late talkers, late walkers, late bloomers...

Julie had three in school: two in elementary and one in preschool. Then came Ayisha. "I love this group because I get to have adult conversations with adult people."

Nods and smiles and "You got that right, girl" comments.

Grace introduced Archie. "He's an only child. Both his father and I are only children as well. I need this group to help me know what's normal and what isn't."

Do not speak. Do not.

Plplplplllllllllll...

Collin motioned to the back. "You saw the triplets. They're why I needed a mother's support group. Everything gets multiplied. I need the sanity this group brings me."

Leave it.

Eliza started to speak, then stopped. She glanced at Collin, then the floor, and finally back to Collin. She didn't bother to hide the bitterness. "You've got this gorgeous home. It's obvious you have money. You could hire three nannies. What do you know about how hard having a kid is?"

There it is. Collin didn't rise to the insult nor explain about family finances. "These are my sons and my daughter. God gave them to me to raise." *Rear.*

Raise. Shut up.

Fine.

"I won't pass my responsibility off to anyone else. I let Grandma and Grandpa babysit, of course. Their brother Rob watches them on the rare occasion when he's not studying for class. I had help in the beginning. My husband and my brother were here. But my brother got married, and my husband went back to work. Now I'm like all the rest of the group, trying to make it through one day at a time. Maybe I could hire a nanny. But these are my children, and God made them my responsibility." She smiled at Eliza. "I need this group as much as anyone else. Maybe three times as much."

Eliza stared at Collin, holding her eyes for several seconds. Collin maintained an even gaze. Not challenging. Not apologizing. Even. Period.

Finally, Eliza nodded. Very slightly. Collin felt, more than heard, the collective sigh of the rest of the mothers. Crisis averted. *Whew!*

Kells waved a hand at Eliza. "Would you like to tell us about your interest in the group? Or anything you think we should know?"

Eliza shrugged. "We have two children. Farley is two and a half, and the Meridian is six months. My partner and I are trying to share the parenting, but she has a higher-paying job than I do, so she is working more hours, and I'm working from home." Her eyes cast to the ground, and her voice became soft. "When I can. Having two toddlers so close together is harder than we thought it would be."

Collin noted the narrowing of Kells's eyes. Collin reached out and touched Eliza's arm. "Having two far apart is no picnic, either. One all alone is brutal. Two so close together is worse." *And three the same age makes you lose your sanity.*

This is not a competition of who has it worse. Stuff it.

Kells moved the meeting forward. "We're going to discuss our 'roses and thorns.' Everyone shares one good thing which happened this week and one bad thing. Once shared, the group will discuss what we've found to help with the thorns. And celebrate the roses. Who would like to go first?"

Tia settled Samuel back in his carrier. "I'll go. My rose is Samuel slept through the night two nights in a row."

Quiet cheers and high fives. Kells spoke for the group. "Fantastic." She chuckled. "But how many times did you get up to check on him to see if he was still breathing?"

Tia shook her head. "Once. Maybe twice. He slept so well. I couldn't believe it."

Kells continued to lead. "And the thorn?"

Tia sighed. Deep, deep sigh. "The thorn is the other nights he didn't sleep at all. He cried. And he cried. And he cried." Tears crinkled the corner of her eyes. "Then I cried."

Kells reached over and hugged the woman. "Oh, honey. We feel your pain."

Collin asked, "Did he finally cry himself to sleep? Or what did you do?"

Tia's shoulders slumped. "I laid him on his side in the recliner with the vibrator on full blast. He went to sleep in about five minutes." Her eyes narrowed. "And I know all about not laying them on their sides. It worked, and that's what mattered."

Collin smiled slightly. "Judgment free zone, Tia. When a baby has colic—or whatever the problem is—anything is fair game."

Winona raised her hand. "Did you move him to his crib after he fell asleep?"

"Move him? Are you crazy? I slept on the floor beside the recliner, so if he managed to scootch off, he'd land on me. Not that he's turning over."

Collin let the group hash out other "baby-calming" and "colic" remedies.

Julie raised her hand. "My rose? Ayisha sat up by herself." General cheers and applause. "Of course, I wasn't there to see it, as I had to be in the back of the house breaking up World War Three between the two older ones, but Paulie told me. He promised me he didn't help her, which I'm still not one hundred percent sure of, but hey, I'll take every milestone I can get."

Kells turned to Grace. "Any updates?"

"Archie is the master of the commando crawl. Which means he's crawled under the bed, under the couch, under the table…" Grace held her hands up in entreaty. "How do you keep track of them? I set him down for one moment, and he's gone."

Tia shrugged. "Bells on his romper."

Grace's eyes widened. Collin nodded. "Hey, don't knock it. Worked for me, too."

Grace laughed. "I'm not going to criticize. I think it's brilliant. We'll stop on the way home and get some."

Kells chuckled. "Ask Collin. I bet she's still got some around here."

"That I'm not using? Are you kidding me? What do you think are on their tennis shoes?"

The joke went over well, but Collin's gut twisted. Not wringer-washer tight. "Hand-washed sweater" tight, maybe. *Do I tell or not? I don't want to scare the group by telling them someone is breaking in while I'm home.*

Or maybe you don't want to admit Collin, the Warrior Princess, had a lapse and freaked out on her own.

Father?

Speak truth.

She waited until the chatter died, and Kells asked, "Who's next?"

"I'll go if no one else has anything pressing they want to share."

Kells looked around at the circle. "Anyone?" No one volunteered. "Floor is yours, Collin."

Eliza quipped, "So is the couch. And the chairs."

Collin laughed. It felt good. She pointed at Eliza. "I like you."

Eliza smiled. "Well, you know…"

"Right." Collin swallowed. *Breathe. Breathe. In. Out. In. Out.* "Uh…my thorn is…I had a flashback freak-out moment with the babies." She closed her eyes. *Breathe. Calm. Relax. You can do this.* "Um…someone got into the house while I was home with the children. I don't know who, I don't know how. But they left a note on the laundry basket. When I realized what it meant…someone had been in the house…I, uh…" *Swallow. Breathe. In. Out.* "I flashed back to...and I…"

Collin brushed the salty water off her face. "I ran to the playroom, gathered the babies in my arms, and held them tight. No one would take them from me again."

She bit the inside of her cheeks. "Except I held them too tight, and I scared them." Tears dripped on her shirt. "Jeff talked me off the edge, and I let them go. But I scared them. And they were…were…were afraid of me. My babies." Her voice broke. "My babies were afraid of me."

Collin laid her face in her hands, wiped away the waterfall. "We talked through it. They forgave me, they hugged me, and by now, they don't even remember it." She looked around the group. "But I do."

Silence stilled the room. Then Eliza stood up, crossed to Collin, and hugged her. Followed by Winona. Tia. Bri. Kells remained in her seat.

The women returned to their chairs. Collin passed a box of tissues around the room. She grinned. "Standard operating equipment."

Laughter accompanied the tears. Once everyone had dried up, Kells asked, "Anyone have anything to suggest?"

Eliza raised her hand. "No, but a question. You said you flashed back. To when? Why?"

Collin looked at Kells, questioning. She tossed her head to the side. "Go ahead. We have time."

Again, Collin lowered her eyes. "When the babies were four months old, Talitha was… kidnapped. They held her for two weeks before finally releasing her unharmed. But those two weeks…" *Breathe. Breathe. Past history. God redeemed it. Breathe.*

Tia cocked her head to the side. "I never heard about this."

Collin nodded. "I don't share it. I don't want the babies to be afraid. When they're older, I'll tell them, of course. One of the kidnappers gave his life to save Talitha's. I want her to know about him and what he did. And God can redeem any situation." *I said it, Father. Did I say it right?*

Well done, child.

Bri's eyes hardened like her voice. "Just like that, you forgive it all, and it's gone?"

Collin shook her head. "If it were gone, I wouldn't have had the flashback." She drew her lips into a straight line. "Or flashbacks. Putting the babies to bed, closing their bedroom door, letting them out of my sight…it's still hard. Every day, it's still hard."

Kells raised her eyebrows. "You might think about counseling. Christian counseling, this time. I've suggested it before."

Collin felt her soul bristle but only smiled. "I hear you, Kells."

Kells nodded. "And your rose?"

"The babies forgave me. I didn't hurt them." Anger ripped through her being. She swallowed it. "Even though someone called CPS on me."

Kells's head jerked around. "Someone did what?"

"Called CPS. Whoever did it saw bruises on the babies' arms and called CPS saying the children had been abused. CPS came out, looked for themselves, wrote it up as a false call, closed the case fully exonerating me, and that should be the end of it."

Kells's eyes narrowed. "When did all this happen? You didn't tell me about this."

"Wednesday, and I haven't had time. Things have been spiraling, and I'm doing the best I can to keep them under control. I'm sorry I didn't tell you before now."

Tia nodded. "I have to agree with Kells. Counseling might help."

Collin nodded. "It did. I mean, I know all the right answers. I know all the proper calming techniques. I know how to refocus, how to separate myself from the past, and remember the present." She raised a brow at the room. "Knowing the truth and operating on it are two different skills. I need to keep working on the 'operating' part."

Eliza seemed to study Collin but added nothing to the conversation. Kells asked, "Does anyone have anything else to add? Otherwise, we'll move on to someone else."

Kells called on Brianna. Her rose, Oscar smiling at her. The thorn, his continued silence.

Kells pushed on past Brianna's report to Winona. Winona shrugged. "I guess my rose is meeting up with Eliza and discovering there were other mothers in the neighborhood. Makes it more fun to walk, go to parks, and have someone to hang with, you know?"

Eliza smiled, but Collin thought it a little strained. Maybe she wasn't as excited about meeting Winona. *But she came. She's here. Which makes it a God appointment.*

I'm not going to tell her that. Not at this point. Love her first.

Winona's thorn would be a repeat of the last week. And the week before. And the week before. "I can't get my husband to help me. Leonard never does anything with Macie. He's missing out on all she's doing." Tears filled Nonnie's eyes. "I can't understand it. I can't. What am I doing wrong?"

Collin started to speak, but Kells interrupted. "We've talked about this before. You're not doing anything wrong. It's him, not you. You have to move past those feelings, Winona. You're like Collin. You know what to do. You have to do it."

Collin kept her tone even. "It's never cut and dried, Kells. We don't always know what to do. Each situation is different. There is no one solution."

Kells shrugged a little. "There is if you let the Lord be your guide. Which again, you know."

She looked around the room. "Did I miss anyone? No? Okay, then my turn. The rose is Allison passed her three-month well-baby check with flying colors. She's hitting all her developmental markers, she's in the ninetieth percentile, and she's making proper baby sounds. I couldn't be happier." The woman fairly beamed.

Collin smiled to celebrate the milestone. "Fantastic. I know you were worried for a bit about her weight."

Kells huffed. "That's my thorn. The pediatrician says she's gaining too much weight, and I need to cut back on what I'm feeding her. All his books and measurements on what is 'right.' Every baby develops at their own speed. Allison isn't overweight. I only feed her when she's hungry."

And she's hungry all the time. Poor kid can't make a noise without Kells sticking a bottle in her mouth.

Shush. Judgment-free zone, right?

Tia suggested, "I had the same issue with my second child. After he was six months old, we switched him to water for some of his bottles. It filled him up without giving him the sugar of juice."

Do not say it. Do not say it. Do not...oh, go ahead.

"Have you tried putting her in her crib and letting her cry for half an hour? Stretching her out between feedings?"

Kells glared at Collin. "Did you ever let yours cry it out?"

Collin nodded. "Uh, yeah, we did. We had to bring the crying one into the other room so as not to wake up or upset the other two, but we did stretch out the feedings."

Kells sneered. "From the looks of Caleb, he hasn't missed many meals."

Told you not to say it.

Collin smiled. "Actually, Jacob is my big eater now. They're all healthy, and that's what matters." She lowered her head at Kells. "Which could be your takeaway. She's healthy and growing."

Kells cleared her throat. "I think we're done for today. There is coffee cake and blueberry muffins, courtesy of Winona. Enjoy."

The erstwhile leader got up and walked into the kitchen. As she passed Collin, she whispered, "After group."

Oh, joy. What did I do now?

What didn't you do?

Yeah, well... Sigh...

THURSDAY AFTER GROUP

Collin rose to her feet and smiled at Eliza. "This is our informal, 'we get to chat' time. Get to know each other a little better. Would you like a refill on your coffee?"

Eliza nodded. "Sure. And I have some more questions for you about the group, if you don't mind."

"I never mind. Come on. We can go watch the littles play, and you can ask to your heart's content." Collin grabbed three muffins. "For the littles. They can split them. And Rob gets the whole one."

Eliza and Collin hung outside the door. Collin whistled softly. A moment or two, and Rob came to the door. "Meeting over, Mom?"

"Social time. Brought some muffins for you all. Split them three and two."

Rob grinned. "You mean I get a whole one to myself?"

"Only if you eat faster than they do. You know the drill."

Rob chuckled. "Oh, I do." He took the sweets and moved back to the center of the room. "Everyone who wants a muffin, go wash your hands. Then sit down at the table." Collin watched him kneel beside Oscar. "Hey, buddy. We're going to eat a snack. You want one?"

The diminutive boy gazed up into Rob's face. After a moment, he nodded one long exaggerated nod. Rob smiled. "Great. Follow Talitha and go wash your hands."

Talitha took Oscar's hand and pulled. "'mon, bubby. We wash hans."

Eliza whispered, "She is so sweet. Little mama."

Collin's eyes beamed. "That's my girl."

"How did it not kill you when they took her? I would have

died." Eliza's voice grew sharp. "Of course, you had the Lord, right? He took care of everything. You didn't have to worry about the outcome. Right?"

Collin stepped back and leaned against the wall. "It did kill me. I died inside each day she was gone." She pursed her lips. "Knowing the Lord doesn't keep bad things from happening. It doesn't keep you from feeling pain or hurt or loss." She eyed Eliza dead in the eyes. "Or fear, or panic, or any other emotion anyone else feels. I felt it all. I still feel it all. What I said about having a hard time closing the door and leaving the babies alone? It still haunts me. I still have to force myself to do it. Every night. Every single night."

Eliza hesitated. "Then what good does knowing God do for you? If you experience everything anyone else does, what good is he?"

Collin breathed in, breathed out. "This is a conversation for another time when we're both free to sit and talk. How about coffee on Saturday? Brunch? Lunch?"

Eliza's eyes dropped to the floor, then back to Collin's face. "Okay. I'll see what my schedule is. Maybe I can slip out while my partner watches the kids."

"What's your partner's name, by the way? Or should I not ask?"

Eliza shrugged. "Pam. We've been best friends since grade school."

Collin nodded. "Pam, then. She doesn't work on the weekends?"

"No. She's a pharmaceutical rep." Eliza huffed. "And she's very good at it."

"It can be a lucrative field once you get your territory established."

Eliza cocked her head. "Really? That's your takeaway on it?"

Collin shrugged. "What else should it be?"

Eliza ducked her head. "I don't know. I catch a lot of grief about 'Big Pharma' and how much they are destroying the world."

Collin shook her head. "Not from me. Can't speak for others, but not here." She waved her hands around. "We're part of the 'filthy rich' who steal from the little guy. It's all in how you want to look at it."

You're not filthy rich. You give...
Not now. Leave it.

Collin prompted, "You had questions about the group?"

Eliza nodded. Her eyes darkened. "Does someone have to believe like you do to be part of the group? Or like Kells obviously does?"

"No." Collin chose her words carefully. "My beliefs are my own. If you want to ask me about them, I'll talk all day. But in this group, there is no one prescribed belief. You can have no belief and still come. Because babies and small children don't care what you believe. They want what they want when they want it. And it's our job as parents to figure out what is best for them. Which is a universal constant across all religious lines." Collin smiled. "A crying baby doesn't care who God is."

Eliza's eyes smiled. She crinkled her nose. "Amen."

Collin laughed. "Okay. Any other questions?"

"No, I think Kells covered most of it." She hesitated. "Is she always the leader?"

Collin smiled. "No. We pass the duty around. We keep the same format, but we trade off facilitating. If someone wants to. No one has to take the reins. We're an all-volunteer army, as it were."

"I like that better."

"We thought it was a good idea." They walked up to the kitchen where Kells stood talking to Tia, Winona and Bri were deep in discussion, and Grace and Julie were refilling their coffee cups. Brianna looked up, smiled at Eliza, and switched partners to talk to the "newcomer." Collin and Winona talked about Macie having new children to play with now she knew Eliza. The woman stared at the floor. "Does Kells seem...short-tempered today?"

Collin guessed the reasons behind the question. "A little. You might ask her about it." Collin put an arm around Nonnie. "There aren't any easy answers, you know. You can't make him pay attention to Macie. You're not responsible for what he does or doesn't do. And you can't 'make up' for his absence. Macie will see it eventually, no matter how hard you try to cover it up."

Nonnie looked Collin in the eyes. Collin saw the water welling in the woman's eyes. "I know what you're trying to do. You can't be both Mommy and Daddy. Stay with the role you're in. If Leonard's behavior goes beyond laziness to neglect, let me know. Then it becomes a different story. For now, enjoy your daughter. These are the fun times. Make the most of them."

Winona hugged Collin. "Thanks, Collin. I appreciate you so much."

"I love you, too. Now go get your child and get out of my house. We're cutting into my nap schedule."

Winona laughed. "I hear you." She moved to the back to retrieve Macie. Brianna left Eliza and got Oscar. The woman's face looked damp as she came from the playroom. Oscar gripped his mother's hand tightly. Bri hugged Collin and whispered, "I heard him say 'bye' to Rob. He actually said 'bye.'" She shook her head. "I should leave him here and let you raise him."

Collin raised her hands in defense. "Noooo! Not happening. I got three. I'll take Oscar, but you have to take my boys in exchange."

Bri shrugged. "How hard can they be? They're angels."

Collin choked. "Excuse me? Angels who decided to help me scrub floors by sprinkling scrubbing powder all over the floor...then adding water? Decided they didn't want to get their clothes dirty, so ran outside in their birthday suits to play in the mud? Then ran back inside to tell me they had to go potty, tracking all the mud inside? Those angels? Yeah, no. You're better off with Oscar." Collin smiled. "But you're welcome to come over with him when you want. You know that."

Bri nodded. "Yes, I do. Thanks, Collin. We'll see you next week."

Kells hung back in the kitchen while the other women packed up and left. Only once they were gone did she glance at Collin. "I think we need to talk."

Rob and the babies came out from the playroom. Collin pointed to the fridge. "Can I get you to watch the posse for a little longer? Maybe give them lunch? I promise I'll cook you something to take back to the dorm with you."

Rob laughed. "It's okay, Mom. You don't have to bribe me to hang with my babies. Right, little ones?"

Three heads nodded with enthusiasm. "Wight. Rob hang babies." Caleb cocked his head. "What hang mean?"

Rob shepherded his brothers and sister to their low table. "It means I get to stay with you for lunch."

Collin pointed to the living room. She and Kells went back in; Collin sat on the floor again. Curling into a ball felt the safest. Right now, she felt in need of a safe place. Thirty-something or not, it still felt protected.

Kells sat across the room from her. She picked a straight-back chair. *One she can lecture from, no doubt.* Collin drew in a slow breath and calmed her being. "What is it, Kells?"

"Two things. First, you need counseling. No more questions about it. No more discussion. You need to go." She dug in her oversized satchel and handed Collin a card. "This is the best Christian counselor I know. Talk to him. He'll get you straightened out." She smiled to take the sting out of her words. It didn't. "You've let this go too long. It's affecting your whole life, and as your friend, it's my job to tell you."

Collin kept her tone even. "How has this affected my life? What do you see?"

"It's a lot of little things. But the bottom line is you've lost your faith in the Lord. You don't trust Him anymore."

Collin's gut surged. "Excuse me? I don't trust Him?"

"No, you don't. If you did, by your own admission, you wouldn't have problems putting the babies to bed or leaving them alone. That's a lack of trust, Collin. And lack of trust is lack of faith. When did you have a real quiet time?"

Collin pointed to the kitchen. "We have three children under the age of three. Quiet time is the half-hour between when they go to bed and we go to bed. If you're asking do I still read my Bible and have prayer time, the answer is yes."

Kells wouldn't let it go. "When? When's the last time you sat down to read the Bible?" Her tone became accusing, and Collin questioned the intention.

"Last night. When we put the babies to bed. We always read a Bible story to them."

Kells sniffed. "It doesn't count."

Collin felt her gut tighten. "It's time in the Word, Kells."

"It's a children's Bible story. It's not the same. It doesn't count."

"We'll agree to disagree. What else?"

Kells hesitated. "People don't call CPS over nothing. The bruises must have been bad for someone to think you were abusing your children."

"I explained. CPS came out, did their own investigation, and exonerated us. There was no abuse."

Kells shook her head. "That's not what I heard."

Collin held up her hand. "Would you like to see the report? I have a copy of it in the office."

Kells waved her off. "No. I don't need to see it. I said I heard different. And others are going to believe it. Collin, can you see how you brought this on yourself when you didn't go to counseling like I told you to? If you had, you wouldn't have freaked out and bruised the babies in the first place."

Collin bit her tongue, the sides of her mouth, and anything else she could clamp down to keep from tearing Kells into little bitty pieces parts. "What is this about, Kells? What are you upset with me about?"

"I'm upset you won't go to an approved counselor. I'm upset this group will only attract outsiders from now on. No one from the church will want to come out to a parenting group with someone they think has abused her children. You'll only get people like Eliza."

Here it comes. "What's wrong with Eliza?"

"You heard her. 'My partner.' You know what that means."

"I know what it means. She's sharing parenting with another woman. Maybe they belong to them by birth. Maybe Social Services or some adoption agency believed she and Pam were capable of providing a wonderful home for not one but two children. They were allowed to adopt, and the two of them are doing the best they can for the children."

"Two women together can't raise a child properly. It's not right." Kells leaned forward.

Collin chose her words carefully. Not because she thought she'd offend Kells, either. "The law states they can. God loved Eliza and Pam so much He died for them. Who am I to exclude them from this group? Or from His love? I have no problem with Eliza or Pam coming to group."

"I do." Kells sat back, her eyes guarded. "And you should, too."

"What do you propose, Kells?" *You know what she proposes. Yeah, but I'm going to make her say it out loud. So she can hear herself say it.*

"I don't want her to be part of the group."

Collin drew in a small breath, let it out. "Eliza is welcome in my house, Kells. Just like you or anyone else."

Kells sat back. "You're making this hard, Collin. Harder than it has to be. I'll have the meetings at my house. Your house is bigger, but it's too neutral."

Collin pursed her lips. "You mean I don't have Scripture verses on every wall, crosses over every door, and pictures of Jesus in each room. Right?"

Kells glared at Collin. "I'm not ashamed to call Jesus my Savior."

"Jeff and I aren't either. We agreed to keep the house 'neutral' so visitors would ask us about what we believe based on our lives. Not our décor."

Kells ignored the comment. "I'll have it at my house. Eliza can figure it out on her own she's not welcome."

Collin shook her head. "Have it your way. You can write the email to the moms telling them they will meet at your house from now on and the reason for the change. And I will refer all phone calls to you. Happy?"

Kells snapped. "No, I'm not happy. I don't want to break up the group. I want us to keep meeting like we have been for the past two years."

"Except no outsiders. This wasn't a 'church' group when we started, remember?"

"But we wanted church people. People we had something in common with."

"We have something in common. We're all mothers of small children. That's what we're here for."

"There are exceptions."

"Would you like women to submit an application from now on? So you can vet them for their theological beliefs?" *Easy, there. You're getting angry. Tone it down.*

I don't want to tone it down. I'm tired of this bigotry in the Name of…

Kells interrupted Collin's internal arguing. "Maybe we should." Kells's tone had a snap to it. "Maybe then we could get mothers who aren't whiners like Winona. 'My marriage is so awful.' Well, then do something about it."

Collin settled herself more firmly on the floor. "What do you want her to do, Kells? You haven't made any viable suggestions she can use."

"Yes, I have. She needs to get out of the house more. She needs to come to church and get involved in a group. She needs to quit whining how bad her marriage is and fix it."

Deep breath. "Nonnie has tried. Remember the uproar she reported when she took *his* car and went to the Bible Study? He told her she didn't need to be around other women. They would talk her into leaving him. For no reason, of course."

Kells shrugged. "I'm not sure she has a reason. It can't be as bad as she says. It's not like he's ever hit her."

"You don't have to hit someone to control them. Or make their life miserable."

Kells snorted. "I've heard all that before. I'm not sure I believe it."

Collin swallowed hard. "Is there anyone else you would like to be rid of? Or do I guess?"

"Brianna. Everything is 'Oscar can't do this' and 'Oscar can't do that.' They should have sent him back to the adoption agency."

"Back to Haiti?"

"Yes. There are a million babies here who need parents. No one should go to another country to adopt. We need to take care of our own first."

Collin sat forward. "When's the last time you spoke to an adoption agency, Kells? Do you know how much agencies are charging people to adopt 'our own'?"

Kells shrugged it off again. "It's not the point."

"It's exactly the point. Couples are being charged forty to fifty *thousand dollars* to adopt a child here. If there are so many children waiting to be adopted, why is it so expensive?"

Kells pointed to Collin. "You're dodging the issue. It's not about the women in the group. I care about you. You're my friend. We've done this group for years now. I know you. And you need to get your life straightened out." She hesitated, then added, "You do, and you might find out who is really leaving those notes."

Collin's eyes narrowed. "What do you mean?"

Kells leaned towards her. "Someone comes and goes, and

nobody sees anything? How? Unless someone in the house is putting the envelopes out themselves."

"Who are you accusing? Jeff? Or me?"

"Jeff would never do anything like that. I know him too well."

"So you're saying it's me? I'm putting them out there? Why?"

Kells sat back. "You may not even realize you're doing it. It may be something buried deep, and it's finally coming back. You said your background has been sketchy. Maybe this is your subconscious asking for help. Counseling will give you those answers."

Breathe. Slowly. But do it. "I appreciate your concern, Kells. I will make an appointment to talk to this counselor. I will examine my relationship with the Lord. And I will see what we can do to make reading more a priority." She lifted her chin. "But I won't exclude Eliza from coming to the house and the group."

Kells sighed. "I think if you do all the other things, Eliza won't be a problem." She stood. "I have to go. Call me after you talk to Dr. Bliss."

"I doubt I can get in to see him before next week."

Kells waved her off. "You'll be surprised. If you call him this afternoon, he'll be available sooner than you think. He lives to help our people."

Kells gathered Allison, her giant quilted shoulder bag, her coffee mug. She stuck her head in the kitchen. "Bye, babies. Bye, Rob."

Rob rose from the table, but Kells waved him off. "No need. I'll see you later." Collin walked her to the door *to make sure she's gone*...watched her walk to her car. A deep metallic blue sedan sat across the road. A man in a dark blue three-piece suit leaned against the back bumper. He saluted her. Collin shook her head and returned to the kitchen. She sank down on the barstool. "Well, that was a joy." She lowered her head and banged it softly on the counter.

Rob swallowed his sandwich. "Now what?"

Collin didn't lift her head. "Kells think I've fallen out of fellowship with the Lord. All my problems are from my lack of faith. Oh, and I'm putting out the envelopes myself."

Rob raised his eyebrows. "She said what?"

Collin waved him off. "Ignore it. I'm going to. What she

thinks of me doesn't bother me. It's what she thinks of Eliza which will sink this group. Or not."

"Yeah? What's that?"

"She has a problem with Eliza and her partner raising children." *Do not start. No grammar police. None.*

Rob chewed on his sandwich. "What's her partner's name?"

"Pam."

"I see. Yeah, I can see Kells having a problem with them. Sad, but there it is." He finished up his lunch, helped the babies clean their plates off the table into the sink. Then he shooed them to the back. He eyed Collin. "If you stop the group, can I still come over and play with my posse? And raid the fridge?"

Collin slipped an arm around his shoulder. "Yes, you can. This house is always open to you, Rob. It's your home. You know it, right?"

He smiled at her. "Gotcha. Course I know it. I'm counting on it once I finish school. Gotta have someplace to hang 'til I get my corner office."

Collin shoved him. "Get out of here! Go put the babies to bed for their nap. I'll rustle up some meals for you to take back to your dorm."

"You got it." Rob disappeared.

* * *

Jeff got home about five. He sat in the car for several moments, letting the song finish before heading into the chaos. *I love my family, Lord. All of them. Is it wrong to want a few moments of quiet time?*

"Jesus went up to the mountains to pray....Jesus spent the night in prayer...Jesus went to the garden where he was accustomed to going for prayer..."

Jeff breathed out a long sigh. "Okay, I hear You. It's not wrong. You knew what it's like. I'll take these moments, then I'll go face the family."

Your disciples.

"Right." Jeff gathered up his briefcase, his papers, his lunch, and exited the car. He walked through the garage into the kitchen.

The babies were lying on the floor in the kitchen, intently

watching Braydon and his assistant double-checking the cameras. More accurately, the children were watching Braydon's assistant's assistant: a large German Shepherd. The dog lay on the floor, at attention, watching the babies watching her. Quite the tableau.

Collin greeted him with a kiss and a whispered, "How was your day?"

Jeff motioned to the children/dog combination and matched his tone to hers. "How long has this been going on?"

"Half an hour. The dog is amazing. The babies have crawled all over her, and the dog doesn't even move." Collin smiled. "I could get used to a canine babysitter."

Jeff waved a finger at her. "We promised. Not until the trio is old enough to care for the animal. Neither of us needs more responsibilities in our lives."

Collin ducked her head to the side. "Truth. But look at them. All four of them. They love the pup."

"Did Braydon say why he brought her? Besides entertaining the trio?"

"She's trained to sniff out anomalies. Once she gets used to the 'regular smells,' she can alert on anything which doesn't 'fit.' He's going to run her through the house every so often and see if she comes up with anything."

"Okay, I see. But he's not leaving her here, right? He's taking her back with him. We can't handle a dog and the trio, Collin."

Collin lowered her head. She couldn't keep the disappointment from her voice. "I'm sorry. I had a bad day. Kells and I had a bit of a falling out."

"Over what? You two have been friends for years. What happened?"

Collin took his briefcase. "Go change. Relax. See if you can entice the trio away from the dog. Supervise Braydon. We can talk later."

Jeff kissed her. "Love you, milady."

"Love you, Jeff."

He walked to the back (unnoticed by the littles) and changed into comfortable clothes. He ignored the urge to stretch out on the bed. *Five minutes. Just five minutes.*

Which becomes ten, then fifteen, then you sleep for an hour or so... Don't start.

Jeff rejoined the group in the front of the house. Braydon was explaining to Collin details about the camera system. Collin grabbed Jeff by the arm. "Here. Tell him. My brain has been fried since the babies were born."

Braydon grinned at her. "The way I hear it, your brain has always been fried."

Collin glared at Jeff in mock anger. "Are you the one sharing state secrets?"

Jeff shook his head. "Not me, mon. You should ask Erin. Your twin talks more than I do."

Collin scowled. "I'll ask him." She smiled at Braydon. "Don't believe everything our brother tells you. He does like to embellish a story."

Braydon chuckled. "I'd noticed. Here, Jeff, let me explain the system to you." Braydon began the run-down of what camera covered what area. How to turn them on. How to turn them off. Most importantly, "Who do you want to monitor them? Us, 24/7, or you when you have time?"

Jeff tried to absorb everything. After several minutes of deep reflection, Jeff made his decision. "I still want to do at-home monitoring first. Set the cameras so Collin and I are the only ones to see the video. Yeah, it's harder this way, but I'm not one hundred percent comfortable with someone else watching my life."

Braydon nodded. "Understood. No, there is no hundred percent safe Wi-Fi or phone network. We'll do it your way and see if we can catch the culprit."

The assistant with the dog looked up at Jeff. "Remote monitoring is safe, Mr. Farrell. No, it's not a thousand percent, but it is safe. No one is going to hack our system. Not with it being monitored around the clock. If you let the office do the watching, it's like having an on-duty guard all the time. It really is safe."

Braydon motioned to the woman. "This is Trisha." He grinned. "One of my better sales associates."

Trisha stood up and shook hands with Jeff. "Sir. You have such adorable children. We want to give them the best protection. Letting us do the monitoring gives you an extra layer of security. Since all our feeds are monitored by humans, we can catch things live, not hours later. And we can have the police en route before you even know there is a threat. Let us do it for a month. If you're not happy, we can easily switch you back to a closed circuit. It's up to you, sir."

Jeff looked to Collin. She shrugged, looked away, then looked back and nodded. Jeff chuckled. "Okay, Trisha. We'll try it for a month."

Trisha beamed. "Great choice, Mr. Farrell. You won't regret it. Your children will be safe and secure. No one will get to them."

Lord, I hope this doesn't make it look like I'm not trusting You to protect us. Jeff smiled. "Thanks. I appreciate the help."

Trisha touched the shepherd, bringing her to her feet. The dog sat rigid beside the woman, eyes laser-focused, waiting for a command. Trisha looked from Collin to Jeff. "With your permission, I'd like to run Gretchen through the house into all the common areas. It will give her a baseline of scents to recognize."

With Gretchen moving, the spell broke, and three little people came to their feet. Suddenly they made a mad bull-rush of, "Daddy!" "Daddy home!" "Daddy, we see puppy!" The littles grabbed him from all sides. Jeff kneeled down and surrounded the trio with his arms. "Hi, babies. I see the puppy."

Caleb nodded. "We has puppy."

Jeff shook his head. "No, Braydon has the puppy. The puppy is here to work. Not to stay forever." Of course, a child's concept of 'forever' didn't match his own, so he let it go. Not the time.

Braydon finished his work and wiring. He waited as Trisha made Gretchen familiar with the kitchen, the playroom, the children's bedroom, the office, Jeff and Collin's bedroom, the bathrooms, living room, dining room, porch…they were very thorough.

Not thorough enough. Braydon caught Trisha's eye. "I didn't hear the closet doors being opened. Run her through again."

Trisha nodded. Jeff passed the trio off to Collin and followed Trisha and Gretchen. *I like watching dogs run their paces. Saw plenty of them when I worked as a paramedic. A lifetime ago.*

Trisha took Gretchen back through Jeff and Collin's bedroom, the spare bedroom, the office…opening every door and cabinet. Gretchen sniffed, then moved on. Nothing of interest. Trisha smiled at Jeff. "You don't have to follow us. I'm sure you have work to do."

Jeff shrugged. "Not really. I'm fascinated by working dogs."

Trisha scowled. But only a little. And only someone paying attention would have caught it. And Jeff did. *What's that all about?*

Which left only the trio's bedroom. Trisha walked Gretchen in, opened the closet, and stood back. Gretchen sniffed, sniffed again. Immediately she sat at attention, her brown eyes fixed on something only she could sense.

A chill ran up Jeff's spine. *Is there something?* Trisha waited a moment, called Gretchen off. The dog refused to move. Trisha called again. Gretchen whimpered, moved a paw forward, but did not come off whatever she smelled.

Braydon appeared at the door. "Did I hear you calling Gretchen out? Did she find something?"

Trisha shook her head. "I think the children's smells are new to her."

Collin's brother eyed the dog. He jerked his head. "Let's see what she's on." He waved to the dog. "Get it, girl."

Gretchen jumped to her feet and raced into the closet. She stood up on her hind feet, pointing her nose to a box on the shelf. Jeff looked at Braydon, shrugged, and brought down the box.

Gretchen sniffed all over the outside, then the inside of the box. She nosed and poked and prodded, giving out little whimpers. Jeff only saw the empty box. *What does she smell?*

After a minute or two, Braydon called Gretchen off. He placed the box back on the shelf. He turned to Jeff. "Whatever she smelled, it's gone now."

Jeff narrowed his eyes. "Interesting. Wonder what she thought was in there?"

"Don't know. She's not much on talking to me about what she finds."

Jeff chuckled. "Yeah, I get it. Okay, we'll leave it alone." He patted Gretchen on the head. "Thanks, girl. I appreciate your help."

Gretchen hung her tongue out and gave Jeff a doggy smile. Jeff grinned. "Yeah, I like you too."

The group walked to the kitchen, where Collin had the littles pulling out pots and pans in preparation for cooking dinner. A great deal of banging and clanging and laughter accompanied the effort. Jeff grinned. *That's my trio.* He followed Braydon outside as his brother-in-law packed up his equipment and staff. Jeff bumped fists with Braydon. "Thanks, man. I think this is going to help ease Collin's mind. I know it will mine."

Braydon nodded. "It's what we do. Peace of mind."

The man climbed into his truck and drove away. Jeff walked back to the kitchen and the chaos. Collin had the littles sitting on the floor, each with their own bowl. She had given each child a portion of biscuit mix and some water. The trio happily mixed the mess, hands covered in dough.

Caleb held his hands high. "We make bissuts!"

Joshua mirrored his brother's action. "Good bissuts."

Collin warned, "Keep the dough in the bowls, please. Mix it well."

Jeff eyed Collin. "Are we going to eat the biscuits?"

She laughed. "I have a separate batch for dinner. This is entertainment and education."

Jeff took a seat at the coffee bar to watch. "Does this go on often?"

"Every time I cook. I want them to learn. And to have fun. Maybe they'll remember it later. Maybe not, but hey…I tried."

Jeff grinned. "Yeah, you did."

Collin directed the littles to put their biscuit dough on the table. Each child rolled their dough into a shape somewhat reminiscent of a circle. Collin helped them roll the dough flat, cut out the biscuits, and put their thumb or finger in the middle, so they knew which "bissut" belonged to who. She put the mess in a cake pan and set them in the oven.

As she worked, she asked, "How was your day?"

"Same as usual. Erin finished the blueprints for the new housing project for downtown. We'll present it to the city council next month. We're hoping we get approval so we can get the houses built and occupied before winter."

"That would be fantastic. If we can get some of the families off the streets and into decent, affordable housing, it will make a huge difference to them."

"I know. Rob's been invaluable with the planning. Knowing the streets the way he does, he's made suggestions I would never have thought about. He's becoming quite the manager."

Collin raised a finger at him. "Don't fill his head too proud. He's still thinking he's going to snag a corner office right out of school. He needs to work up to it."

Jeff pulled a corner off a piece of roast beef Collin carved. "If he keeps coming up with ideas like he did with this project, I'll put him in the office tomorrow. He's sharp, Collin."

"Which is why we adopted him, remember?"

Jeff chuckled. "Oh, and he saved your life, and you saved his. You two were a package deal from the first time I met you."

"Joined at the hip."

Collin set the meat, carrots, potatoes, and a pan of biscuits on the table. "Go wash your hands and come sit for dinner."

Jeff supervised the cleaning of the hands, then shepherded the children back to the kitchen. Five bodies sat. "Hands folded. Heads down. Joshua, it's your turn to pray."

Joshua closed his eyes tightly. His face and body scrunched up. "Jesus, tank you for food. Tank you for mommy an' daddy. Tank you for sissy an' budder. Love you. Amen."

Collin smiled at her offspring. "Thank you for the very nice prayer, Joshua." She served the littles their meals.

Jeff helped himself to pot roast and veggies. "What happened with your day?"

Caleb waved his fork. "Wob come. We pay cars. Wob make tower. Car crash it down."

Joshua would not be outdone. "Wob be dinosor. He chase us. Eat us. We won fast fast, but he catch us."

Talitha chewed her food with deliberation. Only after she swallowed her small mouthful did she report her activities. "I pay Oscar." She looked at Jeff, cocking her head to the side. "Why Oscar not say words?"

Collin answered their daughter. "Oscar likes to be quiet. Some littles are like that. He'll talk when he's ready to. You played with him anyhow, right? And you understood what he wanted, and he knew what you were saying."

Talitha nodded once. "Yes. We pay. He pay kitchen wis me. We make cookies." The littlest Farrell beamed. "We make good cookies!"

Collin smiled. "Whether he uses words or not, he's still a little who wants to play. Thank you for playing with him."

Jeff ducked his head toward Collin. "What about your day?"

Collin shook her head. "After bedtime."

Jeff's shoulders tightened. "Are you okay?"

"I'm fine. Some opinions were expressed, and I need some help processing them."

Jeff raised an eyebrow. "That bad, huh?"

Collin gave him a tight-lipped smile. "Yeah."

The meal finished, Jeff supervised the bathing and putting on of pajamas. The trio then went to the playroom, picked up the toys, threw away anything torn or broken, then went back to the living room for story and family time. Jeff wrestled with the boys and Talitha. They read another chapter of "The Man in the Yellow Hat" with his monkey George. He and Collin put them to bed. Prayers, kisses, and they were done.

He and Collin walked back to the family room. He plopped on the couch, inviting Collin to sit beside him. He put his arm around her shoulders. "Now, tell me about your day."

His phone whirred. Erin. He picked it up. "Talk to me, Erin."

"Do not put this on speakerphone."

"Not a problem. What's up?"

"Mayor Carmack came in the office late. I showed him the blueprints. He wasn't interested. Said he'd heard Collin had been accused of abusing the children at church. I assured him no such thing had ever happened. Told him the real story. It didn't fully satisfy him from the sound of it. Said the council might have reservations about using our firm with this hanging over our head. I told him Collin had been exonerated. But he didn't seem to think it would make much difference. Apologized and said we might expect opposition at the council meeting. He told me to warn me, of course. No way would he ever believe anything like this of Collin. But public perception…"

Jeff breathed normally. "Okay, I hear you. Thanks. Tell Vy we send our love." He disconnected the call. "Don't ask about the call. Tell me about your day."

Collin studied him, then sighed. Her face grew taut, her eyes down. "We had a new woman join us today."

"That's good, right? What's her name?"

"Eliza. She has two little ones, two and a half, and six months."

Jeff coaxed her on. "And?"

"And she has a female partner named Pam. They are raising

the children together."

Jeff nodded. "I see. Let me guess. Kells had a problem with her?"

Collin huffed. "More than a problem. She told me after she did not want Eliza to come, we should have applications to join, and only the ones she approves should join."

"And you told her what?"

"I told her Eliza is welcome in my house anytime, and she should be part of the group. Kells said she'd take the group elsewhere if I let Eliza come over."

Jeff's eyes narrowed. "There's more to this, isn't there?"

Collin drew in a deep breath. "She said my 'break' is proof I'm out of fellowship with the Lord, and I need to go to her Christian counselor to get my act together. She also said I'm the one putting out the envelopes. Maybe I don't know I'm doing it, but I am. And getting my life 'right' will correct all the other stuff. If I get right with Jesus, all my problems will go away, and I'll agree with her about Eliza."

Jeff sat in silence. He lay his head on top of Collin's. "Lady, if anyone has fellowship with Jesus, you do. Kells is out of her mind."

Bitterness laced Collin's tone. "According to her, no Christian will want to come to the group anyhow, seeing they meet in the home of a child abuser."

He sat up. Anger welled in his gut. "You were exonerated."

"According to Kells, it won't matter. The accusation stands." Collin shook her head, her eyes down. "She also said CPS doesn't come out for no reason. There must have been more to it."

Jeff put his arms around Collin's waist. He pulled her into his chest tightly. He breathed slowly. "I don't care what Kells thinks. I don't care what anyone thinks. You are not a child abuser. You are not out of fellowship. You are walking with the Lord as He leads. Welcoming Eliza is exactly what Jesus would do. Love first."

Collin lifted her head. "Something good did happen. Oscar said 'Bye' to Rob. Brianna couldn't believe he actually said a word."

Jeff smiled. "So it wasn't all bad. I'm happy for Bri. Oscar needs time, that's all. He's a bright boy. He's watching everything. Soaking it all in. When he's ready, he'll talk. Probably in complete sentences."

Collin chuckled. "Won't Brianna be surprised?" She stretched. "Talitha played with Oscar. She's such a little mother."

"Yep. And she'll be mothering her brothers one of these days."

"Yeah, I don't think it's going to happen anytime soon. Those boys are both strong-willed. I think Joshua will be the ring leader, though."

"Probably." Jeff paused. "What are you going to do about Kells and her accusations?" *What am I going to do about the mayor and his?*

"I called her counselor for an appointment to talk to him. He had an opening on Monday. Someone canceled. So I'll go and talk to him, see what he has to say. But I will let Eliza come to the group if it meets here."

Jeff caught his wife's eyes. "And if they don't?"

"Then God can take care of them, and Eliza and I will start a new group. An inclusive one. Like Jesus would."

Jeff hugged her. "There's my warrior princess. Do not let Kells or anyone else judge you. I'm not sure I would have gone as far as making an appointment with the counselor, but it won't hurt to see what he says."

"Right. And it will shut Kells up."

Jeff hugged Collin tight. "I love you, milady."

"I love you, Jeff Farrell."

They rose and went to check the monitors. The trio were in their beds, asleep. Collin lay her hand on the monitor; Jeff lay his on top of hers. "One more day, Lord. Leave them with us one more day. Thank You for every breath we have with them. We love You."

Arm in arm, they walked down the hall to their bedroom.

SATURDAY MORNING

Collin met up with Eliza at the Brown Cow Café at ten in the morning. Eliza looked both nervous and happy. Collin guessed the nervous had to do with asking questions about the faith, while the happy had to do with being out without children. It had always made Collin happy anyhow.

She hugged the woman, then slid into the booth they'd been assigned. The server took their orders for coffee. Pastry would wait for a bit, thank you.

Collin asked, "So, what did you think of the group?"

"I liked it. I think it's a place I'll enjoy coming. And I think the girls will fit in fine."

"First impressions can be tough. But it seems like all the littles had a relatively good day. And we adults were on our good behavior."

Eliza gave Collin a side-eyed look. "That's Kells's good behavior?"

Collin gritted her teeth. "Well…she's been off lately. No one is sure why. She's not usually quite so…"

"Acerbic? Mean? Cutting?"

"Right. All the above. She's usually a wonderful friend. I'm not sure how much is postpartum depression she's trying to hide or what. I have a rule about questions like this."

"Which is?"

"Ask her yourself."

"I don't know her well enough to ask her."

"I do. And I need to. I haven't, but I need to." *Note to self…call out Kells. Gently.* Collin moved to other topics. "Tell me about yourself. You said you were working from home. What do you do?"

"I'm a freelance copy editor."

"Ooo! Nice."

"If you can keep the work coming in."

"How long have you been doing it?"

"About five years."

"Then you must have a clientele built up which likes your work."

Eliza blushed a bit. "I have some people who think I do a good job for them."

"Good. It's a tough field, I know. A lot of 'what can you do for me now' kind of things. You must be one of those artistic types who can think fast and see things as a creative whole."

Eliza laughed. "Eh. Some of it is natural. Some of it is learned."

"But I bet yours is mostly natural, right?"

Eliza shrugged, trying to brush off the compliment. "Some of it."

Collin smiled. "How long have you and Pam been together?"

Eliza lost her smile. Her eyes lowered. "We've known each other since grade school. We moved in together after college."

Collin pressed very lightly. "I'm not searching for ammunition, Eliza. I'm a stranger on the street trying to get to know you and the people important to you. I have no agenda and no ax to grind. Okay?"

Eliza sat back and relaxed. A little. Very little. "It's tough. I've found this area less accepting than others."

"You mean this end of town?" The woman nodded. Collin smiled. "So I've noticed. We had a few 'exceptions' taken to Rob moving in. But once people got to know him and knew he would be a permanent fixture at the house, they got over themselves."

"So they all accepted him?"

"I wouldn't say they all accepted him. I'd say no one has raised any objections of late."

Eliza huffed. "Of late. How did you deal with the ones who did?"

"We went with Rob to their homes. Introduced him and ourselves. Assured them we would be good neighbors. Asked them what we could do to not make their lives miserable. No loud parties after ten…no mowing grass before seven a.m. No working on cars in the garage and revving engines to see if they were loud enough…you know, the typical stuff."

"And they were satisfied?" Eliza's eyes held disbelief.

"Like I said, for the most part. We don't have issues with anyone now."

Eliza's eyebrows raised and lowered. "I didn't think that's how Christians handled things. I thought you got in people's faces and told them this is how it is, like it or not."

The server came by. "Pastries?"

Collin nodded. "Sure. I'll do a cream puff. I need the sugar to keep up with the triplets later."

Eliza smiled. "None for me."

Collin's eyes raised of their own accord. "You're going to sit and watch me eat? That's not allowed. You have to have something. Even if it's invisible. Your fork has to move."

Eliza chuckled. "Fine. I'll have a scone. A mini-scone."

The server left. Collin bowed her head. "Thank you." She stared at the floor. "It still bothers me to eat when someone else doesn't. Old hang-ups die hard."

Eliza gave her a look of curiosity. "You had a hang-up about it?"

Collin shook her head. "I've had hang-ups about a lot of things. Been in counseling most of my adult life trying to unlearn them." She smiled. "I'm a work in progress still." She shrugged. "I'm breathing. I'm a work in progress."

Eliza tilted her head to look at Collin. "May I ask why?"

"Why am I a work in progress? Or why do I have hang-ups? Or why have I been in counseling?"

"Yes. All of the above. In any order you want to answer them. If you want."

Collin pursed her lips. "Well, let's start with I had an abusive childhood. Moved from there to trust issues. Acceptance of myself issues. Issues with believing I was worthy to be loved or could love anyone." Collin shrugged. "I had a lot of issues. So I went into therapy and counseling and have been working on myself ever since." She smiled. "But I have a wonderful Counselor, and he helps me."

Eliza's eyes widened slightly. "Who is he?"

"The Lord. And Dr. Sujit." Collin laughed. "Both will show me issues and then give me strategies to overcome them."

Eliza shook her head. "How does God show you an issue?"

"Usually by putting it right in front of me, so I have to admit it's a problem. Then He and Dr. Sujit will help me overcome it. Mostly. Some of the time. When I listen and practice what they tell me."

The server returned with the pastries. He set them down then left. Eliza continued her questioning. "So God speaks to you? Just like that, God speaks to you?"

Collin raised her head to stare at the air for a moment. *How do I explain this?*

Intelligently would be nice.

Oh, be silent.

I always am.

Collin turned back to Eliza. "God has ways of speaking without speaking in an audible voice."

Eliza shook her head. "I'm way behind on how he speaks. I'm still at the point of God speaks. Why would he? Who are we to him? I mean, we're nothing compared to him. Why would he even care?"

Okay, back it up. Collin studied Eliza a moment. "What do you know about God? Or what do you believe about Him?"

"What you pick up in school. Some kids went to parochial schools and knew everything but lived like they didn't. Some were radical about him not being real." She snorted. "So were some of the teachers."

Collin reached over and bumped knuckles with Eliza. "I hear you."

Eliza smiled but continued. "I guess I settled somewhere in the middle. Maybe I believed God existed. But the idea he cared about us as individuals? Knew we even existed? I couldn't go there."

Collin looked over Eliza's head and froze. *He's here. The man in the suit. How can he be here?*

She looked closer. Not the same man. Same suit. *I'm seeing things.*

Eliza touched Collin's arm. "Are you okay? You froze, there."

Collin nodded. "Um, yeah. I'm fine. Saw someone I thought I

recognized." She retraced her thoughts. "Knowing God cares about us is the turning point in faith, Eliza. Coming to a place where we accept He is the Creator of all that is and was and will be is step one. I can walk outside at night—or I could, if there weren't so many lights—look up and believe something greater than myself created the universe."

The man in the suit walked past Collin's table. He smiled at her as he went by. Collin ignored him. He tapped her table, saluted her. "Mrs. Farrell." Then walked out.

Collin dipped her head to pull her face into something other than revulsion or panic. When she could resume looking human, she lifted her head.

Eliza's face echoed somewhere between disbelief and caution. "Who's he?"

Collin shook her head. "I don't know. My current nightmare, I think." She pulled herself together. "Where were we? Stars, right. Okay. You see the stars and recognize something bigger than yourself." She chuckled. "Rob and I went to West Virginia a few years back. It's where we met Jeff. We went up to an abandoned airfield. You want to talk about dark? And stars? Lying there, looking up, I felt like if I rolled over, I'd fall off the edge of the world." She shook her head.

Eliza set her fork down. "I've had a similar experience." Eliza gazed at Collin side-eyed. "Just like that, you're going to say the man is your nightmare and go on talking about God?"

Collin took a bite of her cream puff. "Yes, I am. Because it's God Who gets me through the nightmares." She thought hard. "You can accept God. But you doubt He cares about us."

"Right."

Collin pointed her fork at Eliza. "When Meridian was born, how did you feel about her?"

"What?"

"The first time you held her. How did you feel about her?"

Collin watched Eliza's eyes look off, maybe to an event only Eliza could see. The woman nodded to the vision. "I loved her. More than life itself. I loved her."

"And wanted to give her the very best of everything life had to offer, right?"

"Right."

"And would do anything to protect her. Right again?"

Eliza came back from her memory. "Right." She trailed off as if not following Collin.

Collin kept asking questions. "Did she know you loved her? Did she know you at all?"

"Not right then. Not at the beginning."

"But later. As you protected her and provided for her and carried her and sheltered her…did she figure out you loved her?"

Eliza eyed Collin sideways. "I see where you're going with this."

"If God is our Creator, it's natural for Him to love His creation. And want to care for it and provide for it. And do what is best for it. Even when we don't understand."

Eliza's eyes narrowed. "Explain."

Collin swallowed half the cream filling on her puff. "When I took the triplets for their shots, their vaccines, do you think they understood the pain they experienced from the shot was for their good?"

"Maybe not."

"Maybe? Joshua screamed like a banshee. Which set Caleb and Talitha screaming, and no one had touched them yet." Collin shook her head.

Eliza smiled. "I can see that."

Collin nodded. "Yeah. Or what about the boundaries you put on the baby? Are they for her good? Or because you want to be mean and arbitrary?"

Eliza grinned. "I guess it depends on who you ask."

Collin grinned as well. "Uh, got that right. And it ain't gonna change any time soon, believe me. From the time they learn there is a 'no,' they will be drawn to it like a June bug to a light. But because we love them, we set boundaries. We protect them, we defend them, we provide for them. We also teach them to stand on their own. We watch their accomplishments, and we celebrate with them. When they fail, when they turn away from us, we hurt. We do everything we can to bring them back into a relationship with us."

Eliza shook her head. "You talk like God is a human being, and has feelings like we do. But he's God."

"He is God. And He does know the hurt of a broken

relationship with His children. So He came to Earth in the form of His Son, Jesus. Who walked and talked and experienced everything we do. All of it. The good, the bad, the ugly."

Eliza held up her hand. "I know the rest of the story. He died in my place, and I have to live like Him and obey all the rules so I can one day go to Heaven. Right?"

"Wrong. He died in our place. He doesn't demand anything from us." Collin shifted in her seat. "Back to the parent-child relationship. Your child has thumbed his nose at you. Said they don't want to be your child anymore. Run off to do their own thing. Do you cut them off? Turn your back on them? Or do you do everything in your power to bring them back?"

Eliza shook her head. "Which is the 'die in my place' part. What about what happens next? The 'obeying all the rules' part?"

Collin drew inside herself. "God said there are only two rules. First: love God with everything in you. Second: love your neighbor. That's all the laws God gave us."

Eliza sat back. "That's it? That's not what I hear."

"I know. And it's sad you do hear so much else. God wants us to live for Him. Which means accepting Him as our God and King through His Son Jesus. Learning to love Him is a lifetime experience. And why we have the Scriptures." She smiled. "The Owner's Manual."

Collin took a breath. "In it is everything we need to know God, to do His will, to be His children, to live the lives He wants us to live."

Eliza snorted. "And we have to have someone explain it to us. So we live according to what they say God says."

Collin looked down. "Which is the beauty of having the Scripture to read for ourselves. We can know. We can read. We can experience God all by our lonely little selves."

Eliza looked at her watch. "I've got to get home. I appreciate you taking time to explain it to me."

Collin smiled. "I appreciate you taking time to listen to me ramble." She stood. "I'm not an expert. I'm me. Collin Farrell. I know God loves me. He sent Jesus for me. I accepted Him, and everything else is God and me trying to get through the day." She hugged Eliza. "We can do this again, and you'll get to talk."

Eliza hugged her back. "I'll see you at group."

They paid, walked out. Eliza went to her car and drove off. Collin went to her car. Parked directly opposite her sat a metallic blue sedan. *The* man in the three-piece suit smiled at her. Saluted. Pulled out and drove off.

Collin closed her eyes. "God, protect me. Protect my babies. Please. Whoever he is, whatever he wants, keep us safe. In Jesus's Name, amen."

SATURDAY NIGHT

Saturday evening, Collin, Jeff, and the babies received a knock at the front door. Jeff got up from the couch and answered it. Collin could hear the low rumble of voices but couldn't make out words or speakers. Jeff walked into the family room trailed by Pastor Thomas and two men Collin didn't recognize. Jeff made the introductions. "Collin, this is Burt, and this is Paco. They are on the leadership team. Gentlemen, Collin."

Collin nodded to the men in turn. *My accusers come to see me face-to-face?* She stomped the attitude and smiled. "Gentlemen, welcome." She pointed to the babies sitting on the floor. All three were in their PJs and had their stuffies in hand. "It's storytime. And then bedtime. Have a seat."

Pastor Thomas nodded his head. "We'll be brief, and then we'll get out of your hair."

Burt cleared his throat. "First, I…we…want to apologize for the visit you got from Greg and Samuel. They took it upon themselves to 'handle the problem,' but they certainly did not speak for leadership." He cleared his throat again. "We…I also want to apologize for not supporting you when the abuse accusation first surfaced. You and your husband have been active members of the church for years. We should never have suspected you…"

Collin cut him off. "Being 'active members of the church' doesn't exclude me from abusing my children. I saw it all the time when I worked in Social Services." She smiled without mirth. "The problem was you didn't ask us about it first. Face to face." Collin looked from man to man. "Like Paul instructs us to."

Jeff moved to stand beside Collin. "This whole thing could have been cleared up then and there."

Pastor Thomas nodded. "And should have been. As it is, I continue to get calls asking how I could let this happen? What's wrong with our screening protocols that a child abuser volunteers with children? What am I doing about it?" He looked at the men. "We're committing character assassination."

Paco held out his hands, palms up. "What can we do to correct this?" He turned his eyes to Collin. "How do we make it right?"

You grovel and... "You're right, of course. We do need procedures to make sure this doesn't happen. But the first priority has to be speaking to the individual involved. Before anyone in the congregation is told."

Pastor Thomas snorted. "We're still trying to track down who spread the accusations."

Jeff growled but added nothing helpful. Collin understood the sentiment.

Burt stepped forward. "I—we, the leadership board—suggested Pastor Thomas call this out in all three services over the next two weeks. You were found to be unjustly accused..."

"No. Someone will think you're covering up." Collin repeated the request she made to Sierra. "Tell the congregation we were exonerated." She smiled, her lips tight. "Explain what the word means. But make it clear there is absolutely no wrongdoing. Not 'charges dropped' not 'found not guilty' but exonerated. No wrongdoing, period."

Collin turned to Thomas. "Will you agree to that?"

"I understand your reasoning, and I agree. Saying it from the pulpit may make a difference. Maybe it will silence the rumor mill."

Jeff started to comment but again held back.

Paco added, "A public apology isn't out of the question, either. If you think it will make a difference."

"I don't need a public apology." Collin held each man's eyes in turn.

Thomas disagreed. "I think we should. And I think it should be done at each service. Then no one misses the point. Whispers and rumors will kill a church. This body of believers needs to know we won't tolerate the behavior."

Burt's head snapped to stare at Thomas. "'Won't tolerate'? What do you expect to do about it? We're all guilty of something or another. Are you going to dictate what is and isn't acceptable behavior?"

"I meant we won't tolerate privileged communications being violated. We're supposed to be able to hold confidence. If we can't, we've got deeper problems than a rumor mill."

Burt shrugged. "Fine. I understand what you're saying. I don't know I agree, but I understand."

Caleb climbed into Collin's lap with a book. "Mommy read?"

The boy snuggled down into Collin's arms, making himself as comfortable as possible. Collin kissed the top of his head. "Sure, buddy. Let's get your brother and sister and go to the bedroom. I'll read to you there." She picked the toddler up, nodded to her visitors. "I have to leave you, gentlemen. I have a story to read."

The triplets kissed Daddy goodnight. Collin set Caleb down and pointed to the back. "Everyone in bed. First one under the covers gets to say prayers."

Six feet padded down the hallway. Collin followed. *I prefer the babies' company. I have a feeling things are going to go south with the adults. Even without me there.* She took up her place in the rocking chair. "Now, what are we reading tonight? How about more of 'The Man in the Yellow Hat'? With his monkey George. You like that one."

* * *

Jeff watched Collin head down the hall. He squashed the jealousy he felt…he'd much rather read to his children than listen to what would shape up to be a prolonged fight. *Excuse me, disagreement. Whatever.* Thomas and Burt were still discussing the breach of confidentiality and how to deal with it. Jeff waited until the two men paused to ask his question. "I'd like to know how it got out. Who spread the story?" He turned to Burt. "How did you hear about it? And what did you hear?"

Burt shuffled in his chair. "Pilar told me. She called me from Bible Study and said someone had abused a child in the nursery, and CPS had been called."

Thomas raised a finger in the air. "Did she mention names?"

"No. And I didn't ask. I worried more that the incident had even happened. Which is why I called you, Pastor."

"Did you ask her where she heard it?"

"It came across as a prayer request. The women have prayer time. Some participants are too shy to pray aloud, so they will write their requests down. One of the facilitators will then read the request."

Jeff's skin crawled. "Someone wrote Collin had abused her children and CPS had been called, and they shared it with everyone?"

Burt couldn't meet Jeff's eyes. "I'm not sure it came across quite so direct. I asked Pilar about it when she came home, and she said someone made it a matter of prayer, and no one is supposed to share prayer concerns outside of the meeting."

"Thirty women heard a prayer request stating Collin had abused the babies, and you expected it to stay in the meeting?" Jeff bit his tongue. *Don't say it. Don't say it.*

Thomas countered, "It wouldn't have mattered if it had been thirty men. The result would have been the same. To 'pray about it better,' it had to be shared, right? We're supposed to have leaders with discretion who will not share those names, regardless. Who facilitated?"

Burt's eyes narrowed. "Whoever did it made a mistake. You're talking like this happened deliberately. Someone had a lapse in judgment, at most."

Jeff swallowed the anger. But still asked, "Was it? Who wrote the note? Does anyone know? Did anyone bother to find out?"

Burt shook his head. "I doubt it. They always maintain the privacy of the person making the request."

Breathe. Breathe. Lord, help me. "But no one protected Collin's privacy. Or her innocence." Jeff rested his hands in his lap to prevent the shaking.

Paco held up both hands. "Mistakes were made. The note should never have been read aloud. We agree there." He pointed to Burt. "You called me. Told me there had been an incident in the nursery. Which is what I responded to. And yes, I should have checked the story out myself. I didn't." He looked at Jeff. "And for that, I'm guilty. I admit I was wrong."

Jeff nodded, accepting the apology. "What I want is to make

sure this doesn't happen to anyone else. And Collin's name is cleared."

Burt ducked his head. "I think that's what we need to focus on. Finding out who wrote the note won't get us anywhere."

Jeff's gut twisted. *Why is he so adamant about not looking for the guilty party?* "I still want to know who started the rumor. And why."

Thomas leaned forward. "Jeff, I understand your feelings. You want to protect Collin. I can tell you the volunteers in the office at the time were all people who know Collin well. Brianna took the call. She and your wife are close. I would never suspect her of giving out information so personal. We'll do everything we can to make sure people know the rumors weren't true. CPS exonerated Collin, and she has the full backing of leadership. Pushing to find the guilty party makes it look like a witch hunt, and you're being vindictive. It doesn't help Collin, and it doesn't bring any glory to the Lord."

Here he goes again. I have to be the godly one... Collin suffers, and we have to pretend we...

Jeff pulled up short in his thoughts. *I'm sorry, Lord. Of course, we want to honor You. I'll let it go. You did for me. I can for someone else.* "What matters in the end is Collin and I want to do things His way. Forgiveness. We will choose it."

Thomas smiled. Jeff noted Burt relax in his seat. Paco nodded in agreement.

Before anything else could be said, Collin came out of the room. She had an unopened envelope in her hand. Her face looked as pale as the envelope. Her hands shook as she gave it to him. "Caleb found it under his blanket."

Jeff tore open the cover, read the single sheet of paper. *One lives.* He immediately pulled out his phone and called Braydon. As soon as the man answered, Jeff demanded, "Check your monitors. Someone left another letter. In our son's bed. This goes beyond harassment. I want this person caught."

Thomas cocked his head. "What's going on? What's this about?"

Collin shook her head, her eyes closed. Jeff caught her hand and squeezed it. He pulled her to his chest, looked over her head to answer the pastor. "Someone has been breaking in here and leaving notes around. It's happening while we're here, not when we're gone."

Burt's eyes narrowed. One more than the other. "While you're home? How is that even possible?"

"Which is what I want to know. They left the first note on the laundry basket Collin carried to the kitchen last week. Another one Monday afternoon. Now this one in Caleb's bed."

"But how do you know they're breaking in while you're here?" Burt's tone carried more than a strain of disbelief.

Collin answered for Jeff. "Because I help the triplets make their beds in the mornings. I would have seen it then."

Thomas frowned. "What did the police say?"

Jeff snorted. "We haven't called them. Not yet. No proof. But now, with the cameras, we can show who it is. And how they're getting in."

Paco asked, "You've got cameras and security?

Jeff nodded. "That's who I called. Braydon is reviewing the footage to see who and when."

Burt motioned to the envelope. "What does it say?"

Jeff took the slip from Collin. *One lives.*

Burt scowled. "Doesn't sound threatening to me."

Jeff laid his hand on Collin's arm. He could feel the tension in her. "Maybe not. But it's what the kidnappers wrote when they took Talitha. 'Choose. One lives. One dies.' Harmless or not, we don't need the reminders."

Burt shrugged. "I guess I could see it from your point of view. Maybe…"

The man trailed off. Jeff guessed the Elder thought nothing more need be said. *If I haven't called the police, I don't believe it's serious either, right?*

Wrong.

Jeff held Collin close but addressed the men. "Thanks for coming out tonight. I appreciate what you've done here."

Thomas shook Jeff's hand. "We'll be in touch about this weekend and how we're going to handle the announcements with Collin. And if you need any help, let me know."

"Thanks, Pastor. I appreciate it." Jeff walked the men out, still holding on to Collin. He would not let her go until he knew she had herself under control.

Only after the men were gone did she speak again. "I'm fine, Jeff. You can let me go. I won't freak out on you."

He kissed her. "I never thought you would."

"Braydon's not going to see anything. I know he's not."

Jeff shook his head. "It makes no sense. Something has to show up. These notes don't pop out of thin air."

"Agreed. But someone wants me to think they do. Or…" Collin trailed off. She gazed at the floor. "Or they want you to think I'm writing them."

"Why would I go there?" Jeff shook his head. "That's crazy."

Collin nodded. "Exactly the point. Maybe someone wants you—or me—to think I'm losing my marbles." She shrugged. "Too late. Lost them a long time ago."

Jeff kissed her. "You have plenty of marbles, milady. Far more than most. You're not going crazy."

She shrugged. "Easy to say now. If Braydon's surveillance doesn't show anything?"

"Then it means his cameras don't catch everything, and we'll have to look harder. You are not crazy, Collin. Don't think it. Not for one minute. Got it?"

Collin stared into Jeff's eyes. He put all the assurance and confidence he could into the return gaze. Collin dropped her gaze, hugged him around the middle. "I love you, Jeff."

"I love you, Collin." They retired to the kitchen.

SUNDAY

Sunday morning. Pastor Thomas waited until after the praise band had finished the worship music, then called Collin and Jeff on stage. The assembly buzzed slightly. Pastor Thomas stepped up to his podium. "I want to clear the air about our brother and sister in Christ. There is a rumor flying around saying Collin Farrell abused her children. The rumor is false." His voice took on a stern tone. "Someone in this congregation spread the news CPS had been called. We will never condone character assassination in this body of believers. Collin met with CPS, and they wholly exonerated her of any wrongdoing. There was no abuse. There is no danger to anyone's child. Mrs. Farrell will continue to volunteer with the children in the nursery and preschool areas."

He looked over the room. "If anyone has a problem with this, come to me, and we'll discuss it. My office is open. I'll be happy to talk to you." He turned to Collin and Jeff. "Thank you for serving this congregation. I'm sorry for the unfounded accusations you have had to endure." He hugged Collin, shook Jeff's hand, and the Farrells walked off the stage.

Jeff whispered to Collin, "That went about like I expected."

"You think it will stop the rumor mill?"

"Doubtful. Whoever started this won't give up this easy."

Collin shook her head. "It's sad."

"Yeah, it is." They kissed briefly, then Collin headed to the preschool area while Jeff returned to the service. The man in the three-piece suit saluted her as she passed him. *Not now. Not today.* She nodded and moved on. Collin checked into the room, pulled on her name badge, and entered the play area.

Kells was in the middle of teaching the lesson. The children were sitting on individual mats, listening to the story. Or mostly listening. Collin noted a few with thumbs in their mouths, lying quietly. Others were inching their mats closer to each other so they could still play, or fight, or annoy each other. Children.

Kells looked up in surprise as Collin slipped into the back of the room. The woman finished reading the story. She pointed to the wall. "Anyone who wants crackers sit against the wall. No fighting. Hands to yourself." Kells stood. Her eyes narrowed as she approached Collin. "What are you doing here?"

"It's my weekend to volunteer. I'm on the schedule." Collin kept her tone even. Kells would not rattle her today.

Kells looked at the schedule. "I thought they took you off. At least for the month."

"You missed the first part of service. Pastor Thomas called Jeff and me forward and apologized for the false accusations flying around. He said anyone who had a problem with it should talk to him."

"He did? I didn't hear about that."

Collin nodded. "You will. He promised us he would announce it at every service."

Kells cast a sideways eye. "Do you know how the Elders voted about this?"

Collin kept the triumph from her voice. "God brought the Elders to their senses. Jeff and I did nothing wrong. End of story."

Kells brought the hand wipes out to wash each child's hands before giving them crackers to eat for snack. Only after she finished did she turn back to Collin. "Did you call Dr. Bliss's office?"

"Yes. He had a cancellation on Monday. I'll see him then."

"At least it's something."

"Kells, what is eating you? You've been..." Collin couldn't find the word she wanted. "...on my case since group started. What's got you upset?"

"I told you Thursday. You're out of fellowship, and I can't deal with you until you get back right."

Collin chewed her lip. "I still don't know why you think the way you do. I've never stopped loving the Lord or trying to serve Him. How am I out of fellowship?"

Kells narrowed her eyes and faced Collin head-on. "If you

were right with God, none of the things you're going through would happen."

Collin took two breaths. "Read the book of Job, lately? He lost everything, and God said it wasn't about him. It was about God's sovereignty. We don't get to pick and choose what we want to happen. He doesn't owe us anything. He gave us everything."

Kells cut her off. "Don't lecture me. I know what the Scriptures say. God will never give us more than we can handle. And He doesn't punish the righteous. I don't know what you've done, but I know if you were walking with Jesus, your child wouldn't have been kidnapped, and you wouldn't be having the depression and flashbacks you do. Christians do not get depressed. They don't suffer from depression, I mean."

Collin turned her back on the woman. She waited until she could speak civilly before turning back to face her accuser. "I'm sorry you feel that way. It's not the truth. What do you want me to do here, now? You want me to leave? You want to handle all these children yourself?"

Kells looked at the floor. "No. I need you to help since they didn't assign someone else. After this weekend, I'll make sure the schedules get switched around."

Collin stared at her ex-friend. "We made a good team in here. I will miss seeing you."

Kells began wiping the children's hands a second time after the crackers were finished. Collin got out the little carpet cleaner and made short work of the crumbs. She put on music which allowed the children to jump and bend and stretch and clap and have fun. And also, wear them out for naps after lunch.

Before the alligator finished chomping, parents arrived to pick up their offspring. Several more fathers came than mothers. Strange. *Maybe they want to avoid you.*

Makes sense. In a twisted kind of way.

One mother picked up her two sons, smiled at Collin. "I'm so happy Pastor put those vicious rumors to rest. Why anyone would think you could abuse your own children is beyond me." She leaned in and kissed Collin on the cheek. "Don't let the bad guys get you down, Collin. Keep your head up." Collin watched the woman's eyes and noted she glanced over at Kells before she left. Didn't say hello, didn't say thank you, didn't say a word. *Okay, what is that about? She and Kells used to be friends, too.*

In short order, the children were returned to their parents, the second shift of volunteers arrived, and Collin and Kells left to attend "big church." Collin knew the triplets would be staying for the second service, as they always did when she served. But they enjoyed the playtime. And yes, it wore them out for a long nap after.

Collin met Jeff outside the sanctuary. His eyes were dark, his face drawn. Collin drew in a deep breath. "What's wrong?"

Jeff shook his head. "Not now. Not here. Later."

Not good. He's angry about something. Which is a bad sign. Who said what to him?

Collin walked with Jeff to the front of the sanctuary and their accustomed place: second pew back, center section, all the better to hear and see and not be distracted by littles or anyone else. She pulled her Bible and a notepad out of her backpack. Taking notes helped her retain the information longer. *And you need all the retention tools you can find.*

I do not. My focus is fine.

Squirrel.

Where?

Collin shut the voices down. She turned her attention to Pastor Thomas. He again called them forward and again pronounced them innocent of any wrongdoing. After they took their seats, Collin whispered, "Was it worth the try?"

"No. Not in the least."

Collin's head snapped to eye her husband. To hear him so bitter and frustrated over a simple question…someone must have really set him off. She grasped his hand and squeezed it. Jeff squeezed it back, breathing slowly. *Good. He's coming back.*

For how long?

As long as it takes. Leave me alone.

Again the voices retreated to her subconscious. Collin focused on the morning's teaching from Matthew and the Beatitudes. The old words washed over her, reminding her Who she served and why.

Service over, Collin and Jeff made their way to the children's area to pick up the trio. There were more calls of, "Good to see you," and, "I knew it wasn't true," and, "I'm glad Pastor Thomas cleared all that up." Collin didn't notice anyone avoiding eye contact or going out of their way to avoid speaking or seeing Jeff and her. Could have been any regular Sunday.

The excited trio talked about what they had heard and done, and Jeff and Collin caught an earful of animated jabbering. Then home, lunch, and nap. The littles settled into sleep while Collin and Jeff had adult "we time."

Collin joined her husband on the couch. "Now you want to tell me what made you mad?"

Jeff shook his head in disgust. "I heard the Johnsons talking. Said they heard it's all true, and Pastor Thomas is only trying to cover it up, so it didn't make him look bad."

"One couple."

"Except they were standing with three other couples, and not one of them said, 'Hey, let's ask the pastor. There's Jeff. Let's ask him.' No, they all wanted to hear what they wanted to hear, and nothing will change their minds."

Collin breathed in, breathed out. "I worked with Kells. She shares the same opinion." Collin leaned back against the seat. "What do you want to do, Jeff? Do we leave the church because of the whispers? Or stay and fight them? Or live through them, anyhow. Pastor Thomas and the Elders are behind us. No one else's opinion matters."

Jeff stared at the floor. "I know, Collin. It's the injustice of the thing." He raised his head. "But they unjustly accused Jesus. I guess we should be honored we get to suffer with Him."

Collin shook her head. "I'm not sure we can claim that yet. But we can use His as our example of how to act."

Jeff grinned. "Can I call them out as snakes and vipers, then?"

"Not aloud you can't. Not yet." Her mood lightened. "We'll let it go and see how long it takes the grumblers to find another target."

"A month."

"Probably right. I'm not going to give them any more time or energy. I have a life to live, and I'm going to live it."

"Sounds good. What should we do with the rest of our day?"

Collin unbuttoned the top button of his shirt. "I have an idea."

Jeff kissed her. "Yeah?"

Collin nodded. "Yeah. A nap." She pulled Jeff to his feet.

"Sleep while the babies sleep. Anything else has to wait until they're actually in bed for the night."

Jeff chuckled. "I hear you. A nap would be good. There's a ball game I want to watch. I'll fall asleep out here, and you can have the bedroom to yourself."

"Sounds like a winning plan. At least for now."

Collin walked alone to the bedroom.

And found another envelope lying on her pillow. She closed her eyes, steeled herself, opened them. She picked the envelope up by the corners, careful to not smudge any evidence. Maybe the Elders considered this harmless, but Collin had no such illusion. She slid the note out.

"One dies. And you deserve everything which happened."

Which happened... Deserve everything which happened... Collin's mind crashed into the memories of Talitha's kidnapping. Her baby taken. Her brother nearly killed. His fiancée taken in broad daylight. The notes. The despair. The emptiness...again and again and again. Collin sank against the wall. *Why? Why? Why is this happening?*

I am with you.

Collin breathed. Breathed again. Reached over and took hold of the rubber band on her wrist. Pulled it. Snapped it hard.

The sting broke the spell of the past. Brought her back to the present. *Someone has threatened my babies again. Someone wants to drive me insane.*

Short drive.

The derision in her head snapped her as well. Sane. She needed to be sane for the babies. She would be sane for them. She would be strong. They would not win.

Collin looked back at the letter on the floor beside her. The two sentences drew her back. *"One dies. And you deserve everything which happened."*

What happened? In the end? We got Talitha and Vy back. Erin lived through it. No permanent harm done to any of them. We didn't deserve to get them back. But God brought them back. The writer hasn't got a clue.

Collin pulled herself off the floor. She steadied her breathing, steadied her emotions. She carried the letter in and handed it to Jeff. "We've had another visitor. "

Jeff took the page. His eyes burned. His jaws tightened. His fists clenched. He pulled out his phone and dialed. "Braydon? Someone came in while we were gone. Yeah. They left another note. This one's a threat. Please check your video feeds. Maybe you can see who the perp is."

He hung up. Collin watched his hands shaking. She took the letter from him and placed it back in the envelope. "I know you want to shred it. It won't help."

"I want to shred whoever is leaving these. How are they getting in here? And why? What is this all about?"

Collin squeezed his hand. "Hopefully, Braydon will have some answers."

They waited. And waited. And waited. Jeff's phone squawked. He answered it. "Talk to me, Braydon."

Jeff listened. His face darkened. "Nothing at all? How is it possible?"

More listening. "I'm not doubting you." Pause. "I'd like to review the feed. Not saying I don't trust your people or you. But for my own satisfaction. You understand. Uh-huh. Right. I appreciate it, man. Talk to you later."

Jeff put his phone away. Collin eyed him until he gave her the report. "Nothing on the feed. Nothing outside. The house never changed."

Collin stared off into space. "How are they doing it? How are they getting in? And not being seen on the cameras?" She looked up at Jeff. "You don't think I'm doing it, do you?"

He shook his head hard. "No. Never. I know you. Even at your worst, you'd never do this. Someone outside...someone inside...I don't know how, but we're going to figure it out. I promise, milady. We will figure it out."

Collin hesitated. "When do we call the police?"

Jeff looked away. "When we have something solid to give them. With nothing on the cameras, what are they going to do? What are they going to say? We have to have something besides the notes." She watched his jaw tighten. "I'm sure they won't find any fingerprints, even." Jeff's eyes held hers. "Do you agree?"

"Could we file a report? At least then we have it on record. Maybe they don't come out immediately, but we have the record. We're doing something."

Jeff appeared to think about it. Finally, he nodded. "I'll call it in."

Collin listened as Jeff made the call, made the report, heard his, "I understand. Low priority. We wanted to get in the queue, that's all. Yes, if anything else happens, we'll certainly call."

As he hung up, Collin reached up and kissed him. "Thank you."

He kissed her back. "I'm sorry. I used to hate hysterical phone calls, which were nothing. Always made me feel like we were being called away from someone that needed help."

"I understand, my love. I do. The last thing I need is to be thought of as a hysterical female." *I already feel that way. Don't need others thinking it, too.*

Collin looked at the letter. "What do we do in the meantime?"

"Keep the babies safe. Watch. Listen. Do all the things we know to do."

It came out as a whisper. Or prayer. "Trust the Lord." Collin went internal, marshaling her defenses.

Jeff put his arms around her. "Yes. We trust Him. And we face whatever His plans are. And we keep believing He is for us. He is good, He is God, and He loves us."

Collin let her control melt. "Right. It's what we do. We believe Him. Even when it hurts."

"Even then."

Collin pointed to the family room. "Go stretch out and watch your game through your eyelids." She grinned. "Like you normally do."

Jeff huffed. "Not always."

"Most the time."

He chucked her under the chin. "Watch it, lady. What are you going to do?"

"Take the nap until the babies wake up."

He kissed her. "Love you."

"Love you."

Collin waited until Jeff had disappeared up the hall. She listened for the TV and heard the sound of his recliner creaking. She walked into the bedroom, retrieved a pillow and a small blanket, then moved back to the hallway. She stopped at the babies' door.

She closed her eyes. I'm sorry, Lord. My head is screaming I'm not trusting You. But my gut tells me I need to be here. I need to do this. Just now. Not forever. Just now. I know You understand. I love You.

She settled down on the floor, lying across the door opening. Nothing and no one would pass her. Not without tripping over her. She pulled the blanket over her shoulders and closed her eyes. *Fifteen minutes. Twenty tops.*

MONDAY

Monday morning. Collin sat in the office of Dr. Bliss, filling out the appropriate papers. All three hundred and fifty-four of them…

Okay, that might be an exaggeration. But there were enough to try her patience. And her memory. She finally finished the last one, stepped up to the reception desk, and handed the clipboard back to the girl behind the counter. "I think I got them all filled out. As good as I could."

The receptionist smiled. "I know there's a lot of them. But it helps Dr. Bliss help you." She flipped through the sheets, stopped. "You didn't fill out the insurance information, Mrs. Farrell. We can't bill…"

"We're self-pay."

"You're sure? We can bill every insurance. Dr. Bliss makes sure the codes match what the insurances will cover. He's never had a claim rejected, either."

Collin smiled. *Be pleasant. Be calm. Be patient.* "No, we are self-pay."

The woman held out a laminated card. "Dr. Bliss does have a sliding scale for people who self-pay. Maybe it can help you."

Collin looked at the scale. At the low-end, people got fifteen-minute sessions with an associate. Mid-range got half-hour appointments, also with an associate. At the high-end, you got the entire hour with Dr. Bliss. Collin sighed. *Fleece the flock.* She handed the card back. "Bill us the full amount."

For the first time, the woman looked uncomfortable. She hesitated, then smiled again. Weakly. "I'm sorry, Mrs. Farrrell, but self-pay clients have to pay at the time of the appointment. I hope it's not an inconvenience for you."

Collin pulled out her credit card. "Do you take plastic?"

"Dr. Bliss prefers checks. He doesn't get billed the recovery fee from the credit card companies."

Collin put the card away and pulled out the checkbook she carried. *See? There is a reason I carry it. Haven't written a check in years, but I still carry it, in case. Like today.*

Collin wrote out the check, waiting for the receptionist to give her a total. The woman gave her a figure. Collin didn't flinch. Outwardly. *You have got to be kidding? To sit with someone and listen to them talk for an hour, and you charge how much? Our tenant houses charge less for a month.*

Lest her displeasure spill into her actions, Collin took a seat by the window to wait for her turn. She looked out at the well-tended landscaping. Several small birch trees framed the building. Rose bushes lined a walkway. Hummingbirds dive-bombed anyone and anything which crossed their territorial lines. Pansies and violas were planted along the side of the building. *I can't wait 'til the littles are old enough to help plant a garden. A real garden with real vegetables and fruits we can eat. Should be fun. And delicious. Homegrown tomatoes...yeah. Those.*

"Mrs. Farrell?"

Collin looked up. An older gentleman, perhaps early sixties, held open a door and pointed inside. "I will see you now."

Collin left her garden and entered the room. Bookshelves lined the walls. Books filled the shelves. *Of course, they do. But does anyone actually read them?*

Quit being snide. Best behavior, right?

Collin took a seat in a straight-back chair directly across from the hand-carved wooden desk. She resisted the urge to run her hands over the beautifully inlaid maple and oak top. *Hands to yourself. Hands in your lap, even. No twisting. No tells.*

Dr. Bliss sat in his chair behind the desk. "What brings you to see me, Mrs. Farrell?"

Collin got straight to it. "A friend insisted I see you. She's concerned about me and felt it in my best interests I see you."

"A friend insisted you come, and you came? Must be a powerful friend." Dr. Bliss scribbled on the calendar on his desk. Curly cues. Boxes. Doodles.

Collin cleared her throat. "Not powerful. A woman whose opinion I value."

"And why did she feel you needed to see me?"

Collin breathed slow. "About three years ago, someone kidnapped my daughter. She was four months old. We got her back after two weeks. Last week, an intruder in the house triggered a flashback in me, and I panicked. I grabbed my children and held them tight, convinced someone wanted to steal them from me again."

Collin lifted her chin. "My husband talked me off the ledge, the children forgave me, and I dealt with it." She paused. "The intruder left threatening letters. I had a flashback after the second letter. The third letter, I ended the trip down memory lane on my own." She held up the rubber band on her wrist. "My reminder."

"So, three years ago, someone took your daughter. But they returned her. Unharmed, yes?"

"If you call almost freezing to death, being left without food and water for an entire day as unharmed, yes." *Back it down a bit, okay? No need to let him know there are still triggers which upset you.*

Dr. Bliss scribbled some more. "But they returned her. The kidnappers. Were they caught? Tried and convicted? Serving prison time?"

Collin breathed in and out. "Two of the kidnappers were murdered by the third for releasing my daughter and my sister-in-law. The police captured the third, and he is serving life for the double murders. So yes, he is serving prison time."

"Are you a woman of faith, Mrs. Farrell?"

Collin caught the man's eyes. "If you mean do I know Jesus as my Lord and Savior, the answer is yes. Do I try to follow Him in everything I do? Yes. Does He hold my life? Yes."

Dr. Bliss shrugged. "One may know Him intimately and still not live a life of faith."

Collin shook her head. "I don't understand what you mean. To follow Him is to place your faith in Him. Always. Every day. In everything. How much more intimate can I be?"

"Tell me, Mrs. Farrell. Have you forgiven the kidnappers?"

"Yes."

"But you're still having flashbacks?"

"I had several in the beginning." She swallowed. "I spent two weeks in the hospital. But I worked the program, and I got better." She lifted her chin. "This was the first episode I've had in two years. I reacted badly to the threat to my children."

Dr. Bliss held up his hand. "The perceived threat, correct?"

"A stranger in my house leaving messages in envelopes is not a perceived threat, Dr. Bliss. It is a very real threat to the safety and well-being of my children."

"But you don't know the intruder's intentions. You don't know if they are a threat."

"If they are in my house without my consent, they are a threat."

"I see. Tell me again how you are a woman of faith?"

Collin swallowed hard. "My faith in the Lord is absolute. His charge to me to nurture and protect the children He gave me is also absolute. Someone breaking into my house when the babies and I are home represents a danger I must address." *I'm getting a bad vibe here.*

"Would you say you trust the Lord implicitly?"

"I trust Him to have my best interests at heart. I trust Him to do what His sovereign will is. I trust Him to carry me through fire and flood and the shadow of death. Yes, I trust Him."

"Yet by your own admission, you didn't trust Him to protect your children from an intruder in your home."

Collin laid her hands on the desk. "Trusting Him implicitly does not mean I do nothing. I trust Him to protect me, but that doesn't give me license to go play in traffic. I trust Him to provide for my children's daily needs. It doesn't mean I don't prepare meals and feed or clothe them. I have my responsibilities from Him."

"Do your responsibilities and His ever overlap?"

Collin sat back in the chair. *Distance is good. Less chance of hitting him.*

By accident.

Not exactly.

Behave!

"If you're asking do I get in the way of what He's doing in my life, yes, there have been times. I've thought He wanted to do one thing, and it turned out He had something else in mind entirely.

Absolutely I've had those moments."

Dr. Bliss frowned at her. "Is everything always about you, Mrs. Farrell?"

She shook her head. "No. There are lessons for everyone in any situation. I've seen God move in miraculous ways when I was only an onlooker. But I still drew lessons from the experience."

"So God can work in other people's lives without your help?"

"Of course."

"But you don't trust Him to work in your children's lives without you."

"I trust Him to work. I trust He has worked. I trust He will work. But I won't leave my children unattended or unprotected because I 'trust God' to care for them."

Back it down. Back it down.

No! This is ridiculous.

Stay calm. Hear him out.

Collin growled, but internally. She lifted her chin slightly. "There is God's part, and there is my part. I overreacted with my part. Overcoming the trauma is still a work in progress for me. And the Lord."

"But if you've forgiven the kidnappers, there should be no more trauma. Mrs. Farrell, your problem is your lack of faith."

Dr. Bliss lay his pen down and directed his full attention to her. "If you loved Jesus more, you wouldn't be having flashbacks. I am going to give you exercises to help strengthen your trust in Him. When you are anxious, repeat over and over, 'I love You, Jesus. I love You.' Spend less time thinking about yourself and more time focusing on Him. Give Him room to work in your life and the lives of your children. If you believe He loves you, He won't let anything happen to those children."

He sat back and stared at her. "Would you have stopped your daughter's kidnapping if you could?"

Collin's hands shook. She sat on them. "My brother nearly died trying to prevent it. Yes, if I could have stopped it, I would have."

"Do you see how you were working against God? He wanted your daughter for some purpose of His own. Trying to prevent her from being taken might have been in direct opposition to God. He needed her, and you fought Him. Your brother's nearly being killed could have been God's way of telling you to stop."

Collin stood up. She didn't try to hide the shaking of her hands or the tremble in her voice. "Dr. Bliss, we're done. Thank you for your time."

"Mrs. Farrell, you're here for an evaluation. I can't certify your mental state if you don't complete the session."

Collin glared at him. If she could have lasered him into non-existence, she would have. "You do what you have to do, Dr. Bliss." She turned and walked out.

As she moved past the reception desk, Collin called sharply, "Have a wonderful day."

You could have said it more nicely.

I didn't have to say it at all. Shut up. All of you. Shut up!

Collin walked to her car, climbed in the front seat, closed the door, locked it, then dropped her head to the steering wheel. Hot tears splashed on her hands. "Who does he think he is? God never caused Talitha to be kidnapped! He's not the author of evil. How can that ignorant, self-important, ego-maniac think for one moment..."

She choked on all the things she wanted to say but couldn't get out at once. All of it. She leaned her head back and growled, "AAARRRGGGHHH!" Collin shook her hands and arms out. A shudder ran up her spine. She closed her eyes. "Lord, forgive me for what I'm thinking right now. You know I love You. You know You are the center of my being. It's all about You. Help me. Help me put this in some sort of perspective. Or understand it. I don't. I don't."

Collin turned on the car, turned on the radio and its preset Christian radio station. Listening to worship music calmed her soul. Ten minutes and three songs later, she put the car in drive and headed to Lacey and Harmon Farrell's house to rescue her in-laws from her children. She called.

"Hello, Collin, dear. Done so soon?"

"Uh, yeah. The appointment ended early. Is there anything you need while I'm on the way?"

"No, but thank you. You know, you could leave them here for a little longer. Say, 'til after lunch? We're having a great time. Harmon's got them painting the garage."

"Nooooo!"

"Now, Collin. They're in paint shirts and bare feet. Wash and wear, I promise."

"It's not that. They'll want to paint their room, or the house, or the carport."

Lacey laughed. "It's good for them. They get to play and have fun. All four of them."

Collin grinned. "Yeah, I know about the biggest kid. Tell Pop Harmon I love him, and I'll see him when I come back for the triplets after lunch."

"Go enjoy your morning, dear. We love you."

"Love you too, Mom Lacey."

Before she could cut off the call, another came in. Kells. Collin sagged, then looked at the clock. Why would she call now? She knew Collin's appointment ran from nine to ten. It was only half-past. She couldn't know Collin had left, could she? Could she?

She picked up the call. "Kells."

"Did you see Dr. Bliss?"

"Yes."

"Did he mention your lack of faith?"

"We discussed a few things, yes."

"You don't agree with him, do you?"

Collin stared at the phone. "Why would you assume that?"

"Because I know you. You're too proud to admit you're wrong."

"And you're convinced he'd tell me I'm wrong. Is that what you're saying?"

"Of course."

"Why?"

"Why what?"

Collin turned the corner into a coffee shop parking lot and stopped the car. She needed to be able to think and not drive. "Why do you think he would tell me I'm wrong? And about what?"

Silence. "I know you. You disagree with everyone about anything if it gets close to you."

"Um-hum. Have you written the email to the ladies saying the group is going to meet at your house because you don't want Eliza to come?"

"No. I'm not going to. I'm going to tell them you have a stalker after you and your children, and your place is no longer a safe place to meet. And you chose to drop out rather than pack up all three children to come to my house. And Eliza chose not to come anymore."

"How are you going to handle it with Nonnie?" *I'm ignoring the stalker part. We will get back to it, believe me.*

"It's not like she and Eliza are best buds. I doubt if the matter will even come up between them."

"Nonnie isn't stupid, Kells. She's going to ask Eliza why she isn't coming."

"Then I'll tell her Eliza wanted to meet with you one on one, and she's with you instead of the group."

"So it's safe for Eliza to come but not for anyone else? What happened to the 'you're putting the letters out yourself' theory?"

Silence again.

"You can't have it both ways, Kells. I don't understand any of your actions right now. We're friends. What's going on? What's this all about?"

"Nothing is going on on my end. It's all on you. You're the one…"

Collin interrupted. "Tell me, Kells, why did you call me half an hour before my appointment should have ended? How did you know I left the office?"

Silence. "I…I didn't. I called to leave a message so you would call me."

"Right. But you expected to hear my voice. You weren't caught off guard by me answering. You knew. How?"

"This isn't about me. This is about…"

Collin's eyes narrowed. "No. You've made it about you now, and how you could possibly know what I spoke to with Dr. Bliss and how long my appointment lasted. Someone in the office has breached confidentiality. Seems to be happening a lot lately. Any ideas who? Or why?"

"You're accusing me…"

"I'm asking you. Did you talk with Dr. Bliss or his receptionist or anyone else in his office about my seeing him?"

"Today?"

"Any day, Kells. I don't know what you're pulling, and I sure don't know why. But I will get to the bottom of this. And I will protect my children, my husband, and myself from any and all threats." *Foreign or domestic.*

"The only thing threatening you is yourself. You…"

Collin hung up the phone. She put the car in motion and headed toward the bakery close to the Lacey and Harmon's house. She could get a coffee and pastry, relax, clear her head, and pick the babies up after lunch. *Good plan.*

I can make one every now and then.

Collin's phone beeped again. She looked at the number and picked it up. "Nonnie? Hi."

Winona's voice had a tremble in it. "I'm sorry to call you, Collin, but I didn't know who else to call."

"What's wrong?" Collin pulled into a bookstore parking lot. Empty lot.

"Leonard…he got physical with Macie. They were playing, and he… he…" Winona began sobbing.

Collin gripped her phone. "Is Macie okay?"

"She's at the hospital. She broke her leg." Winona snapped. "*He* broke her leg. I think he did it deliberately."

"Are you at the hospital?"

"Yes."

"Where is Leonard?"

"He's here, too. He's in talking to the doctor. They wanted to know how she broke it, what happened, what we were doing, where we were."

Collin pointed the car towards Children's Hospital. "I'll be there in ten minutes." She hesitated. "Nonnie, are you going to tell them he hurt her on purpose?"

Silence. "I don't know what to do. I'm afraid. If he hurt her, will he hurt me too?"

Collin gritted her teeth. When she could speak again, she kept her tone even. "Have they interviewed you about it yet?"

"No. Not yet. Leonard said he wanted to be the one to explain what happened."

"When they talk to you, tell them what you saw, Nonnie. You don't have to accuse him of anything. Tell them what you saw. It should be enough for them to look into it deeper."

"He's going to know I reported him." Nonnie's sobs choked

her words.

"He's going to know you told the truth. And protected Macie. Are you still in ER?"

"Yes. They may have to take her to surgery." Nonnie whispered, "My baby. In surgery. My poor baby."

Collin swallowed. She started to speak, but a caution warned her. *Get the facts. Get all the facts.* She turned the corner onto Children's Way and pulled into the ER parking lot. "I'll be right in, Nonnie. Which bay are you in?

"Fourteen."

"Tell the desk you're expecting company. And to let me in."

"I will."

Collin hung up again. *Lord, I don't know if this is You, but I'll take it as such. Keep me neutral until I know all the facts. And thank You. I think.*

The security guard waved her on through, and Collin went in. She pulled back the curtain on bay fourteen.

Nonnie sat on the bed holding Macie. The little girl slept, probably anesthetized. Leonard hadn't come back to the room yet. Collin wrapped her arms around Winona.

The distraught woman accepted the hug and burst into tears. "My baby. My poor baby! Look at her. Look at the bed. It's so big, and she's so tiny. She doesn't belong here. She should be home with me." She looked up at Collin. "I don't want him to be near her. I don't want him in the house ever again." Nonnie hugged Macie. "She'll never be able to run or play or dance... He's ruined her life. What if she's in pain forever from this? What if she can't walk again?"

Collin rested her hand on Winona's arm. "You're not thinking clearly, Nonnie. Macie will be fine. It's a break." She tossed her head. "I've broken about every bone in my body, and I'm still walking."

Winona snapped. "But you're an adult. She's a baby. How is she going to walk?"

Collin stepped back. "She'll walk fine, Nonnie. And I broke my leg—or had it broken—when I was younger than Macie. She'll be fine. Babies adapt."

The curtains parted. Leonard came into the room, accompanied by a doctor and a uniformed police officer. Leonard glanced at Collin and smiled. A weak, apologetic smile. "Collin. I didn't know Nonnie called you. I'm sorry she dragged you into this."

Collin's eyes widened, then narrowed. "Dragged me into what?"

The police officer motioned to Winona. "We'd like to speak to you, ma'am. Will you come with me?"

Winona's eyes became saucers. A deer in headlights. She turned toward Collin. Her lip trembled as she stood. She handed Macie to the doctor. He laid her on the bed, tucking blankets around her. Winona took a deep breath, nodded, and walked out with the officer.

Leonard dropped onto the bed and began stroking Macie's hair. He kissed her gently. "My poor girl. She doesn't deserve this."

Collin stepped closer to the bed. "What happened? Nonnie says her leg's broken?"

Leonard nodded. "I had the day off and went outside. I heard Macie let out a scream. It sounded like pure terror." Leonard's voice shook. He looked at his hands. "I said I would always protect her. But I didn't. I couldn't. Not from this." He glanced at Collin. "Not from her own mother."

Collin went still inside. *Get the facts. All the facts.* "What did Nonnie say happened?"

Leonard hung his head. "Macie wouldn't go to sleep for her nap. She wanted to play with me since I was home. It threw her off her routine, I know. But Nonnie...Nonnie had been losing her temper with Macie all morning. She yelled at her constantly. I walked outside, thinking that maybe if she didn't see me, Macie would lie down. But the yelling continued. I could hear Macie crying...then she screamed. I ran into the house. Nonnie told me Macie fell...but the doctor says the break had to have a great deal of force behind it. You don't break the hip bone by falling off the bed."

"Hip? Nonnie said it was her leg."

"X-rays show the hip's broken. The doctor thinks Macie had to be thrown violently. Poor little baby."

Facts. Get the facts. Listen. Do not judge. Do not choose sides.

"It must have been awful. Did you call an ambulance?"

Leonard shook his head. "No. I didn't want to wait for one. Nonnie held Macie in her arms, and I drove here." He closed his eyes. "I broke so many traffic laws. But I didn't care. All I cared about was getting Macie here where they could help her."

Collin leaned against the bed and held Macie's tiny hand. She bit her lip. "I'm sorry this happened."

Leonard eyed Collin. "Has she said anything in your group about being stressed out?" He dropped his gaze. "Never mind. I'm sure the police will ask you all those questions. They're going to do a full investigation." He shook his head. "I never thought she would hurt our baby. Never."

Collin squeezed Macie's hand. "We don't know the stresses people live with. Or which ones make them snap." *Don't ask. Don't ask.*

Ask.

Collin smiled. "Tell me about Macie at home. What makes you smile?"

Leonard beamed. He stroked the sleeping toddler's head. "The way she dances through the house. She doesn't walk, she dances. She's so full of life." He touched the pink cheek. "She's picking up books and reading them to me." He looked up at Collin. "Every night before she goes to bed, she sits on my lap and reads a book to me." He shrugged. "Okay, so she turns the pages and turns the book upside down. Sometimes we read the book back to front. But it's sweet father-daughter time." He looked at the floor. "I wish Nonnie took more time to be with Macie."

Collin kept her voice gentle. "Maybe she's tired from chasing her around all day."

"Maybe." Leonard sounded less than sure. "That's why I hired a housekeeper to come in three days a week, so Nonnie wouldn't be so stressed."

Collin kept her voice to mild surprise, not the all-out shock she felt. "You have a housekeeper coming in?"

"Yeah. She does laundry, cooks meals, runs the vacuum, does other light housekeeping."

Laundry is not light housekeeping.

Yeah, tell me about it.

"I see. Sounds like Nonnie has help, then."

Leonard shook his head. "I have to work overtime to pay for it. But Nonnie insists she has to have the help. I don't mind the extra hours, except it takes me away from Macie."

Lord, I can't sort this out. None of what he says matches what Nonnie tells us in group. I'm being deceived, but by who?

The doctor came back into the cubicle. "We're going to take Macie to surgery now."

Leonard held up his hand. "You can't. Not until they're done talking to Nonnie. She'll never forgive herself or me if she doesn't see the baby before she goes to surgery."

"We have the team waiting."

"Please? Five minutes?"

The doctor pursed his lips. "Five minutes." He exited the curtains.

Leonard looked at Collin. "Am I right? To make them wait? I'm not hurting Macie, am I?"

Collin shook her head. "You made the right call. I'd be ballistic if any of mine went into surgery, and I didn't get to kiss them goodbye."

Collin's gut constricted. Her eyes lost focus of the now, back to the then. *Talitha! Not my baby! No! Don't take her!*

Collin closed her eyes to the shadows. She drew in several life-giving breaths. She snapped the rubber band. The shadows receded. Collin opened her eyes.

Leonard's head cocked. "Are you okay, Collin?"

"Yeah. Old data. Pay it no mind." She gave him a wan smile. "I'm fine."

Leonard nodded. He looked where the police had taken Winona. "I'm going to tell them she needs to say goodbye to Macie. They can talk to her more after the baby's in surgery." He glanced at Collin. "Will you stay with her?"

"Of course. She's not going anywhere. I promise."

Leonard pushed the curtains open, walked to the interrogation room (or the spare room, whichever image you prefer,) and knocked lightly. Collin turned her attention to the sleeping child. "Oh, Macie. Jesus loves you. He's going to be with you in surgery. And you're going to be just fine. He's going to hold you and carry you and keep you in His arms." She stroked the toddler's cheek, brushed the hair back from her eyes. "Auntie Collin will stay with you until Mommy and Daddy come back. You are loved, little one. More than you know. But one day, I pray you will."

The door opened again, and Winona and Leonard came out arm-in-arm, desperately clinging to each other. Nonnie's face was white and drenched in tears. The doctor and a police officer followed close behind them. Collin stepped back and made way for the parents to say their goodbyes.

Nonnie picked the little girl up and crushed her to her chest. "My baby. My baby. My poor baby. Oh, honey, Mommy is so sorry you were hurt. I love you."

The doctor had to coax—and practically tear—Macie from her grasp. He handed the child to her father, who kissed her. "I love you, Macie. We'll be right here when you get back. Be strong, little one. I love you."

He handed the child to the doctor, who laid her out on a gurney. Nurses helped strap the toddler to the rolling transport, then wheeled her down the hall.

Nonnie collapsed on the floor. "My baby. My baby."

Leonard kneeled beside her. "She'll be fine, Nonnie. She's strong. She's our love. She'll be good." He drew her to her feet. A nurse smiled. "I'll take you to the surgical waiting room. The doctor will let you know when she comes out of surgery and when you can go see her."

Leonard touched Collin's arm. "Thank you for coming, Collin. Will you wait with us?"

"I can't. I have to pick up my three. But we will pray for you and Macie. God has her. Hold on to Him."

The shattered couple followed the nurse down the corridor. Collin picked up her satchel, threw it over her shoulder, and walked out into the bright sunshine. She pushed all thoughts of who, what, why, and how to the bottom of the awareness. Now she wanted her three and the life and joy and happiness they were experiencing with Gamma and Gampa. Anything else would have to wait.

TUESDAY

A knock at the front door, followed by someone trying the handle. Collin looked up from the cookbook she read. Who?

A voice. "Collin, open the door. It's Kells."

Collin uncrossed her legs, rose from the floor, and went to the front door. She opened it and stood back to let Kells in.

The woman struggled to carry in her satchel, the baby, and two large cloth bags. Collin glanced from the bags to Kells. "You want some help there?"

"Please. I'm going to drop something, and I don't want it to be Allison."

Collin went to grab the bags, but Kells stopped her. "Get the baby. She's the heaviest."

Collin grabbed the car seat from the pile and swooped Allison away from her mother. "Whee!" She flew the baby into the dining room, set her down on the table. "There you go, Princess. All safe!"

Allison chuckled and cooed and babbled. Collin leaned in and kissed the chubby cheeks. She turned to watch Kells walk in, set the bags beside the couch, and sink down. The woman let out a deep sigh. "Finally!"

Collin eyed Kells sideways. "What's going on, Kells?"

The woman sat up and motioned to the bags. "I went through drawers in the nursery and found a shirt which belonged to Caleb. Decided I'd bring it back. Then I found Talitha's pants. The deeper I looked, the more stuff I found." She locked eyes with Collin. "I didn't realize how connected we've been over the years. Finding all this stuff reminded me. I'm sorry, Collin. I was out of line. Will you forgive me?"

Collin broke into a mile-wide smile. "Of course. Done. Over. I'm so glad to have you back." She hugged Kells. There might have been a half-hitch hesitation in the return embrace, but Collin ignored it. Filed it away. "You want to talk about it?"

"No, I'd rather know what Dr. Bliss had to say. Honestly. What did he say to you?"

Collin felt her stomach tighten. She calmed herself. "He said much of what you believe. A Christian shouldn't have problems. If I'd been 'right' with God, my baby wouldn't have been taken." Anger seeped up from the depths, tensing her muscles. Constricting her throat. Narrowing her eyes. Collin fought it back. Calm. She would remain calm.

"He went so far as to tell me trying to keep Talitha safe from the kidnappers was fighting against God's will. And Erin's nearly losing his life might have been God's punishment for us interfering in His plans." *Breathe. Breathe. Slowly.*

Kells's eyes widened. Her mouth "o'd." Her hands shook. "He said what? He actually said those words?"

Collin nodded. "That's when I walked out." *Breathe. Breathe. He's gone. You're here.* "I'll take a lot of insults. But being told I'm wrong to protect my child isn't something I'll stand for. Or sit for."

Kells nodded. "I hear you. I'm so sorry, Collin. I can't believe a psychiatrist would actually… I mean, maybe you misunderstood him?"

"I did not mistake his words, Kells. It's what he said. Not implied. Said."

Kells sat back. "I'm sorry. I'm sorry he would say anything so off." She hesitated, looked at the floor, then looked back at Collin. "I can see what he means, though. We're always kind of fighting against God. We may not know it, but we do."

Collin swallowed the bitterness from her tone. "Protecting and caring for our children is a God-given responsibility. We do not fight against Him when we obey Him."

"You're right. Did he say anything else?"

Collin smiled through pursed lips. "He agrees with you. Christians who are walking with the Lord shouldn't have problems." Sarcasm won. "They should walk from victory to victory with no care in the world."

Kells looked down. "But you don't believe him."

"No, I don't. I live a different reality than you do, Kells. I'm happy you don't have to contend with the issues I do." Swallow. "Read Corinthians. Paul talks about everything he suffered. All the jailings. All the beatings. Every one of the apostles was murdered except John. They were walking in the Lord's will when it happened."

Kells looked out the window beside her, then turned back. "We can agree to disagree. Can we talk about Eliza?"

Collin held up a hand. "Let me check on the littles. It's been ten minutes, and they shouldn't be unsupervised too long."

Kells indicated the bags. "I'll put these in the nursery. You can sort them out later."

Collin grimaced. "Story of my life. Sorting laundry."

Kells laughed. "You had to have three at once. It's easy to tell Allison's from mine."

"For now." Collin moved down the hall, Kells behind her with the bags. Kells stopped at the nursery, put the bags on the floor, and closed the door. She followed Collin to the playroom and called, "Auntie Kells is here."

Immediate excitement, and three bodies burst out of the room to be the first to get attention. "Aunnie Kells! Aunnie Kells! Aunnie Kells!"

Kells kneeled down to capture the trio in her arms. "Hi, babies." She hugged and kissed each one.

Collin watched the interaction. *This is the Kells I remember. What happened to her?* She directed the littles. "If you can be very good and listen to Mommy, you can come in the family room and see baby Allison while I talk with Auntie Kells."

"We be good, Mommy." "Yes, Mommy." "See baby Ason?"

"Uh-huh." Littles in tow, Collin and Kells walked back to the family room. Kells took Allison out of her carrier and set her in her lap so the trio could see her, touch her ("gently"), and generally fawn over the baby. Allison loved the attention and laughed and babbled. Collin got the trio occupied with books, then went back to talking "adult talk" with Kells.

"You wanted to talk about Eliza."

Kells leaned back in her chair. "I still don't like the idea of her coming to the group. I don't like her agenda." She held up her hand to stop Collin's protest. "But I'll agree to let her come if we don't talk about her partner or their living arrangements."

Collin took a moment to settle herself. "We don't talk about anyone's living arrangements, Kells. Eliza won't be any different."

"We talk about whose job it is to do what."

"Which we disagree on, too. Who are you worried she'll influence? None of the littles are anywhere near old enough to understand there's anything different with Eliza and Pam."

Kells ducked her head. "I know. I want to protect my child, above all."

"When Allison is old enough to understand she needs protection, you can have a discussion with her about lifestyles. But we're so far away from there, it's not even an issue."

Kells shrugged. "Yeah, I know. I think I figured it out." She pursed her lips. "So we will have group here on Thursday, and everyone is welcome."

Collin smiled. "That's what I wanted to hear. Thank you."

Kells reached out and hugged Collin. "I do, too." She hesitated. "Have you seen any more envelopes?"

Collin nodded. The brightness left the room. "One. But the monitors still don't show anyone coming in. Someone left it Sunday while we were at church."

Kells shook her head. "I can't imagine how anyone gets in and out without leaving some kind of trace. It's almost impossible, isn't it?"

Collin felt the yank in her soul. "Almost. But not quite. The fact they're doing it means it's not impossible."

Kells shrugged. "And the police still have nothing?"

"We filed a report on Sunday. No one has come out to investigate it yet. Low on the priority list. Our security team ran a sniffer dog through, and she had a hit in the babies' closet. Something had been there. It's a matter of time until whoever it is slips up, or the dog finds something."

Kells's head perked up when Collin mentioned the dog. "You had a dog come through the house? And it got a hit? How?"

"The dog is trained to smell out anomalies. Smells which aren't part of the natural landscape, as it were. She spotted something in the trio's closet. Whatever she smelled had disappeared by then. But there had been something. Braydon is going to run her through occasionally to see what she comes up with."

Kells's tone came out flatter than Collin expected. "That'll be informative."

Collin side-eyed her visitor. "You still think I'm putting the letters out myself?"

"I didn't say you were knowingly doing it. I thought it might have been a possibility."

"It's not." Collin watched her tone. "I appreciate all you wanted to do is help me, Kells. And you care about my family and me. I'm not off my rocker and planting threatening letters."

Kells met Collin's eyes. "I never thought you were off your rocker." She looked down. "I'm sorry I complained about Winona and Bri. I was having a bad day, I guess."

Ya think?

And you wanted to pass it on to everyone else?

"I promise I won't tell them anything you said." *And I'm not going to tell you anything further about any of them.* "You might keep Nonnie and Leonard in your prayers, though. Macie broke her leg and is in the hospital. I'm sure they would appreciate all the support you can give them."

Kells sat up in interest. "Macie broke her leg? How?"

"I don't know the details. Nonnie asked me to come to the ER, and I stayed until they took Macie back for surgery. Nonnie called me later to say she came through the surgery fine but will have to be off the leg for a while. She's pretty distraught over the whole thing."

Kells pressed. "She didn't say what happened? Did Macie fall? Off of what?"

Collin shook her head. "I don't know how it happened, and Nonnie wasn't clear about the details. It didn't seem the right time or place for me to push her about it, either. You can ask her yourself the next time she comes. Or you can call her."

"I'll call her. The way she idolizes her baby, I'm sure she's a basket case."

"I wouldn't know."

"You don't think Leonard hurt the baby, do you? The way Nonnie talks about him all the time, I wouldn't put it past him."

"That's unfair, Kells. And you said yourself you don't believe half what Nonnie says about her marriage. You can't have it both ways."

Kells shrugged. "Yeah, I guess. I'll give her a call." She stood. "I should get moving. I have errands to run, and you were first on the list." She hugged Collin. "I'm glad we're okay again. Thank you for being understanding."

I don't understand anything about you, Kells. "I'm glad we're still friends. I appreciate you coming over today. And dropping off the trio's clothes. I can't believe there were two bags full! I'll have to go through them all."

Kells laughed. "I wouldn't bother with it right now. You've got plenty of other things to do."

Collin nodded. "The trio and I have to make a cake for Daddy."

"Is it his birthday?"

"Nope. We just want to bake a cake. They love to help me in the kitchen."

Kells smiled. "I can't wait until Allison is old enough to help. Mommy-daughter time is going to be special." She paused. "But what do Jeff and the boys do?"

"Oh, they have plenty to keep them busy. But whatever they do, Talitha does as well. She's not going to be left out of anything looking like fun."

Kells shrugged. "She'll start wanting to do 'girl' things pretty soon."

Collin let the dig fly by without comment. She walked Kells to the door, kissed Allison goodbye (after the babies all said their goodbyes,) and watched her friend walk down the path back to her car. She watched until Allison had been safely strapped in the back seat, and Kells pulled the car out of the driveway onto the street.

Collin turned to the trio. "Well, again, time with Kells proves interesting. I wonder what else will happen today?" *Unicorns and rainbows? Flying lizards?*

"Mommy, I hungy."

She sighed. "Of course you are. It's been what, an hour since you all had a snack?"

Three bodies jumped around her. "Nack! Nack! We wan nack!"

"Fine. Go sit at the table." Six feet pounded into the kitchen.

Collin sighed. "Life."

* * *

Jeff set his phone down with extreme care. Better than throwing it across the room. Which would be his first inclination. "Those stupid, ignorant people. How can they look at themselves in the mirror? Believing some rot about Collin abusing the kids? And me trying to cover it up?" He closed his eyes to let the fire die. Instead, it retreated to a slow simmer. "They don't want to do business with a firm which has a director who's a child abuser. Fine. I don't want to do business with them, either. God, Father, this is ridiculous! You can't let this continue! You have got to prove her innocence!"

The office monitor buzzed. Erin. Jeff hit it harder than he intended. "What?"

"Don't yell at me, bro. I'm on your side."

Jeff backed it down. "Sorry. What do you need?"

"Wanted to tell you the count from my desk. I've got three wanting to know if it's true, one wanting to 'hold up' on a contract for unspecified reasons—except we all know the reason—and four offering support. They heard the rumor, dismissed it, heard about the exoneration, believe it, and will be there to fight with you for Collin."

Jeff breathed slowly. "Thanks for the encouragement."

"Jeff, Collin's my sister. You know how I feel. I know the Lord has something in mind for all this. We don't know what, but He will bring good out of it."

Jeff grumbled. "I know, bro. I wish I could see it now, not have to wait in hindsight."

"Right. It would be easier. But not how He usually works. You're the one who taught me. Obedience and faith."

"If they were coming after me, I could handle it. I think. But coming after Collin? That's what really gets me."

"I know. I know." Erin walked into the room, his arm crutches tapping the floor. "Easier to defend someone else. We might doubt ourselves, but we'd never doubt the other person."

Jeff glared at the desk. "I'd still like to know who blew this all out of proportion."

Erin chuckled. "I don't. I'd probably lose my religion and go ballistic."

Jeff shook his head. "Not you, man. I know you better."

Erin's phone sang. He answered it. "Yes, love of my... right. When? Where? How long?" Erin's face paled. "I'll meet you there. I love you, Vy."

Jeff waited. *Lift him, Lord. Whatever this is.*

Erin fumbled his phone in his pocket. "Vy...had an accident. Car hit her broadside. She's okay, but the baby..."

Jeff stood. "You want me to drive?"

"No. You stay. I'll call you from the hospital." Erin's eyes brimmed with moisture. "Pray, please."

"You got it."

Erin disappeared out the door.

Jeff hit his knees. "Lord, please. They were so excited about this baby. If there's any room in Your will, please, protect its life. Save it, Father. For Erin and Vy. For Your glory. Please? But Your will, not mine, be done. Amen."

He hung his head as the Spirit played Jeff's recent conversations and attitudes back to him. Jeff nodded. "I'm sorry, Lord. Forgive me for grumbling and complaining. You are in control. Of all of it. I gave You my life, and You have it. If it serves You to take it all down, then let me walk before you with nothing. If the accusations against Collin bring good somehow, then we will accept them and still praise You. I'm sorry I've been acting like a spoiled child. I love you, Father."

His phone rang. "Yes, Mr. Crommarty. What can I do for you?" He listened. "I'm sorry to hear that, sir. The accusations are false. CPS came out and visited our home. They examined our children. They exonerated Collin of any possible wrongdoing and declared the call a fake. Yes, I have the report. Yes, I'm happy about it, too." He listened. "I can understand, sir. It looked bad, I know. We knew the truth would come out. I understand you want to wait before we move on the contracts. I do. Thank you for considering us to begin with. Right. Have a good day, sir."

Jeff disconnected the call, sat the phone down. He breathed slowly and deliberately. "You have this, Lord. You have all of it. Your will, not mine. I love You."

He returned to examining the proposals left on his desk. All two of them.

* * *

After dinner, Collin had the chance to sort through the clothes Kells brought back. She carried the bags into the family room so she could watch the littles and their father play and wrestle before bedtime. As usual, Jeff presented the babies with a challenge, and they had to figure out how to accomplish it. Tonight's challenge: take off Daddy's shoes. The boys went for a frontal attack while Talitha tried to sneak in from behind. Jeff would tire them out.

Before she could dig deep, the back door opened. Erin let himself in. Collin took one look at her brother's face and hugged him. "I'm sorry, Erin."

Erin nodded. His eyes stayed focused on the floor. "Yeah. We lost the baby." His voice choked. "Vy is going to be fine." Erin fumbled for his words. "They're going to keep her overnight. Lots of bruises from the lap and shoulder belts. Flying glass. Vy said a pedestrian crossed against the light. She stopped to let him go. He stopped, then saluted her. And then a dude ran the light and hit her broadside."

Erin's voice maintained the same soft, even tone. "Never even stopped. Backed up and kept going. The pedestrian gave the license number to the police. But they can't match the plate to the car which hit her. They're still looking."

Collin felt a shudder up her spine. *Do not say anything. Erin and Vy have enough going on. You don't need to drag them into your fantasies. You have no way of knowing if this is the same guy or not. Leave it.*

Erin looked up at Collin and Jeff. "God's been telling me over and over 'forgive.' Forgive someone who murdered our child?" Tears dripped down Erin's cheeks. "It's all I got. All I can do." He lowered his head again.

Collin whispered, "How is Vy taking it?"

Erin shrugged side-to-side. "She's hurting. But she's getting the same message I am. 'Forgive.' What else can she do? What else can either of us do?"

Jeff offered, "Grumble and complain and attack God. It's what I did. I'm sorry you heard me today."

Erin managed a small smile. "Well, maybe it might have been my motive. I didn't want to sound like you."

Jeff rested his hand on Erin's shoulder. "Wise man. What can we do? How can we help?"

Erin shook his head. "I need to get back to the hospital. But I wanted to tell you in person. I needed to, I guess." He looked at Collin. "I needed a hug."

Collin hugged him again and again. "I love you, A-One. I'm so sorry."

He nodded. "I know." Jeff hugged him as well. Erin punched Jeff lightly in the arm. "Thanks, bro. Okay, look, everything is fine. It is. God has this. I don't understand it, but He does. So I'll leave it with Him."

He lifted his head. "And I know we have a baby in Heaven waiting for us." He smiled, but tears glistened in his eyes. "A baby girl. We'll come up with a name later." He looked at the floor. "I gotta go. I love you." He reached down and patted each triplet on the head once. "Uncle Erin loves you." He managed to untangle himself from the embraces and slipped back out the door.

Collin felt the catch in her throat. She hugged Jeff, dropping her head on his shoulder. "Oh, Jeff. I'm so sorry for them. It hurts."

"Yeah. I know. He's got the right attitude. Unless he's just saying the words."

Collin shook her head. "No. You know Erin. He says it, he means it."

Jeff nodded. "About God, yes." He smiled. "Not so sure about everything else."

Collin shoved him. "Funny man. True, but still. I love you, Jeff."

"Love you, Collin."

Collin went back to emptying the bags Kells brought. She looked inside and cocked her head. Neither bag felt full. One had only a handful of pairs of toddler jeans, and the other had an assortment of shirts. Some of which didn't even belong to the trio. Were obviously Allison's. *Is she losing her mind?*

She emptied the bag, and a half-chewed piece of something unidentifiable fell out. Collin picked it up gingerly. Teeth marks marred the surface. Sharp teeth. Small teeth. Not a child's tooth.

Collin's eyes narrowed as she studied the object. She turned it over and over in her hand, then called, "Jeff? Look at this and tell me what you think."

Jeff twisted himself free of the littles' attack and took the mystery item from her. He repeated Collin's turning it over and over, held it close to examine the teeth mark... Finally, he looked up. "I got nothing. I'd say an animal chewed this. Something with a small bite. But very sharp teeth."

"That's my impression. Wonder what it's doing in Kells's bag with the clothes?"

"You'll have to ask her."

Collin huffed. "I'll put it on the list of other questions I need to ask her. She apologized for sniping at me."

"Nice."

"I thought so. Until she started grilling me about what Dr. Bliss said."

Jeff shook his head. "Someone ought to report him."

"To who? He's a psychiatrist. He can have weird ideas. It's called 'therapy.' Right?"

Jeff grumbled under his breath. Collin caught the inflection, if not the words. "Excuse me?"

Jeff repeated to be heard. "It's not what I call it. But it's over. No more seeing therapists. Not those, anyhow." He reached down, caught a male child in his arms, and gently swooshed him to the couch.

Not to be left out, child number two shouted, "Me too, Daddy. I fwy too!"

Two more children flew onto the couch, careful not to land on each other. "Gin! Do gin!"

Jeff chuckled. "No, we're done for tonight. We'll play tomorrow. Now it's bedtime. Go get your stuffies."

Little legs trotted down the hall into the nursery. Talitha came back, hugging her penguin. Collin listened for signs of trouble from the back. Joshua didn't disappoint. "Yion! Yion! Mommy, canna fin yion!"

Caleb's cries joined his brother's. "Mommy! Canna fin bear! Bear gone."

Collin rose from her chair. "I'm coming." She motioned to Jeff. "Pick a book."

The toddlers were tearing their beds apart, looking for the missing stuffies. Blankets flew across the room. Pillows became airborne as well. Nothing would be spared in the search for their bedtime companions.

Collin held up her hands. "Everyone stop. You'll never find them like that." She pulled the covers back to their respective beds, smoothed them out, and assured herself no stuffie hid beneath the blankets. Pillows were replaced, turned, and also declared stuffie-free zones. Under the bed?

Collin got on her hands and knees beside Joshua's bed. "Lion? Are you under here?"

Far in the corner, all the way to the wall, she made out a lump which might have been a lion. She had to shimmy under to retrieve it but dragged the lion back to its owner. "Here, Joshua. He was hiding."

Joshua caught his lion in his arms. "Yion! You no hide."

How did it get back there? The trio doesn't play under here. And I know I put him on the bed after we made it this morning. Same with Bear. Hmm.

Collin moved to check for the missing bear. But he wasn't under the bed. Or under the dressers. Or in the hamper. Not in the drawers, either.

Caleb's lower lip trembled. "Where bear? Mommy, where bear?"

"I'll find him, Caleb. He's got to be in here somewhere." *I know I saw him on the bed. I know it. Caleb moved him for nap. Then put him back after. He's got to be in here.*

Talitha and Jeff came in. Talitha crossed to her brother and handed him her penguin. "Here, bubby. You seep pengin. I gib you."

Caleb swatted the animal to the floor. "No pengin. Wan bear! Wan my bear." A full-on tantrum began winding up.

Jeff pulled Caleb to his arms. "Caleb, Sissy wanted to help you. She wanted to give you her stuffie. It was a very brave thing for her to do. You need to say sorry."

Caleb couldn't handle it. "No! Wan bear! Wan bear!" His heart broke, and Collin's did too. She shook her head. "I don't know where he could be, Caleb." She opened the closet door and looked on the floor. No bear.

Jeff jerked his head up. "On the top shelf."

Bear sat above all the commotion, perched on the topmost ledge, inside the open cardboard box. Collin's breath caught. "What is he doing there?"

Jeff stood, released Caleb, and pulled down the stuffie. He checked it over, turning it back to front and back again. Finally, he gave it to Caleb. "Here, buddy. Here's Bear. Let's go read a story, then it will be time to go to bed. Okay?" He looked at his beaming son, hugging his bear tight enough to squeeze all the stuffings out. "Apologize to Sissy."

Caleb dropped his head. "I sowy, Yiya."

Talitha nodded. "S'okay, bubby. I okay."

Collin read a look in Jeff's eyes she didn't like. An almost angry, but not quite, look. An almost pensive look, but still not quite right, either. Whatever his mood, she didn't like not being able to decipher it. As they walked up the hall, she asked, "What is it?"

He shook his head. "Later."

Collin kept her eyes on him. He read the story of Elisha and the bottle of oil that never ran out. He put the book down, looked at the back of the house. "I have an idea. How about if we have a slumber party tonight?"

Puzzled looks met him. "What summer potty?"

Collin raised her eyebrows. "Say what?"

Jeff nodded. "Yeah. Let's all sleep in here tonight. It will be like we're camping. Camping's when you sleep outside in a tent all together in one place." He smiled at the toddlers. "Mommy and Daddy will sleep in here with you, and it will be just like camping. It will be fun."

Collin threw an aside for Jeff's ears alone. "Fun for who?"

He threw one back at her. "Go with it."

Collin nodded. "Okay, then, let's go get some blankets and pillows and make our beds out here." She eyed Jeff. His eyes narrowed, but he nodded.

In short order, the littles were bedded down on the floor around the family room. Jeff carried in blankets for Collin and himself. Collin followed with the pillows. She dropped them on the floor beside the couch. "I guess a night on the floor will be character building."

"It will be something. I'll explain after sleepy heads close their eyes."

It was actually kind of nice sitting on the floor beside the littles, stroking their hair, their hands, their foreheads, humming to them until they fell asleep. It felt peaceful. It felt warm. It felt...

"Safe. They'll be safe in here."

Collin turned to eye her husband. Jeff motioned to the back of the house. "The box we found the bear in? It's the one Gretchen, the Shepherd, alerted on." He sat back against the couch. "I don't know what's going on. But I can bet Braydon won't see any trace of an intruder from outside."

"Are you going to call him?"

"In the morning. I'll have him bring Gretchen back tomorrow and see if she gets a hit on the box like before."

Collin stared at her son's stuffie, cuddled close in his arms. "Or on the bear."

"Yeah. Thanks for going along with this. You can have the couch."

"No. You have to work tomorrow."

"I'm the boss. I can take any day off I like. And I like to take tomorrow off."

Collin chuckled. "Don't tell Erin you're the boss. He's of the opinion you're co-owners."

"We are. But someone has to be the Big Boss. I'm older. I get the title." He grimaced. "And the headaches."

Collin lay her head on his shoulder. "I love you, Jeff. Thanks for having this sleepover."

He kissed her. "You're welcome." They snuggled down protectively, surrounding the littles. No one would disturb them tonight. Tonight the whole family would sleep soundly. God willing.

WEDNESDAY

He did, and they did, too. Collin woke before the babies. She looked across the mound of bodies to see Jeff lying with his eyes open, staring at the ceiling. She smiled and kept her voice soft. "Wondering how you ended up here?"

He rolled over to look at her. "For a moment. Then I remembered I proposed this." He sat up and groaned. Quietly. "Why I thought it was a good idea is beyond me. First order of business is a visit to the chiropractor."

"After you call..."

"Braydon. And he brings Gretchen out. I know. Something or someone is in this house. It's the only thing to make any sense."

Collin shook her head. "But it doesn't. How can we not see it? Or hear it? There is no invisibility cloak. No magical ability to whoosh from one place to another. I don't get it."

"Neither do I. Which is why I'm going to have Braydon put cameras on the inside of the house."

Collin drew internal. "You are?"

Jeff turned to face her. "Yes, we are. We're going to have complete control of when they are on and when they aren't. But I want eyes on the 'empty' rooms. I want to know what's sneaking around with us."

Collin closed her eyes, drew in a breath, then nodded. "Agreed. As long as we can cover them when we want. I don't want prying eyes watching my children."

"We'll put caps on the cameras. But we have to remember to take them off when we leave the room. It won't do us any good to have them and not use them."

"Agreed. I'll be mindful of using them. I will, Jeff. I want to catch this person—or whatever—now."

Jeff threw back his covers, stood, and pulled Collin to her feet. "Coffee. I'll make it. And bring it to you. You can sit and watch the trio sleep."

Collin elbowed him out of her way. "I'll make coffee. You watch them sleep." She grinned. "You're fair game sitting on the floor. Once I bring the coffee in, we take the high ground and no wrestling."

"I hear you."

"Good. I'm not cleaning coffee stains off you, the trio, or the carpet." Collin headed to the kitchen, started the coffee maker, then looked at the cabinets. Family breakfast on a Wednesday? *Oh, why not. Give you practice making those teddy bear pancakes.*

Collin whipped up the batter and let it rest while she carried a cup of coffee to Jeff. The littles were still sleeping. Collin studied their positions. It could best be described as a 'puppy pile.' Caleb had wrapped himself around Talitha, using her back for a pillow. Talitha had hold of Joshua's arm. Joshua lay on Caleb's legs.

The baby pile. They slept like that in the crib, too. All of them on top of each other. Erin and I moved Joshua and Caleb out. They were waking up, but Talitha wasn't. We left her in the nursery...

...and then the kidnappers came.

Collin sensed the past rising in her awareness. It threatened to wash away the now, to plunge her back into the terror. She reached over and snapped the rubber band around her wrist.

The sharp sting put the memories to flight. Her vision cleared. Jeff eyed her. Collin smiled. "I beat it."

"I see you're using the rubber band again. When did you start?"

"Last week. After the second flashback. Something said I might need it."

"Did you?"

"Besides now? Yes."

Jeff kissed her. "You're doing fine, milady. You're here."

"And I'm going to stay here, too." She motioned to the now-writhing pile of body parts. "Wake them up. We're going to have pancakes."

"On a Wednesday?"

"It's an underrated day. Why not?"

"Let's do it."

Collin returned to the kitchen and began making round teddy bears from the batter. She had enough for two each. If she limited herself to one...and she needed to lose a pound or two, right? Still some baby weight hanging around the middle. Maybe five pounds. Maybe ten...

Collin snapped the rubber band hard. From the family room, Jeff called, "What did you do that for?"

"A reminder."

"Ookay..." His voice didn't sound sure. Neither would hers if she explained it. *Let it go.*

Without the musical score, okay?

Riiight.

Sleepyheads rubbed eyes and faces and stumbled into the kitchen to sit at the table. Collin poured milk. She waited.

Caleb looked at his glass. "I hab brown mik?"

"Not this morning. We're having pancakes. You get brown milk with snack."

Talitha looked at her fork. "I wan boo fork."

"Sorry, honey. It's in the dishwasher. You'll have to use the purple one."

Joshua sat up, indignant. "Puple one my fork. Sissy not hab it!"

Talitha jerked the offending cutlery away from him. "No! I hab it. Mommy gib me."

Joshua teared up. "Mommy! Yia hab..."

Jeff held up his hands and thundered, "Wishing bones!"

Three heads snapped around, too amazed to continue their protests. Jaws hung open. Jeff motioned with his hands. "Let's all calm down. You each have a fork. You each have a spoon. You can each eat breakfast with what you have."

Talitha eyed her father side-eyed. "Why you say bones?"

"To get your attention. And it worked, too. Mommy has teddy bear pancakes for you. Everyone put their hands in their laps."

Hands disappeared from the table, out of the way of the still-warm pancakes. Once everyone had been served (Collin served herself the scrunched-up practice bear), Jeff directed, "Caleb, I think it's your turn to pray."

Little heads bowed in absolute earnestness. "Tank Jesus

Daddy fin bear. Tank Jesus Mommy make pan-cakes. Tank for food. Tank sissy an brudder. Amen."

Collin poured syrup into small cups for the littles. They could tear their bears into bitesize pieces, dunk them in the syrup, and not waste an entire bottle. She noticed Caleb had a dark red semi-circle on the back of his hand. She watched him eat. Whatever had happened, it didn't seem to bother him. She reached out and caught his hand. "Caleb, how did you get this boo-boo?"

Caleb cocked his head. "George bite me."

"George?"

"George bite me."

Collin looked at Jeff. "First George scratches him, now George bites him?"

Jeff looked at the mark, rubbed it, shrugged. "It could be anything." He tousled his son's hair. "George is a story, Caleb. In a book. He's not really here in the house."

Caleb nodded large. Jeff shook his head. Caleb shook his head. "No George ina house."

"Right. No George in the house. Your mind is making up stories. It's a good thing, though, Buddy. You keep making stories."

Collin dismissed the uneasy feeling in her gut. *It's nothing. Let it go.*

You say it too often.

You don't do it often enough.

Collin finished cleaning up the kitchen. Jeff put in the call to Braydon. Collin listened to the one-sided conversation as best she could, with three littles clamoring for attention.

"Yeah, me again. Hey, can you check your cameras last night? You won't find anything, I know. But we had something weird...okay, weirder than normal for this house... We'd really love to get Gretchen's input on something... No, I'm not going to tell you what. I don't want you putting thoughts in her head."

He chuckled in response to his brother-in-law's comment. "Yeah, well, that's true."

Collin walked with the triplets to their bedroom so they could get clothes. The door had been left ajar. Collin looked in, then threw her hands across the opening. "No! Wait. Do not go in." She turned and screamed over her shoulder, "Jeff!"

The room had been torn apart. Beds lay stripped of coverings. Blankets and sheets were piled in the middle of the floor. The countertops had been swept clean of all contents. Shredded books littered the carpets. The curtains slashed.

Collin sank to the floor to keep the babies out. Her eyes glazed. *Another nursery. Fire. Explosion ripping through the room. Her heart ripped from her chest. Again. Again. A...*

Jeff's voice. Strong. "Collin. We're here. It's safe. We're all here."

A sharp snap on her wrist. She jerked back to awareness. Jeff had used the rubber band to retrieve her brain. Collin looked up at him, swallowed hard. "You can't leave, Jeff. You can't leave me by myself. What happens if..."

Jeff pulled her to her feet and closed the door. He smiled at the triplets. "Hey, I've got an idea. Everyone in the bathroom for a bath."

"Baf! We has baf!" Six pudgy legs ran down the hall. Jeff put his hands on Collin's shoulders and turned her. "Go draw the bath. I'll get clothes. I'll call the police. Braydon will be here in the next half-hour, and if he's not, I'll roast him." He hugged Collin. "We are going to beat this, milady. We are. Hang with me."

Collin nodded. Her hands shook. Her whole body vibrated. *I will not lose my mind. I will not lose my mind. Lord, please. I can't. I can't. Not again. Help me stay on top of this. I don't want to be back in the hospital. Catatonic. Unthinking. Unfeeling. I can't. I have to take care of the babies. Please. Keep me...make me sane. Father, I beg you. Please.*

Peace. Be still. Peace. I give it to you. Hold it.

Collin drew in a deep breath, held it, let it out. She walked down the hall to the bathroom where three nekkid bodies sat in the empty tub, waiting for the most magical of moments: when the water came on. Collin chuckled. She turned on the water, made sure it was a safe temperature, then plugged the drain. They would play until their skin wrinkled if she let them. Maybe today, she would.

Jeff walked into the bathroom with an armload of clothes and his phone in his hand. He wrangled the clothes to Collin while still maintaining his grip on the phone. Music said he'd been placed on hold. He whispered, "I think I got enough of everything."

"Pants, shirts, pull-ups. Sock and shoes optional."

He nodded. "Got it all." He lifted his phone. "Yes, I'm here. I need to report a break-in. Someone trashed my children's nursery. No, they weren't in it at the time. Sometime in the night. Yes. Please send someone soon."

He waited. "I know this isn't high priority. But my children are under three. If they had been in the room, we'd have a different scenario. Please."

He listened. "Thank you. I appreciate your help." He pocketed the phone. "Dispatch said they'd try to get someone out in the next couple of hours. He assured me they would take it seriously."

Collin bathed the triplets, let them play longer than usual, then got them out and dressed. About the time she finished, she heard the backdoor open and Braydon call, "Anyone here?"

Joshua's eyes exploded like a fourth of July firework. "Unka Bwaydon!" Cheers and chubbies ran down the hall to greet him. Collin hung the towels and joined them.

The triplets sat on the floor in front of Gretchen, touching the puppy gently, stroking her fur, generally in awe again. Gretchen licked Caleb's head.

"She lick me! She lick me!"

Collin gave Braydon the stink-eye. "No comments about liking how he tastes. His imagination is wild enough as it is."

Braydon nodded. "I won't make kids afraid of dogs. It's never smart." He had Gretchen lay down so the littles could hug her, one at a time. Then he brought her to her feet. "What have you got?"

Jeff shook his head. "No. I want you to run the house. The whole thing. See what she finds."

Braydon pursed his lips. "It's easier if they know what they're looking for. Gives them something to go on."

Jeff agreed. "And if we knew what it was, we'd give her the information. We don't. We just know something is here."

Braydon shrugged. "Fair enough." He and Gretchen took the long way around, through the kitchen, down the hall, through the back bedrooms, to Collin's room. Nothing out of the ordinary caught the dog's attention. Nothing in the living room. Nothing in the den, nothing in Jeff's office. But the family room...

The bags Kells brought caught Gretchen's nose. She snuffled and sniffled and alerted and whined and whimpered. Braydon looked from Collin to Jeff and back again. Collin raised her eyebrows. "I don't know. Kells brought back some of the kids' clothes in them."

Braydon turned the bags inside out. The unidentified piece of leather fell out. Gretchen pounced on it. She didn't pick it up, but she brushed it with her nose. She moved it around. She did everything but eat it.

Braydon called her off. "Good girl. We'll leave it for the police." He looked at Jeff. "What else you got?"

Jeff led the way down the hall to the nursery. Gretchen pulled at the leash, excitement in her step. Braydon called her back. "Easy, girl. Easy." His eyes narrowed as he looked to Jeff. "Babies' room?"

Jeff opened the door. He stood back.

Gretchen came to a full alert. She whined and wiggled and made it clear she wanted to be let go, now. Braydon continued to hold her back. He eyed the destruction. "You call the police?"

"Yeah. They're coming this morning."

Braydon closed the door. "I don't want Gretchen to contaminate a crime scene. If they let her after they've got their pictures, I'll turn her loose and see what she comes up with. But they need to be here first."

He ducked his head to Collin. "But we know the rest of the house is clear. That's something."

Collin dropped her head. "It is if you don't mind sleeping on the floor in the family room."

Braydon hugged her. "Understood. We're going to get this figured out, Collin. We are."

Collin closed her eyes. She whispered it. "Before I lose my mind?"

Braydon kissed the top of her head. "You're not losing your mind, sis. We'll prove it. Sooner or later. Hang in there."

Three adults, three children, and one canine retired to the kitchen to wait for the police to arrive. Braydon talked about where he would put cameras inside the house, what angles they would cover, and how to keep them from turning on when the Farrells didn't want them on.

Collin started on her third cup of coffee when the police arrived. The triplets sat in wide-eyed awe as the uniformed men came into the house. Officer Roper and Officer Tomke introduced themselves to the three adults. They were also introduced to Gretchen.

Officer Tomke shook Braydon's hand. "Thanks for not running your dog in there before we got here. I know the temptation is to see what she can find, but it helps us."

Braydon ducked his head. "I train service dogs with Franklin County. I know some about where and when they're supposed to be."

Both uniformed men kneeled down to be on eye-level with the triplets. Officer Roper asked, "And what are your names?"

Collin thought Caleb's head would burst from wonder and amazement. Joshua found his tongue faster. "I Jo-u-a. I bigger."

Caleb came back to life. "No! I Cayeb. I bigger."

Jeff held up his hand. "You're both bigger. Stop fighting."

Talitha stepped forward to stand before the patrolman. "I 'yitha. I yiddle one."

Collin swooped her up. "Yes, this is Talitha, our littlest one."

Officer Tomke smiled at the triplets. "So nice to meet you all."

Jeff caught his children's attention and pointed to the officers. "If you are ever lost, or get separated from Mommy and Daddy, look for someone in a uniform like these men have. They will always help you."

He eyed his brood. "You understand?"

Three heads nodded. Three voices echoed, "Yes, Daddy."

Officer Roper smiled. "Nice to be considered the good guys."

Jeff shrugged. "Paramedic. Ten years. You'll always be the good guys."

Tomke pointed at Jeff. "You're the heroes."

Again, Jeff shrugged. "Eh. We do what we can."

Collin nudged her husband. "Can you investigate the nursery, please?"

Jeff ducked. "Ookay. I hear you." He led the men (and Gretchen) down the hall to the back. He opened the door and stood back.

Collin watched the officers look in quickly, then step back. Roper drew his weapon. They entered the room. She couldn't see what they did next. She could only wait for a report.

About five minutes in, she heard Roper say, "Bring the dog in. Let's see what she finds."

The whining and whimpering and growling evidenced Gretchen found something to interest her. But after another five minutes, men and dog came out. Officer Roper closed the door. He turned to Jeff. "We'll get forensics out here to dust and take samples."

Collin eyed the man sideways. "What do you think it is?"

"I can't say, ma'am."

Collin queried him. "You have an idea, but you can't say it? Or you don't have any idea?"

He raised his eyebrows. "I don't have any idea. Forensics may give us some clues." He glanced around the house. "Do you have someplace you can go for a while until we get this scene processed?"

Jeff nodded. "My folks' place. I'll get you the address and phone numbers where we can be reached."

Collin touched Jeff's arm. "I have group here tomorrow. After the stand I made last week with Kells, I really don't want to cancel." She addressed the police officers. "If we seal this room off, can we still live in the rest of the house?"

Braydon cut her off. "Collin, you don't know who or what is in here. You don't know how they even got in. This is not a house you want to stay in."

Collin felt confusion and fear swirl around her. Panic joined forces with the mingling emotions. "I don't want to leave! I…"

Jeff caught her arms. "Collin, think. It's about keeping the babies safe. That's what matters."

She stared at him. His eyes bored through the darkness threatening to bury her. Collin reached over and snapped the rubber band on her wrist.

The sharpness brought her mind back into focus. "I'm sorry. You're right. We'll have to evacuate the premises and invade your parents' house. I'm sure they'll love having us descend on them for a while."

Jeff smiled. "You know they will." He put his arm around Collin's shoulder and faced the officers. "You'll let us know when it's safe to return?"

"Of course."

Collin managed a smile. "Thank you for coming out so quickly. I appreciate all you do." She didn't ask permission to go into the room for more clothes. Grandma had a limitless supply, it seemed.

She did have the littles collect their stuffed animals from the living room. As Caleb walked past Gretchen, the dog whined and alerted. Braydon stopped the boy. "Hold on, Caleb. Can the puppy see your bear for a moment? She won't take it, and she won't hurt it, I promise."

Caleb hung back for a moment, sheltering his bear in his arms. Braydon kneeled down. "Please, buddy? It's important."

Caleb thrust the bear out with both arms to Gretchen. "Here, puppy. You see bear?"

Gretchen nosed it and whimpered and tasted it and moved it around. She pushed it with her head, then sat at attention.

Collin shook her head. "Uh, no. You are not keeping the bear as evidence. No way. You can come to Grandma's house and take prints and fur samples. But you are not taking this bear from Caleb."

Jeff echoed her sentiment, if less belligerently. "Our son can't sleep without his bear." He shrugged to the officers. "And neither will anyone else if he doesn't have him."

Officer Tomke chuckled. "I understand. Trust me. I have kids. We'll dust it for hair now. Not much chance of getting prints off him anyhow."

Collin held up her hand. "I have what you need." She went to the utility closet and pulled out a lint roller. She handed it to Officer Tomke, who pulled off several layers before being satisfied he had an "uncontaminated" section of tape. He 'dusted' the bear top to bottom and back again. He smiled at Collin. "Done. We will have to keep the roller, though."

"Not a problem. I have multiples."

* * *

Collin and company packed the van. Jeff called his folks. They were happy to have the family come for as long as it took to sort out the mystery. Come on down!

Only after the family had arrived, unloaded, and got settled in did Collin ask Lacey, "Can I have my mother's group meet here tomorrow? I know it's short notice, but I don't want to lose the continuity."

You don't want to lose face.

I don't want to lose Eliza. Hush.

Lacey beamed. "A room full of babies? How fun! Of course, you can. What do you need to set it up?"

"Nothing, Mom Lacey. You already have the perfect place. We can use the playroom and the backyard if it's nice enough. Rob is our designated 'childcare assistant.' I'll call him and tell him to come here."

She made all the calls, giving the women the address for the temporary change of venue. Everyone assured her it wouldn't be a problem.

Kells's voice smirked over the phone. "Did the threat of the invisible stalker make you change locations?"

Collin bit her tongue. And her lips. And the inside of her mouth. She kept her tone smooth. "No. Not the invisible one. The one which trashed the nursery while we were sleeping last night. The police are investigating now." *Do not mention the bags.*

Or the dog.

???

Trust me.

Collin took the internal hint. "I don't want to lose anyone in the group. We all need it. Mom Lacey is more than happy to have babies to cuddle and love on. She's also happy to have someone to bake for. And she makes a wicked pot of coffee. Everyone else has agreed."

"You called the others before you called me?" The snip in the tone intensified.

"I called you first. Your line was busy. Your voicemail box is full. I can't talk to you if I can't reach you."

Kells sniffed. "You should have waited 'til I said yes or no."

"Next time, Kells."

"Fine. I'll see you at your in-laws' house tomorrow." Kells ended the call.

Collin stared at her phone. "I'll be so happy when your month of being leader is over, Kells. You are not yourself." She gazed out the window.

The man in the suit gazed at the house. He saw her looking. Smiled. Saluted. Got in his car and left.

Collin froze. Everything in her went rigid. Still. Unmoving. *Snap the band. Snap the band.*

Nothing responded. Nothing reacted. Collin stood.

"What's wrong? What happened?"

"I don't know. She seemed fine, then...this."

"Bring her in the living room. Sit her down."

"Collin. Collin. Can you hear me, lady?"

She turned her head. She saw nothing. Only the man in the dark blue three-piece suit. Smiling. Saluting.

Something snapped at her wrist. It didn't phase her. Nothing phased her. She would feel nothing. See nothing. Fear nothing.

Wet and warm bathed her face. She closed her eyes. The bathing continued. A soft voice, sweet and comforting, spoke. "It's okay, Collin. It's okay, dear. It is. There's nothing here to hurt you. Nothing to hurt the babies. They're safe. They're playing in the backyard with Grampa. And their daddy. Take a deep breath, honey. One deep breath."

Collin obeyed the voice. She took a breath.

"Deeper, honey. Take a deep breath. One all the way to your toes. Breath in."

Collin tried again. The effort of breathing down to her toes shattered the plaster casing holding her. She shuddered. Again. Again.

Mom Lacey wrapped her in her arms. "Hold on there, sweetheart. Hold on to it. You're coming back. You're safe. You're here. We're all here."

Collin shook. Earthquake shaking. Vibrate the house shaking. Lacey held her. "It's okay. Get it out of your system. Shake it off. All of it."

Collin breathed in. Breathed out. Tears boiled down her cheeks. Flooded her chin. Sogged her neckline. She buried her face in Lacey's shoulder. "I'm so sorry. I'm sorry."

Lacey held her, crooned to her. "No apologies. None. You're fine. You are. I love you. We all love you."

Collin listened to Lacey's voice for several moments. She lifted her head, slapped the tears away, stared at the carpet. "I...I..." She met Lacey's gaze. "I saw something. Outside. I...I got scared. The babies…"

Lacey squeezed Collin's shoulder. "The babies are fine. They're outside playing with Grampa and Daddy. When you're ready, we'll go out, too."

Collin nodded. She gathered her muscles. Gave orders to her bones. Assembled the brain cells. With Lacey's help, she stood. Put one foot in front of the other. Then the other foot. Life returned to her systems. She nodded to Lacey. "I think I'm here. I'm alive."

"I know you are, honey. Let's go join the others and tell them what you saw."

Panic screamed, *No! If we talk about it, we'll freak out again!*

Resolve answered, *We won't. We're here, now. We'll tell Jeff. And it will be okay.*

But do we remember what we saw?

Collin swallowed hard. She had to. She had to. It mattered. She had to.

She did. Collin walked into Jeff's embrace, kissed the worry off his face, out of his eyes. She breathed deep. "I saw the man in the suit outside on the street."

Jeff cocked his head. "What man?"

"The man in the suit. I've seen him at church twice now. Then I saw him outside on the street Thursday after group. He was there when I got coffee with Eliza. And again now. He always smiles then salutes me." She looked at Jeff. "I don't know what he wants. But I don't trust it's good."

Jeff's eyes narrowed. "I have to call the police. If he's hanging around, following us, stalking you, they need to know about it. Now."

He pushed her away carefully, pulled out his phone from his pocket, and dialed. "I need to speak to someone about a stalker who's bothering my wife. Yes, I can wait." Collin heard the mutter, "Spend half my life waiting on the phone…"

Collin kissed him on the cheek and then went to join her offspring and their predecessors.

THURSDAY

Kells came to group with Brianna. Oscar head-butted Rob again, then grabbed his face and kissed him. Rob hugged the diminutive boy. "I love you too, Oscar."

Brianna's eyes widened, then filled with tears. "Why not me? Why doesn't he talk with me?"

Kells brushed by Brianna. "We'll talk about it after group starts. Let's get the room settled first."

Collin hugged Bri. "Glad you're here, Bri. We will talk about it in the group. And with Rob. I'll see what magic he has. Maybe it's because Rob's a guy like Oscar."

Bri dropped her head. "He doesn't do it with my husband, either."

Collin shrugged. "We'll see what it is."

Grace came up the walk with Archie in his carrier. Collin caught hold of him. "You're gonna have to get wheels on this thing soon, Grace."

"Tell me about it. He's heavy!"

Tia came in with Samuel. Winona came in alone and subdued. Collin kissed her, but didn't pry. "I'm praying for all of you, Nonnie."

Nonnie nodded. Tears lined her eyes, ready to fall at a wrong word or a moment's notice, whichever came first. Eliza appeared down the street, making her way to the house. She looked lost and hesitant. She held a car seat with a cover over it in her arms.

Collin called out, "Yes, this is the place. Come on in, Eliza."

The woman doubled her speed. She smiled at Collin. "Oh, good. I wasn't sure."

"Yeah, this is my mom and pop-in-law's place. We're using it this week. I'll explain why we needed to move later. Come on in and get settled. Introduce your beautiful little girl to us."

Collin leaned in and kissed the child's face. The baby was obviously of mixed parentage. Eliza hesitated, then lifted her chin. "This is Meridian. She's six-months-old, and the light of my existence. Her sister—her step-sister—is in preschool like I told you last week."

Eliza unstrapped and untangled the baby from the carrier. About then, Lacey Farrell stepped into the room. She took one look at Meridian and put out her arms. "Baby! Can I hold her?"

Eliza's eyes widened slightly, narrowed, then returned to normal. "Sure. You are?"

Lacey held out her hand. "Lacey Farrell. Gamma to the triplets in the back of the house."

Collin motioned to Lacey. "This is Mom Lacey. To everyone. If she doesn't know it about babies, it's not worth knowing."

Lacey waved a finger at Collin. "I never said I knew everything. I said raising three sons and a special needs daughter has taught me a great deal about things like patience and perseverance and persistence, and how to clean almost any surface. But it's a far cry from everything." She motioned with her head. "The rest of the group is in the kitchen getting drinks. You want me to hold her while you get a beverage?"

Eliza smiled. "Thank you. It'd be nice."

Lacey snorted. "Nice, nothing. I love the smell and feel of a baby." She corrected herself. "A clean, dry baby."

Eliza laughed. "I hear you."

Lacey took Meridian into the reading room where the group set up. Collin and Eliza went into the kitchen. Eliza shook her head. "She makes you feel welcome, doesn't she?"

"Yes, she does. Mom Lacey loves everyone. And lets you know it up front."

Eliza's eyes narrowed ever so slightly. "She didn't have a problem with you and her son adopting Rob?"

Collin drew the inference immediately. "Because he's a person of color? No. Not a problem. She and Harmon, Jeff's father, are the ones who suggested it. Strongly suggested it. Insisted on it, even. Either Jeff and I adopted him, or Lacey and Harmon would. We beat them to it."

Eliza looked down, then up. "But he's not your biological son."

Collin held Eliza's gaze. "Rob is as much my son as the triplets are. No, I didn't give birth to him. But we raised each other from the streets. He saved my life, I saved his. We were linked at the hip when Jeff met us. Package deal, you know? Jeff wanted the whole package, and that's what he got."

Eliza eyed Collin sideways. "And if he hadn't?"

Collin looked at the floor. "Then I wouldn't be Mrs. Jeffrey Farrell. I didn't have to give Jeff ultimatums. He loved Rob as much as I did. Still does. The littles love their big brother. We're family. Always. Without fail."

Eliza dropped her eyes. "Beautiful sentiment. I wish..." She trailed off, unable or unwilling to add anything more.

Kells stuck her head in the doorway. "Are you two going to join us or make us wait on you all morning?"

Collin shook her head. "We're coming, Kells. We're coming." She and Eliza joined the group.

Lacey ooed and ahhed over all the babies, then left so the women could talk freely. Kells began the meeting again. "Julie called this morning. Ayisha ran a low-grade fever last night. She thinks it's teething but didn't want to take a chance it wasn't and give something to someone else. We appreciate she thought of us first."

Kells motioned to the room. "We should all thank Mrs. Lacey Farrell for allowing us to meet here this morning. Collin will fill us in on why she felt it necessary to disrupt our routine."

Collin held up her hand. "I'll wait to answer. Is there anyone with anything pressing they want to discuss first?"

The women looked around at each other. Brianna raised her hand slowly. She ducked her head. "Why does Oscar relate to Rob and not me?"

Kells offered her opinion bluntly. "Maybe it's the race. Rob looks like Oscar."

Collin shot back, "Babies do not see skin color as the same or different. It just is." She turned to Bri. "Maybe he doesn't feel pressure with Rob. I know how badly you want Oscar to talk. Rob doesn't...."

Kells snorted. "Please. A baby his age doesn't know anything about pressure. They know they're loved, or they aren't." She pointed at Bri. "You need to take him to a therapist and have him tested. Then you'll know. And you'll know what to do about it."

Tia stepped in. "Testing at this age isn't the most reliable. And you'd have to find an exceptional therapist to know what to look for. It's all developmental. He's hitting all the other markers, isn't he?"

Bri nodded without adding to the conversation. Tia continued, "Short of having his ears checked to see if his tubes are plugged, I'd suggest love him the way he is. Stop comparing his developmental progress to anyone else. Boys talk late. Girls talk a lot. Relax and love the baby you have."

Bri hung her head. Tia put an arm around her. "Bri, we did the same thing with our first two. The oldest hit every marker right on time. The younger one didn't hit any of them. But at six and three, neither of them stop talking. Trust me, enjoy the quiet."

Collin moderated the advice. "How much playtime do you have with Oscar? I mean time when you play patty cake, or read to him or sit with him and sing together?"

Bri lifted her chin. "I spend a lot of quality time with Oscar. I make sure we have structure and formative play and brain-building activities. I'm using the latest research on how to give your child the best start in life."

Grace nodded. "The schedule they have you on is fierce. So many stimuli to be presented in specific ways."

Tia cocked her head. "You're doing what?"

Grace and Bri looked at each other, then at the rest of the group. "It's the latest 'how to raise an exceptional child' program. There're podcasts and videos and an entire curriculum you can buy."

Bri's tone sounded defensive. "It's all over the internet and on all the TV networks."

Tia turned to Collin. "May I?"

Collin grinned. "Go right ahead. Please."

Tia put a hand on both Grace and Bri. "You want to know the best thing to do with your curriculum?"

Their eyes widened slightly.

Tia smirked. "Throw it out. Throw out all the junk. Enjoy your child! Every child is different. Every child develops in their own fashion. What works for one will not work for another." She shoved the two women lightly. "Get rid of all that stuff and watch your child grow and be happy with it."

Collin threw in her two cents worth. "Play should be for play. Not an exercise where they *have* to learn something. If they do, great. If they have fun, great. Relax." She reached over to Archie. She handed him a ball. He immediately put it to his face and licked it. Collin caught Grace's eyes. "He just had a learning experience. You didn't have to teach him. He learned balls are round, and you can't eat them."

The boy made as if to throw the ball, but it never left his hand. Grace pointed to him. "See? He should be able to throw the ball."

Tia shook her head. "He learned a pump fake. Okay? He doesn't want to throw it. He'll throw it in time. Right now, celebrate he has the ball."

Kells cleared her throat. "I think we've spent enough time on Oscar and Archie and you two paranoid moms. Who else has something to report? Or ask?"

Collin motioned to Eliza. "Eliza brought Meridian. We're keeping the girls outnumbering the boys."

Eliza raised Meridian's hand so the baby could wave. Three babies waved back (with help.) Eliza took the initiative. "My rose for the week is being able to come today. It's been a bit hectic as our three-year-old changed preschools. But Meridian and I were able to get the time away, so here we are."

Collin made sure to say it. "And we're glad you are." She ignored Kells's narrowed eyes. "The thorn was changing preschools? What made you change?"

"Pam changed offices. She changed territories, too, so she wanted a school closer to where she works. It's farther for me to drive to pick Farley up and drop her off. But Pam can be closer to attend activities and see Farley during the lunch hours."

"Harder on you, but better for them. Very commendable on your part."

Kells glared at Collin. "Women usually yield to what the man wants. He's the head of the household, after all."

Collin pursed her lips. "It should be to be a joint decision. Eliza is working from home, too, so they both have to find a workable situation."

Tia leaned in. "Yeah. My husband wouldn't make such a move without consulting me. He'd be sleeping in the garage if he did."

Kells laughed, but her eyes burned. "Haha."

Eliza ducked her head to the side. "We discussed it. It does take more time out of my day, but it's worth it for Pam to have more time with Farley. Pam works some crazy hours and sometimes takes trips out of town. If she can see her daughter more during the day, it's a good thing."

Kells shifted in her chair. "Winona, where's Macie?"

Collin watched the woman closely. Nonnie lifted her chin. "She's at her grandma's house. My mom's house." Nonnie stared dead at Collin. "Mom wanted to have her come visit for a few days, so we let her."

Collin kept her tone soft. "Good idea, Nonnie. It will give you and Leonard a break. Breaks are good."

Nonnie's eyes never left Collin's. "Yes, they are. It's what we need right now."

Kells's eyes narrowed. She glanced from Collin to Nonnie and back. "Fine. Moving on. Allison continues to be the perfect baby. I have no thorns in my life."

Collin smiled. "That's good. I mean it. It's good to have a period of no thorns. Gives you something to look forward to when you're buried under thorns."

Kells snipped, "If your life is in order, there won't be any thorns."

You keep believing it for as long as you can... "Well, my life fell out of order this week." She spread her hands wide. "As you can tell. Which is why we're here and not at my place. Something—or someone—broke in and trashed the baby nursery. Shredded the sheets and curtains. Overturned the dressers. Pulled clothes out of the drawers and literally tore them up. The police are investigating now."

Brianna gasped. "How horrible! What about the triplets?"

Collin pointed to the back. "They're safe. They weren't in the nursery." She paused, then admitted, "Jeff decided we should have a family slumber party in the family room. We all slept on the floor in there." She paused. "I don't want to think what would have happened if they had still been in there." Her eyes lost focus.

Darkness rose along the edges of the room…

She snapped the rubber band and came back to the present. Collin looked around at the other mothers and added, "The police are checking it all out. We should know later today what they found and when we can move back in."

Kells shrugged. "Seems strange no one ever sees anyone going in. You have cameras don't you?"

"Outside, yeah. We're going to have to take other measures."

"Like what?"

"Like I don't know what. Not yet. Jeff and I will talk about it when he gets home from work. In the meantime, we're staying with Gramma and Grampa and Auntie Leesa. The triplets think they're having a party."

"Doesn't this mess up their routine as far as bedtimes go?"

Collin smiled at Grace. "No. We keep the same schedule here as at home. No matter how Grandpa begs to let them stay up an extra hour."

Talk circulated for another hour. Desserts were served, the meeting broke up. Women and children went home. Winona left without speaking to anyone. *Why did she come?*

So you'd know she wasn't in jail?

I'll buy it. I need to call her, though.

Kells lingered long enough to nail Collin with a parting shot. "I still say if you had your life right, none of this would happen."

Collin pursed her lips and bit her tongue. "I'm happy for you, Kells. My life with the Lord has always been different than yours. He works in different ways with different people."

"His favor rests on His people, Collin. Maybe you need to examine who you belong to." Kells shifted the baby carrier to her left hand, juggled her shoulder bag, and started out the door.

Collin called out. "Kells. Some of those clothes you sent weren't ours. I thought maybe they were Allison's."

Kells shrugged. "Probably not. Nonnie sent the bags to me with clothes for Allison. I thought I'd taken them all out, but maybe I didn't get everything. Talk to her about them."

"I will." Collin's gut tightened. *Nonnie gave the bags to Kells. Maybe Kells didn't have anything to do with it. Maybe the smells came from Nonnie's house. Great. Now I have two suspects to watch.*

Collin walked to the playroom to relieve Rob of his babysitting duties. He hugged her. "You okay, Mom? Mom Lacey told me what happened with the nursery." His face drew into a mask of anger. "I can't believe someone would threaten the trio. What kind of low-life goes after babies?"

"The lowest." Collin snorted. "I only hope the police can find something. Or someone."

Rob nodded. "You aren't going back to the house, though, are you? I mean, if they identify whoever it is, you're going to stay here 'til they catch them, right?"

Collin looked at the floor. "What would you do?"

Rob snorted. "I'd go home. I'm not letting anyone chase me out of my home. The police could catch the perp when he came back at me."

Collin studied her son. "And what about Mom Lacey and Pop Harmon? Would you stay here and maybe put them in danger?"

"No way." Rob stopped talking and stared at his mom. "I see what you're doing. You want me to agree with you, right?"

"So far, you have."

Rob kicked the door frame but lightly. "Low move, Mom."

Collin shrugged. "It's all a consideration. Jeff and I could go back to the house, but if the perp—as you call him—is after the triplets, then they would be in danger here, too. So far, the notes have been directed at me. This attack is probably to get my attention, to show me they are capable of reaching out and touching the ones I love."

Anger burned in her soul. "But it'll be their death. Because no one touches my family." She stopped, swallowed hard. "Except God."

Rob put his arms around her. "He's not going to allow something to happen again, Mom. Not again."

Collin lifted her chin. "I can't say that. I can't. But I know He loves me, and He has me, and whatever happens, His will is perfect." Tears brimmed from her eyes. "I knew it when Talitha and Vy were taken. It's all I had to hang on to."

Rob nodded. "It's all any of us had to hang on to. But it was enough."

"You're right. And it will be again."

"We stand on the rock." He kissed Collin's cheek. "I gotta get back to campus."

Collin kissed him as well. "Go raid Grandma's fridge."

"She already packed me a cooler and a carry-all. I'm good for about a week."

Collin smiled. "Mom Lacey."

"Yeah." Rob kissed her again and then headed out the door.

Collin wandered down the hall to the playroom. Pop Harmon sat on the floor with the trio, building with the wooden blocks. He explained to them concepts of stability and g-force and structural integrity. The triplets stared in fascination as he lay block on block on block. Finally, as he reached the top of his tower, he pulled out a towel and waved it at the building. "And then comes the test: can it withstand the wind?"

The tower stood. Harmon nodded. "A very good tower. But can it withstand three dinosaurs?"

The triplets roared and stomped and knocked the tower all over the playroom. Harmon looked up at Collin. "Guess the answer is no."

Collin hugged the man. "Thanks for playing with them, Pop Harmon. They love you so much."

"I love them, too. I can see them being an important part of my later years."

"Mine, too."

"Mine first."

Collin laughed. It felt good. Good and right and peaceful. She called out, "Okay, dinosaurs. Time to clean up. Lunch is waiting." She didn't mention naptime. Not yet. Save the fight for after they ate. When they were sleepier. Yeah. Don't mention it. Yet.

* * *

Jeff disconnected the call. He jerked to his feet. His chair skidded across the room and slammed into the wall. He clenched and unclenched his fists. *I have never wanted to hit something so bad...* He needed to get out of the office. Away. Anywhere.

The rec center. Find a pick-up game and pound some baskets. Or get pounded. The result would be the same. His tension and frustration and anger would be spent in non-lethal ways.

Jeff walked into Erin's office. "I'm going out. I'm going to find a rec center with a pick-up game and pound the pine. You wanna come?"

Erin eyed Jeff sideways. "That bad?"

"Yeah. You wanna come?"

Erin tossed the pencil he held. "Count me in." He rolled his wheelchair back from the desk. "Give me five minutes to call Vy."

Jeff's fire died. "Take all the time you need, bro."

Erin held up his hand. "No eggshells, man. We're both doing fine. God's will. He's got this."

Jeff nodded and walked back to his office. He pulled out the duffel bag with his "sports clothes," made sure he had a complete change of outfits—including for the shower afterward—then called Collin.

She answered on the first ring. "Afternoon, my love. What's going on?"

"Erin and I are going to a gym to play round ball." A sudden thought nudged him. "You want to join us?"

She hesitated. "I'm pretty rusty. I'm liable to embarrass you."

"You've embarrassed me every time we play by beating my brains out. This could be the break I need to finally beat you."

"In your dreams, Farrell." Her laughter sounded sweet. "Where and when?"

"Um...southside. As soon as we can get there."

"I'll meet you in thirty. Bring your crying towel."

"Always."

Erin rolled into Jeff's room carrying his own duffel. "You talking to Collin?"

"Yeah, she's going to meet us there."

"Oooo...competition."

The men left the building. Jeff's work phone jangled. He ignored it. Life would wait. Roundball called.

* * *

In the rec center café after the game, the three teammates swilled drinks and rehashed the play. Erin chuckled. "Did you catch the look on Godzilla's face when you juked him out of his tennis shoes?"

Jeff cackled. "Oh, yeah. Guess he's never been beaten by a

girl before."

Collin smiled. "My pleasure to further his education. Do not underestimate your opponents." She dipped her fries in her frosty.

Oh, gross.

It's Ohio. Do it.

Erin tossed a French fry at Jeff. "You kept missing the three, man. What's wrong with you?"

"Three kids and a job."

"Excuses."

Collin stretched. "Anyone remember the ibuprofen? I'm going to need it before we get home."

Jeff mocked her. "Oh, poor baby. Stiff already?"

Collin sneered at him. "You could say that. You could sleep on the couch if you do."

Erin looked at his watch. "This has been great. Love it. We need to do it more often. After I teach Vy how to play the game. Then we can really take on all comers."

Jeff's phone buzzed. He looked at the number. "Oh, police. Hang on." He picked up the call. "Jeff Farrell here. Can I help you?"

Collin whispered, "No speaker. Not here."

His eyes flared at her. *Okay, so he knew already. I'm still in Mommy mode.*

Your performance on the court would belie the thought.

Collin smiled with the memory. *Yeah, we weren't half bad. A dude, a chick, and a guy in a wheelchair. And we mopped the floor with 'em.*

Jeff's conversation continued to be primarily silent listening. "Uh-huh. I see. Humph. Really? Interesting.

Veerrry interesting.

Oh, stuff it.

Collin tried to interpret Jeff's face. *Not happening. He's finally mastered the poker face.*

Taught him well, you did.

He finally strung multiple words together. "You'll let us know when you catch it, right?"

Catch it? It?

"Thank you, Officer Tomke. I appreciate your help and your call. Right. I'll wait to hear from you."

Erin's face mirrored what Collin guessed her own looked like. The intense eyes. The slight turn of the head. The total focus. He spoke for her, too. "So? What did they come up with?"

"The hair sample off of Caleb's bear matched the ones in the room."

"And they belonged to who?"

"What. A primate. A capuchin monkey."

Collin gasped. "There's a monkey loose in our house?"

Erin lowered his head and chuckled. "Okay, that's a first."

"For us, yeah."

Collin repeated, "There's a monkey loose in our house?"

Jeff nodded. "They're pretty sure. They think it's in the attic."

Collin sat back in the booth. Her eyes lost focus. "There's a monkey in my house. We have a monkey in the attic." She looked up. "How did it get in? Where did it come from?" *What is it eating? Where is it going to the...never mind. I don't want to know. Not yet.*

Jeff shook his head. "They don't know. They are setting some traps to try and lure it in. If that doesn't work, they'll have to go up and try to catch it themselves."

Collin shook her head. "A monkey. What does it want in my house?"

"Caleb's bear, for one thing."

Collin looked up. Jeff held her eyes. "I remember. The night we found the bear in the closet."

"Right. The box Gretchen alerted on. And then the bear itself."

Collin looked at the floor, the wall, the ceiling, the table. "The bags with the clothes. Had it been in there, too?"

"They haven't found any evidence of it beyond Gretchen smelling it there. But the chance is high."

Collin's head jerked up. "The leather strap thingy."

"They're testing it. Comparing tooth marks. But good chance it will prove to be something the monkey chewed on."

"But what about the notes? Did the monkey put them out, too? How did it know where and when to put them?"

"When they catch it, they'll ask it. For now, it's our prime suspect for all things mysterious."

Erin shook his head. "Only you two. Monkeys in the attic.

News to brighten Vy's day." He pushed back from the table. "I gotta go. This has been the most fun I've had in a long time. We need to do it more often."

Jeff snorted. "Yeah. With all the people pulling out of deals, we can maybe hustle at hoops for a living."

Erin tossed one last fry at Jeff. "See you later." He wheeled his chair out the restaurant door.

Collin eyed Jeff. "What do you mean about people pulling out of deals?"

Jeff shrugged. "We've had some calls after the whole mess with CPS. Having the senior partner of our firm being investigated for child abuse looks bad in some circles. The fact you were exonerated seems to have been missed."

Collin dropped her eyes. "Still? It's been over a week. No one got the memo I've been cleared?"

Jeff reached out and caught Collin's hand. "Listen, milady. We don't need those contracts. We're doing fine without them. I've had more calls come in wanting to do business with us than have backed out. So don't go there."

Collin looked off to the side. She let her emotions settle, then turned back to Jeff. "Right. We did nothing wrong. That's what counts. The Lord will uphold us."

"Right. It's all up to Him."

Collin finished her frosty and fries. "We should get back to your folks' house. Rescue them from the tiny terrors."

Jeff grinned. "Yeah, I guess. I'm sure the tiny terrors are doing fine."

"It's your folks I'm worried about. They need a break."

"They'll never admit it, you know."

"Of course not. Grandma and Grandpa get tired? Never."

Jeff bussed the table. He caught Collin's hand, and they walked together to their respective cars. Jeff kissed her before he let her go. "I love you, milady."

"I love you, Jeff Farrell."

Collin slid into her car, closed the door, laid her head back on the headrest, and groaned. "I am so sore! I'm not going to be able to move tomorrow."

She sat up. "Except I have kids. I don't have the luxury of not moving." She started the engine. "A monkey. A monkey in my attic."

She put the car in gear. A call came in over Bluetooth. "Collin Farrell here. Can I help you?"

"Collin, it's Sierra Tresalyn. How are you doing?"

Collin's stomach tightened. "I'm good if this is a social call. Is it?"

Sierra hesitated. "No. But it's not an official call, either. It's a courtesy call. You have an enemy, Collin. One who is attacking you relentlessly. I'm doing what I can to keep this thing from hitting official channels. But there have been four allegations filed against you for abuse, for neglect. They're also citing you for child endangerment and being an unfit mother. You're mentally unstable. You can't be trusted to care for your children. You're a danger to them. It's vicious.

"We're countering every charge with our report from last week. So far, the higher-ups are satisfied with these being malicious assaults with no basis for truth. But if they keep coming in, sooner or later, we're going to have to come out again."

"And you won't find anything more than you did the last time." *Except the monkey in the attic. Which could take some explaining.* "I know these calls are all anonymous but are they coming from the same source?"

"I can't give you the information. But I can say we're tracking the calls down. This kind of character assassination goes beyond nuisance calls."

"Right. Okay, thanks for giving me the heads-up. Any time you need to come out and see the babies, you're welcome to come. I have nothing to hide." *Except the monkey in the attic.*

Sierra signed off. Collin pointed the car towards the Farrell house. Monkeys in the attic. Child abuse accusations. Threatening letters. What did they all have in common?

Collin gritted her teeth. "No one is going to take my children from me." She pulled the car over to the side of the road. She let the anger melt. Replaced it with stillness. Went to prayer. "Father...Abba Daddy, please. I'm scared. I know You love me. I know You do. I don't want to lose my babies." She breathed slowly, fighting back the tears. "I know You love them more than I could ever love them. And You hold them. They're Your children, not mine. I know. I know You can and will do what You know is

158

best. Help me accept Your will. Whatever it is. In the Name of Your Son, Jesus. Amen."

She blew raspberries at fear, pulled the car back onto the road, and drove on.

FRIDAY

Jeff refused to keep looking at his phone. The call would come when it came. The call which said the monkey had been sighted, caught, removed. And he and his family could resume living their normal lives in their own home. Looking at his phone wouldn't make the call come any faster.

He tossed the device on his desk away from his line of sight. Better. He picked up the first proposal on his desk. A housing development on the east side. Affordable housing, so the story went.

Except the proposal listed the selling prices well above what many in the area could afford. Which was not what Trinity Builders wanted. "Affordable" meant people could actually *afford* the homes. Could buy them. Live in them. Raise families in them. Those are the houses Trinity wanted to build. Not this.

Jeff made a note across the bottom of the front page, signed it, and tossed the packet aside. If the developer could bring the price down a hundred thousand, maybe they could work something. But as it stood, no.

The work phone rang. Jeff picked it up. "Jeff Farrell here. Can I help you?"

He listened to the repeated theme. Then repeated his answer. "I'm sorry you feel that way, Mr. Lyman. None of the charges are true. CPS has refused to even investigate the allegations. They know my wife is a loving, caring mother. These are false accusations. CPS has judged them to be malicious in nature, and the police are looking into who is making the calls."

"No, sir. I can assure you my children are in no danger from my wife or anyone else. Collin will be vindicated through all of this. If you feel you have to take your business to another builder, I understand. I disagree, but I understand. Have a good day, sir."

Jeff hung up. Put the phone on silent. Tossed it next to his personal phone. Returned his attention to the remaining proposal on his desk.

Erin interrupted his study. "Hey, man. Vy got a call at home asking for verification Collin had completed counseling back after Talitha and she were kidnapped. They said they were calling for your church."

Jeff's eyes flared wide. "What?"

Erin nodded. "Yeah. Vy told them to bug off. Or something along those lines. She can be adroit in her word choices."

Jeff chuckled. "So I've heard. She's called you out in some colorful ways a time or two."

Erin shrugged. "I probably deserved it." He lost his smile. "They gave the name of Rancine. Anyone you know?"

"Never heard the name. I'll call Pastor Thomas and find out who it is. And why they're asking personal questions."

Erin's eyes narrowed. "This is getting beyond harassment into criminal. Is there anything we can do to stop this?"

"If we knew where it came from, maybe."

Erin nodded. "We'll have to look into it. I'll see if Vy can pull in some favors from her colleagues."

Vy worked for the DEA. Or had worked until she and Erin married. She still maintained friendships with her former teammates. One thing Jeff had learned: you don't mess with a DEA agent's family. Maybe Vy could get the help they needed to find this slimebag.

Which wasn't the word Jeff wanted to use. The check in his spirit told him he shouldn't have used any word. *Love your enemies. Pray for those who spitefully use you.*

Jeff muttered, "I'll pray for them. Once we catch them, I'll pray for them."

The check became stronger. Jeff grumbled. "Fine. I'm sorry." He sat back. "Lord, I don't want to pray for these people. Or this person. I want them to stop hurting Collin and the children. I want them to get what's coming to them."

He folded his hands. "But You didn't give me what I had coming. You gave me mercy and grace. And You expect me to give them the same. All I can see is the pain this is causing us. Take the pain away, help me walk in this as in Your will, and help me love my enemy." He stopped. "At least let me stop hating them. Then teach me to love them as You do."

Silence followed. Jeff's silence. Silence so God had time to talk to him, to change his heart. To restore a right attitude…

The phone rang. "Jeff Farrell here." He listened. "Great news. Really fantastic news. So we can move back into the house? And use the nursery? Can we clean it up?"

More listening. "Sure." He hesitated. "I hate to ask this, but are your people sure there was only one monkey?" More chatter. "Right. The odds of there being one monkey were astronomical. Two monkeys would be impossible. Right. I appreciate your help. I do. Collin will be thrilled to know we can move in safely. Do you know where it came from? Have there been any inquiries about a lost pet? Zoo animal? Anything? No? Okay, we'll go with it, then. Thanks again."

Erin raised his eyebrows. "Well?"

"They caught the monkey. Had to get it with a net, but they got it. Took it to the zoo vet to have it checked out to be sure it's healthy. It is. Now they have to try to find the owner. Someone has to be missing their pet. These aren't cheap animals."

"But they're exotics. Are they legal in Ohio?"

"I'm not sure. I'll have to look it up." He dialed. "I'll call Collin and tell her we can move home. Should make her day."

"Something needs to."

"I hear you."

* * *

Collin took the call. "Can I help you?"

"Collin, this is Pastor Nick." *Head of volunteer staffing for children's ministries.*

"How can I serve you, Pastor?"

"This is…difficult. I'm sorry to even have to ask."

Then don't. "Go ahead."

"Did you have an appointment with Dr. Bliss this week to evaluate your fitness to be in children's ministries?"

Collin breathed in and out. Several times. "I saw Dr. Bliss. I scheduled the appointment myself to discuss personal issues. No one suggested or referred me or in any way hinted my seeing him had been mandatory."

Hesitation. "Um... I see. That's...different from...from the information I have in front of me."

"What information, Pastor?"

"I'm looking at a communication which says you were referred to him for mandatory prescreening to determine your fitness to continue as a volunteer with children's ministries."

"When did being screened include a psychological evaluation?"

"I haven't heard of it before, but the note references a bylaw passed by the Elders back two years ago."

"Interesting how we are both just now hearing about this. I'd like to see the minutes from the meeting."

"So would I. But until I can dig them up, were you sent for evaluation?"

"No. Absolutely not."

"Collin, I have to tell you, this is getting weirder by the minute. Because I have a form from the doctor's office responding to *our* form asking for the evaluation. And he responded you failed to complete the assessment. Therefore, you were deemed unsuitable for volunteering in the children's programs."

The tension in Collin's body surged. "Who signed the initial referral? And what is the date on it?"

Pause. "I can't make out the signature. It's half a letter, then a straight line. No one I know of signs their correspondences this way."

"And the date?"

"It's dated last month. Around the fifteenth."

Collin closed her eyes. "It's on church letterhead, of course?"

"The referral is, yeah."

"Pastor Nick, no one referred me to Dr. Bliss. I never received any notice I needed to be referred or my seeing him would impact my ability to volunteer. I went to see him on my own. And I walked out on my own." She chewed the inside of her lip. "I do remember him saying something about not completing the evaluation as I walked out. But since I wasn't there for an evaluation, I didn't consider it an issue."

Pause. "Someone is forging documents as from the church? This can't happen."

Wanna bet? Look on your desk. It happened. "I agree. What are you going to do about it?"

"I'm going to find those minutes. Then I'm going to find out whose signature this is. And who they think they are to unilaterally set up something like this."

"Am I still good to volunteer this weekend?"

Pause. "As far as I'm concerned, absolutely."

"Thank you for your confidence in me, Pastor. I appreciate it."

"We appreciate our volunteers. We can't run the church without you. I will not have my people treated this way. Thank you, Collin. I'll let you know what I find out."

"Thank you, Pastor." Collin disconnected the call. "I sure hope you find out who this is. And how deep the trail is they're forging." She sat still for a moment. "What do I do, Lord? How do I fight this?"

Be still. Know I am God.

"Yes, Lord. I will be still and let You work." It's all she could do, anyhow.

* * *

Jeff saved the good news about being able to go back to the house until he got home. Collin met him at the door before the trio could snag him. He kissed her. "How was your day?'

Collin shook her head. Her eyes held a guarded look. Troubled. Hurting. Pensive. How many words could he use to describe what he saw in those eyes? She shrugged. "It's been a day. Tell me about yours."

He walked with her into the family room area. "Let's get Mom and Dad out here. I want to tell them the news, too."

"Oh? You have news?"

"Yeah. You'll appreciate it." *Some of it, anyhow.*

Lacey and Harmon were rounded up from the backyard where the littles were digging in the garden, planting rocks for Gampa. Hands were washed, dirt brushed off, shoes emptied. Finally, everyone sat in the family room waiting for the big reveal.

Jeff put his arm around Collin's shoulder. "The police say we can go home. They caught the monkey."

Collin looked up at him. "Really?"

"Yeah. I guess it came down through the access hole and got into the nursery, then into the rest of the house. Animal Control came out and captured it. Now it's all about finding the owner."

Collin's eyes remained guarded. "Did they think it could have been a trained monkey?"

He studied her eyes. "Trained how?"

"Trained to put out envelopes?"

Jeff drew in a deep breath. "That might explain it. The monkey had a radio collar on. I know capuchin monkeys are trained as service animals. I'm sure it wouldn't be hard to teach one to drop an envelope on command."

Collin nodded. "Which would mean the monkey didn't escape from someone."

"Someone deliberately planted it in the house. I'll call Officer Tomke and ask him about it."

"Thank you."

Jeff hugged her. "It's almost over, milady. Officer Tomke said we could go home. There's no need to keep the 'crime scene' as it is. They have all the photos they need." He saw the objection starting to form and smiled. "No, they do not believe there is a second monkey. One would be surprise enough."

Collin chuckled. "Okay, I had to ask."

"So did I. And the answer was no."

Lacey raised a hand. "Does this mean you're leaving now?"

Jeff hugged Collin. "I thought we'd wait until after dinner if that's okay with you?"

Lacey beamed. "Of course it is. I love having six extra hands in the kitchen."

Collin chuckled. "Yeah, I know how much help they are."

Harmon suggested, "They can always come with me and paint the garage. I've still got two sides yet to do."

"No. No painting! I swear, if they start on their own walls, I will ban you from ever owning a paintbrush again!"

Harmon laughed, obviously not threatened. Lacey left with the littles. Harmon left to watch the littles help Lacey. Jeff sat down beside Collin on the couch. "What happened today, lady? You look shell-shocked."

She dropped her eyes. "I got a call from Pastor Nick. Someone forged a letter ordering my referral to Dr. Bliss as a condition for my volunteering. And since I didn't complete my 'evaluation,' I'm not fit to work with children."

Jeff pulled away from Collin far enough to see her face directly. "Did what?"

"Official stationery and everything. Referenced a bylaw passed by the Elder Board two years ago. They even had a referral form to fill out. Signed and everything."

"Signed? By who?"

"No one recognizes the signature."

Jeff's anger heated to a simmer. "I suppose they could ask the doctor's office to identify it."

"Unless they say it's privileged information."

"It can't be privileged. Unless they don't want to get paid."

"Except I paid for the visit. If he doesn't say anything, he still gets his money."

Jeff shook his head. "No. This isn't something his office can hide. He'll be forced to reveal who ordered the test."

Collin looked at the floor. "You think it matters?"

"You better believe it matters. We're going to get to the bottom of who is making all this trouble."

* * *

Collin suggested one more "summer potty" rather than cleaning up the nursery. It would give her more time to wash everything, figure out what could be salvaged and what needed to be replaced. She left unspoken the fact that she wasn't ready to let the littles sleep alone yet. Jeff agreed. The babies were excited about sleeping with Mommy and Daddy again. Tucked in, story read (no more Man in the Yellow Hat!), prayers said, and the babies drifted off to sleep. Collin and Jeff sat on the couch watching their littles sleep. Collin sighed. "I could sit like this forever."

"I could, too. If I didn't have to work."

Collin chuckled. "I hear you." She laid her head back on the couch. "Are we sure we're not the ones out of God's will?"

Jeff sat forward to stare in her face. "What? We did nothing wrong, Collin. Nothing. Someone is out to ruin your reputation before the church. And to drive you into another trip to the hospital."

Collin looked at the floor. "I don't need help there."

"Stop." Collin looked up. The vehemence in Jeff's tone surprised her. "I mean it, Collin. There is nothing wrong with you. Your struggles after Talitha's kidnapping weren't some failing on your part. It's called PTSD, and no one in their right mind would fault you for experiencing it."

Collin shrugged. "Except people have." She couldn't keep all the bitterness out of her tone. Some of it. But not all of it. "Well-meaning, 'care about me' people are telling me it's not real. Not for a Christ-follower. A 'real' Christ-follower. I shouldn't have mental problems. Or depression. Or any other condition coming from the brain. We've been given the 'mind of Christ.' He gave us a 'sound mind.' Which means all these problems are of my own making. I created them, so I can 'get over them.'"

She closed her eyes. "Don't they think if I could, I would? Do they think I like being this way?"

Jeff cradled her in his arms. "Christ gave us 'sound minds' in broken bodies. A 'sound mind' isn't the same as a healthy brain. Someone who's diabetic is missing a chemical or has an imbalance in their system. Someone with depression or any other mental illness is missing chemicals or has an imbalance in their brain. You can't tell a diabetic, 'If you love Jesus more, you could go without medicine.' You can't tell someone with a mental illness, 'If you love Jesus more, you can think your way out of your problems.' Both people need medication. And a good doctor. And support. Not condemnation."

He kissed the top of her head. "You have done nothing wrong. There is nothing wrong with your relationship with the Lord. Can we put it to rest?"

Collin opened her eyes and nodded. "I will if they will." She stopped. "No. I will. Period."

Jeff kissed her tenderly. "That's what I want to hear. I love you, milady."

"I love you, Jeff Farrell."

SATURDAY

It started off innocently enough. Jeff and the trio cooked breakfast and cleaned the kitchen while Collin folded the blankets and put away the pillows from the family room. They ate breakfast (bacon and eggs; the littles had theirs scrambled). The littles got a bath and then dressed. Jeff took them outside to play in the yard while Collin worked in the nursery.

Most of the bedding could be salvaged. The curtains were a total loss, as were the lights on the nightstands. Collin attacked the room with disinfectant and most every cleaner she had in the house. The temptation to burn it all down and start over niggled at her brain. She ignored it. Yes, it would be faster. No, it would not be better. Too extreme.

She washed bedding and walls and bedframes, shampooed carpets, and laundered every stitch of clothing in the room. Anything she couldn't put in the washer, she scrubbed by hand. Twice.

Why are you doing this? What is wrong with you?

Nothing. I don't want there to be any trace of the monkey left, that's all.

Trace of your guilt, you mean?

Collin ignored the accusation. She wanted the room clean. Spotless. Sanitized. Sterilized.

You're trying to wash away your guilt. You feel like it's your fault there was a monkey, and if you can get the room clean enough, you can absolve yourself of the responsibility.

It isn't my fault someone put a primate in here. I didn't do anything to provoke this.

Didn't you? Are you sure?

No, or I wouldn't be doing this. Leave me alone.
Peace, child. Breathe.

Collin curled up in a corner. So many voices. So many accusations. So many condemnations... *Father, help me. Please.* Tears drained down her face. Ran in rivulets down her neck. Soaked into her collar. *I'm sorry. I'm sorry. Whatever I did, I'm sorry.*

Whatever you think you did, I carried for you. I paid all the price. Lift your head. Be free.

Collin leaned her head against the wall. She sobbed. "I don't understand. I don't get it. I'm doing everything I know to do. I'm trying to please You. Why is this happening? Why can't I love You enough to live like Kells does?"

Like Kells says she does. But does she?

Collin lifted her head. "What?"

Does she?

"I...I don't know. She talks a good story if she's not."

Ask her. Ask her how she's doing. You're friends. Go visit her. Unannounced.

Isn't that rude?

Go.

Collin wiped her face on her jeans. She pushed off from the wall and stood. Moved by a thought, she went into the kitchen and whipped up a batch of brownies. Thirty-minute brownies. The fast kind for unexpected visitors. Or immediately needed gifts.

The aroma of baking chocolate brought spectators in from the backyard. Jeff led the pack. "I smell brownies." It was an accusation.

Collin smiled. "Yes, you do. And if everyone washes their hands, they can have one." She nailed her biggest kid with a stern glance. "One. I'm taking a batch to Kells."

Jeff's eyebrows went up. "Oh? Are you two talking again?"

"We will be." She thought a moment. "Or not. Depends on how she takes a surprise visit."

Jeff chuckled. "Ah, one of those. I'll pray it comes out okay."

"You'll know if I come home with my tail between my legs."

Collin put out a generous brownie for each child (and an extra one for Jeff, just because,) packed up the remainder into a container she could afford to lose, and headed out. Before she changed her mind. Or chickened out.

She refused to listen to the *"this is a bad idea"* voice in her head. She drowned it out with music. When that didn't work, she rebuked it. "I'm going. I'm going. Period."

Twenty minutes later, she pulled into Kells's driveway. Only one car sat outside. Collin knew Kells's garage didn't hold cars. It held paraphernalia for camping, fishing, boating, but not cars. *Wonder where Steve is?*

Collin walked to the door and knocked. *At least I knock. I may be rude, but there are limits.*

She heard Allison raising the roof about something. And heard Kells screaming back. *Ooo...Mama's lost her cool. She's gonna need these brownies.*

Collin knocked a second time. More screaming. From both females in the house. Collin opened the door and stepped inside. "Kells? Help's arrived."

From the looks of the front room, help was overdue. Diapers—some of them used—lay stacked on the couch. Fast-food wrappers papered the coffee table. Soda cans littered the floor. The curtains were drawn tight. From the looks of the dead plants, no sunshine had come in for some time. Days. Weeks, maybe?

Kells walked in from the back of the house. She saw Collin. "Go away. Get out of here!"

Collin opened the container of brownies and held them out. "Here. Eat one."

Kells's eyes were haunted. But she looked in the container, then looked up at Collin. "Your special cocoa, chocolate syrup, chocolate chip brownies?"

Collin nodded. "Yeah. The killer kind."

Allison continued to scream in the background. Kells reached in and took a confection. She popped it in her mouth. After a moment, she looked at Collin. "Go away. But leave the chocolate."

Collin set the container down, reached out, and hugged her friend. "Kells...what's going on? I love you, sister. What's happening?"

Kells waved around the room. "This. I can't stay on top of it. I can't be a single mom."

Collin's stomach dropped. "Single mom? Where's Steve?"

Kells stared at the floor. "Gone. He left the week after I came home from the hospital with Allison. Said he wasn't cut out to be a father." She looked up, fire in her eyes. "Sure fooled me. He sure loved being there to begin with. But once Alli got home, everything changed." She snapped. "We cramped his style. Cut into his free time. He wasn't ready, he said." She glared at the door. "So he walked out. I haven't heard word one from him since."

Collin hugged Kells again. "I am so sorry." She handed Kells another brownie. "Eat. I'll get Alli."

She walked to the nursery and picked up the sobbing child. Alli stopped crying almost immediately. Collin patted her back, bounced her on her shoulder, and generally did what moms do to put a baby to sleep. It took five minutes, but the infant closed her eyes and slept. Collin set her in the crib and walked out of the room.

Kells had helped herself to a few more brownies. Collin took the container away. "That's enough at one sitting. You'll make yourself sick."

"So? At least I'll die happy."

Collin shook her head. "Go take a nap."

"I can't. You're here."

"And I'm going to be here. Go. Lie down. Sleep while the baby is asleep. Do it."

Kells dodged around Collin's arm, snagged one last brownie, and went to the back. Collin shook her head. She went into the kitchen, found the trash bags, and started the clean-up. Once all the garbage had been removed, the room looked halfway presentable. Collin opened the drapes, watered the living plants, disposed of the casualties. She sprayed everything with a disinfectant and then moved to the kitchen.

Again, once the trash had been removed, half the battle was over. She washed the dishes, straightened the countertops, swept the floor. *I'm not mopping. There are limits.*

She moved to the bathroom. Trash. Counters. Sweep. Collin lowered herself to scrub the sink and bathtub. Allison needed someplace to bathe after all.

It might not be perfect, but it looked a thousand times better. And maybe Kells would be able to keep up with some of it. Collin went back to the kitchen and perused the pantry and fridge. Kells needed to grocery shop. Collin made a list of things to buy, including some healthier alternatives to fast food delivery. Still quick and easy, but with less fat. And salt. And sugar. *But that takes all the taste out of it.*

Oh, hush.

She worked and hummed and cleaned and generally lifted her own spirit. What it would do for Kells, she didn't know. Hopefully, show the desperate woman people still loved her. And she could ask for help.

She'd been at it for two hours when Kells wandered in from the back room. She looked at all Collin had done, dropped on the couch, and buried her head in her hands. "Why? Why are you here?"

"Because you're my friend. And Someone cleaned up my mess, too."

Kells stared at the floor. "I'm sorry, Collin. I am. I lashed out at you because…"

Colin finished the statement for her. "…because you were lashing out at yourself. I know the routine."

Kells lifted her head. "I believed it. I believed if I lived right, worshipped right, loved right, none of this could happen. He'd protect me."

Collin sat across from her friend. "There is no 'right' way, Kells. There's only the attitude of our heart. He'll never 'owe' us anything. Not protection, not favor, not blessings. He gives according to His will. And we accept it as it comes."

Kells shook her head. "You accept it. I've watched you."

Collin chuckled. "Not without grumbling and complaining about it first. I'm trying to get past that part. Trying being the operative word. I'm a work in progress like all of us."

Kells looked out the window. "Why did he leave? Why did God allow it?"

Collin reached out and squeezed Kells's hand. "Wrong question. At least for the present. The question now is, what does the Lord expect you to do about it? Or with it, anyhow."

Kells snorted. "I can tell you what He doesn't want. All I've been doing. Nothing. Or as close to nothing as I can get away with."

"Yeah, nothing isn't an option."

"Oh, it's an option. Not a good one, but it is an option."

Collin ducked her head to the side. "Granted. Let's set that aside. What does the Lord require of you right now? What do you need to be doing?"

"Caring for Allison."

"And caring for yourself."

"Eh." Kells shrugged. "Debatable."

"No, it's not. You can't care for Allison if you don't care for yourself as well. So program it into your priorities. You need help. I'm here. There is a church full of women who live to help. Grandmas who are dying to hold a baby. Helpers who get their kicks out of cleaning. I'm not one of those, but I can do it in a pinch."

Collin held Kells's eyes. "Ask, Kells. Lower the walls, kick pride in the can and ask for help."

Kells turned her eyes away. "How can I? He left me. What does it say about me?"

"Nothing. It says nothing about you. It says everything about him. You aren't responsible for his actions, Kells. Only how you react to them. He chose to abandon you and Allison. Your choice is to survive and thrive for your daughter's sake."

Kells's eyes glistened as moisture threatened to spill out. "How? How do I survive? I don't even know where he is."

Collin chose her words carefully. "First, I'd suggest you talk to Legal Aid. Freeze your bank accounts. Open a new one in your name only. For a start."

"How do I do both? If I freeze my accounts, how do I get the money to open my own?"

Collin smiled. "You ask for help from a friend. One who is ready and willing to help you."

Kells choked. "I've been so rotten to you. Why would you help?"

"Because He loved first. All I do is because of Him, Kells. It really is. I owe Him everything. Literally everything. Including my life. I hold nothing back He wants." *Except the babies...and even those you've had to release.*

Talitha's empty crib flashed in her eyes. Collin stared into the blackness. The despair. The heartache. The longing. The fear. It gripped her. Squeezed her heart. Squeezed the oxygen from her lungs. Her baby. Gone. Never to return? Could she live? If God required it, could she honestly say, "Not my will, but Yours be done?" Was it what He wanted?

Tears rained down her face. She didn't try to stop them. She poured out the anguish. And whispered, "Please. Please. I love her so much. I want her back with me. Please. Please."

And over and over, the question came, *If I ask, will you give?*

Broken. Knowing she could only give one answer. Collin whispered it. "Please, please don't ask. Please."

If I ask, will you give?

She closed her eyes. Great sobs wracked her body. She slid to the floor. Facedown, on her knees, there could only be one answer. "You know I love You. Please. Please."

Will you give?

"Yes. I give her to You. You are the Lord of life. You are my God. I give her to you. Now and forever. Take her. Take them all. They are yours. Teach me how to live without them. With only You. I love You."

Someone shook her shoulders. Someone pierced the memory, shattering its death grip on her mind. Kells called, "Collin! Collin. Come back. It's okay. She's safe. She's with you. It's over. It's over. Come back, Collin."

Swimming from the depths, Collin rose through the memory back to the present. The emotions fell away, stripped like a snake crawling out of its skin. Collin lifted her head. She drew in a long, life-giving breath, let it out slowly. She looked at Kells. Nodded. "I'm back."

Kells sat back on the couch. Her face ashen, her eyes tinged in horror. She whispered, "Is that what you went through? All those two weeks?"

Collin closed her eyes. "Yes."

Kells shook her head. "I couldn't do it. I couldn't. There's no way."

Collin smiled, a sad smile through lips she chewed to keep back the tears. "It hurt so bad. But I didn't have any other choice. I had to give her up."

Kells lowered her head. "I'm sorry, Collin. I've been so cruel. I didn't know. I didn't. I don't know what I thought, but I'm sorry."

Collin smiled. "It's okay. I forgive you. Even for the monkey in the attic."

Kells jerked her head up. "The what?"

Collin's eyes narrowed. "The monkey in the attic? The one you let loose in the house?"

Kells shook her head. "I never had a monkey. I certainly never let one loose in your house. What are you talking about?"

Collin explained briefly about "George." Kells's eyes widened in shock. "I never did it, Collin. I haven't been anywhere since Steve left. Honest. I swear, I never had anything to do with a monkey."

"Gretchen alerted on the bags you brought."

"Who's Gretchen?"

"Sniffer dog. She's the one who found the monkey to start with. She found the bags very interesting."

"I got those bags from Nonnie. She brought over some clothes she thought I could use for Allison. But she brought them maybe two weeks ago."

Collin rose from the floor and returned to sitting on the couch. "I'll talk to her about it. Maybe she has a good explanation."

"Maybe. She's not been herself lately. She seemed really quiet in group this last week."

Collin nodded. "I noticed. She didn't say anything. I need to call her."

Kells snorted. "Her, you'll call. Me, you drop in unannounced."

Collin smiled. "But I brought brownies."

"True. And you're going to leave them, right?"

"As long as you promise not to eat them all in one sitting."

"I promise."

Collin tapped fists with her friend. "I'm going to go grocery shopping for you, then I'm going to head home."

Kells shook her head. "No, I'll take Allison and go. We need to get out of the house." She smiled a tight-lipped smile. "I need to learn to be a single mom."

Collin warned, "Who knows how to ask for and accept help. Right?"

"Right." Kells hugged Collin. "Thank you doesn't cover it. I owe you."

"Nope. You owe Him. Pay it forward." Collin hesitated. "I meant what I said about the money, Kells. Not a loan to be repaid. Just a helping hand like I got once."

Kells lowered her head but nodded. "Yeah." She looked up. "You wouldn't know the number for Legal Aid, would you?"

"Actually, I do." Collin went to the kitchen, found some paper and a pen, and wrote the number down. She handed it to Kells. "Call them. They're good people. They'll point you in the right direction. And give you suggestions you might want to follow." Collin sighed. "They're used to dealing with this kind of thing. Far more often than you know."

Kells folded the paper. "Thanks again, Collin. I'll see you at church on Sunday." She smiled. "And try to get there on time, will you?"

Collin grinned. "I'll try. I love you, Kells."

"I love you. Thanks, Collin."

"No problem." Collin picked up her shoulder bag and walked out the front door. She smiled all the way to the car. "Thank You, Lord. I needed that. She did, too, but I needed it more. Thank You."

Collin pointed the car toward home...

...and passed the man in the three-piece suit lolling at the corner. He smiled. Saluted. Got in his car and pulled away, headed in the opposite direction.

SUNDAY

Collin kept her eyes searching the assembly at church for the man in the three-piece suit. Twice she thought she spotted him. Neither time did it turn out to be him. *How hard is it to find a man in a suit at church? We're a 'come as you are' congregation. No one wears a suit.*

She checked the trio in then went to her class. Kells had already arrived with Allison on her shoulder. Collin lowered her head and eyed the woman. "Separation anxiety?"

Kells snorted. "You could say that."

Collin smirked. "Yours or hers?"

Kells sneered. "Don't start. Do not start."

Collin laughed. "You want me to take her?"

"Thank. She needs to diet if I'm going to lug her around on my shoulder." Kells narrowed her eyes. "

"No 'I told you so.' Got it?"

Collin took Allison from her mom, so Kells could get the children settled, start the story, and break up the talkers, pokers, and gigglers. *Must be something in the air. Seems like the kids are more wired than normal.*

Is there a 'normal' for kids this age?

Good point.

Collin bounced and joggled the infant on her shoulder until snack time, when Kells took her back. Allison promptly fell asleep. Music played, parents came, and Kells and Collin parted ways. Collin went to check on the trio. A man in a suit smiled in passing. Collin did a double-take. *Not him. Same suit. Not the same man.*

Am I losing my mind?

Collin lowered her head and walked to the nursery. Amanda

Ruiz greeted her. "There you are. I knew you'd be in to check on them."

"How'd they do?"

The volunteer smiled. "Still in the same clothes. We're making progress."

"So far. Thanks for caring for them."

Amanda's eyes narrowed. "Have to ask…they've been talking about a monkey at the house. Did you get a pet monkey?"

Collin shook her head vehemently. "No. A renegade capuchin monkey found its way to our place. Hid out in the attic and only came out at night. Animal control caught it, and it's gone. For good, I hope."

Amanda laughed. "Which explains it. I thought they were telling a tall tale. Except all three of them were telling the same story."

"Yeah, well…they were telling the truth. About having a monkey. Any exploits they might have embellished are strictly of their own imagination."

Collin stepped aside to let another parent check in their child. She waved at Amanda and headed to church. Two more men in suits smiled at Collin as she made her way to the auditorium. Neither saluted. Collin closed her eyes as soon as she reached her seat. *I do not want to see anyone else. I don't. This is wrong. All wrong. Lord, help me. Please.*

Peace flooded her soul. She lived and moved and had her being in Christ. She would not fear. She opened her eyes, turned to look for Jeff.

The man in the suit sat behind her. *The* man. In *the* suit. He smiled. Saluted. Rose and left.

Jeff slid into the seat beside her. "What's wrong? You're pale."

Collin tried to point out the man, but he'd disappeared. She swallowed. "Nothing. I thought I saw the stalker. I've been seeing people who look like him all morning. And now, I thought I saw him behind me." She held out her hands. "But he's gone."

Jeff spun around to search the auditorium. "I don't see anyone."

"I said he's gone." Collin couldn't keep all the irritation from her tone. "Forget it. I'm going to."

Jeff squeezed her hand. "Hey, lady. I'm on your side, remember?"

Collin dropped her eyes. "I know." *I'm afraid we've both picked the losing side in this battle.*

Service listened to the message on unity and brotherhood and the importance of the Body being one. Considering the past couple of weeks, it seemed timely. *Now, if people will take it to heart.*

As the message ended, Pastor Thomas went off-script. Or so it appeared. He surveyed the congregation. "We have a rumor mill amongst us. I am calling for a dedicated time of prayer tonight at six p.m. We will pray, then, as the Lord leads, we will discuss the rumors we have heard. We will put them to rest once and for all. Those who want to see this body grow in love and unity will be here. I understand some can't. But make this a priority. Come expecting the Lord to meet us. Have a good morning."

He dismissed the assembly. Collin looked at Jeff. "Did you have any idea he planned this?"

"None. But it's time. I hope we have a full turnout."

"Agreed." *Except the man in the suit. I don't want to see him here. Or anywhere.*

They gathered their children and headed home. Collin tried to avoid looking at cars as Jeff drove. *No looking for trouble. Go home. Pretend life is normal. Make it so.*

Collin unlocked the door, opened it. Instead of letting the littles in first, she entered the room before them. *Caution. The monkey is gone. There is nothing here. You have cameras. Nothing can...*

An envelope on the floor in the middle of the kitchen. Collin sagged to the floor. The littles immediately jumped on her. "Mommy! We pay, Mommy!"

She hugged each one, unable to join the fun. Kissed them. Directed them, "Go sit at the table." All the while, she stared at the envelope.

Jeff came in from the garage. Collin saw his eyes widen, then narrow as he looked at her. She pointed to the floor. "I thought this was over."

Jeff's face hardened. He got out a napkin and picked up the envelope by its edges. He pulled it open, read the note. He folded it back in place. Pulled out his phone. Dialed. "Braydon. Check your feed. Someone got in. Let me know."

Dialed again. "I want to report a break-in. Yes, I'll wait."

Collin rose from the floor. Lunch. *Fix lunch for the littles.* She moved to their table and asked, "Do you want peanut butter and jelly? Or do you want bologna and cheese?"

"Blll an' teese!" Three voices in unison.

Collin nodded. Moved to the refrigerator. Pulled out the cheese slices and bologna. Everything done by muscle memory. Her mind frozen. *Lord, we were supposed to be over this. The monkey put the letters out. The monkey is gone. There shouldn't be any more letters. Why? Why is this happening?*

She mayo'd the bread. Assembled the sandwiches. Cut them in quarters. Set them on the table. Made sure to set two in front of Talitha. Poured milk. Stepped back to study Jeff.

Who had toggled calls from the police to Braydon. And sounded not happy. "I don't care if the person monitoring the feed saw nothing. There's an envelope in the middle of the floor which wasn't there when we left. Either your cameras...yeah, okay. Fine. Call me."

Collin stepped into his chest. Laid her head on his shoulder. Whispered, "What did it say?"

He shook his head sharply. "No. It doesn't matter. We're done playing this game." He put the phone to his ear. "Yes, ma'am. I need to report a break-in. Again. Jeff Farrell...right. No, no monkey this time." He stopped. "No. No. I don't want to even think about there being another monkey. Whatever this is, it has to stop."

Collin stepped away and moved to watch her littles eat their sandwiches. Or their "blll an' teese." In separate parts. First the cheese. Then the bologna. Then the bread. Never all at once. Littles. She left them in the care of their father and walked to their bedroom. She pulled the pillows, blankets, and stuffies off the beds, brought them to the family room. She made a space on the floor for them. And one for herself. Sunday naps were routine. She would not upset the babies more than she had to. But she couldn't leave them in a closed room by themselves. Not now. When this was truly over, maybe. *When they're sixteen. Maybe then.*

The exaggerated silence in her head spoke volumes. *I know, I know. Can we get through this, please? Before we talk about my sanity?*

Collin waited by the opening to the kitchen until the children had all finished their lunch. Then she shepherded them to the bathroom, then back to the family room. Caleb looked at the pillows, then at his mother. "We hab summer potty?"

"Yes. We're having another slumber party. Maybe for nap."

"Why, Mommy?"

"Because Mommy wants to watch her babies sleep today. Okay?"

Three heads nodded. "Yes, Mommy." Three bodies climbed under their covers, hugged their stuffies. Two thumbs went into mouths. Three sets of eyes closed.

Well, four sets of eyes closed. Collin prayed, *Lord, I'm sorry. I'm sorry. If I'm not trusting You. I'm sorry. But I have to do this. I do. I can't just do nothing. Not with someone coming in here. I can't. I can't. I love You.*

The answer came back. *There is no condemnation for those who are in Me. I love. I am love. I lived like you, I understand you. Peace.*

Collin curled up on the floor beside her children. Moisture from her eyes dampened her pillow. *Thank You. I love You.* She paused. *I'm not losing my mind, am I?*

Warmth spread through her. *Okay. Thanks. I love You.*

Jeff woke her up when he came in to join her. "I'm sorry. I didn't mean to wake you."

"What did the police have to say?"

"Since there's no sign of a break-in, and our security cameras don't show anything, they won't make this a priority call. They'll have someone out when they can spare someone."

Collin lowered her eyes. "Like never?"

Jeff hugged her. "We're going to…"

Collin interrupted him. "…get through this, I know. Did Braydon call you back?"

"Not yet. He's going to review the footage himself, then call me."

Collin held his eyes. "What did the letter say?" He started to wave her off, but she caught his hands. "No. I want to know. I need to know. Tell me."

Jeff drew in a long breath. He lifted his head. "It said, 'Next time they won't be coming back.' The police still wouldn't come any sooner."

Collin sucked in her lip. Let the fear roll over her and off her shoulders. She would not break. She would not fear. She would not...

She breathed out. "Who hates us? Who wants to hurt us? I don't understand. I don't."

Jeff hugged her again. This time, he didn't say anything. His presence gave his answer. It would have to be enough.

They sat leaning against the couch, watching their tribe sleep. About an hour in, Jeff's phone barked. Softly. He answered it. "Talk to me, Braydon."

Collin watched his face rather than listened to his words. "Really? Fine. No, we have a meeting at church tonight, but you can come as late as five, and we'll still be home... Yeah, no, we need to be there. Special prayer night. You're welcome to join us... Okay, see you in about an hour. Bye."

Collin waited for her husband to explain. He put his phone back in his pocket. "Braydon wants to show us the feed. Wants us to see what he's seeing. You heard him. He'll be here in about an hour."

"The babies should still be asleep."

"I thought so, too." He snorted. Lightly. "But subject to change at any moment."

"Right."

Not quite an hour passed before Braydon's van pulled into the driveway. Collin watched him get out, accompanied by Gretchen. Braydon carried his laptop and had a bag of dog food slung over his shoulder. A big bag.

Collin exchanged looks with Jeff, went and opened the door. Gretchen came in first. Braydon dropped the kibble on the steps. He kissed Collin as he entered. "I'm sorry you're going through this again, Collin. I am." He touched knuckles with Jeff. "But it's why I wanted you to see this for yourselves."

Jeff motioned. "And your associate?"

"Wanted to run her through the house. Then, after you see the video, you can decide about letting her stay or not."

Collin felt her spirit rise. A little. Yes, Jeff had opposed Gretchen. Maybe now would be different. Maybe? She could hope, anyhow.

Gretchen lay down near the baby pile. Braydon set his laptop on the counter, opened it, fired it up. "This is the footage from the time you left for church 'til the time you came home. We'll run through it fast enough so we can get to the important part."

Jeff eyed his brother-in-law sideways. "If it doesn't show anything, how can there be an important part?"

"Watch. You tell me."

Collin crowded in so she could watch as well. Braydon isolated the kitchen camera, showing its feed. He zipped through maybe an hour or two, then slowed it down to real-time. "Watch. Watch closely."

Collin watched. Her eyes fixed on the spot where the envelope had been placed. Nothing changed. Nothing changed. Nothing...

Out of nowhere, the envelope appeared in the exact location she'd found it. Her eyes widened. She turned to Braydon in shock. "Show it again."

Braydon backed the feed up and played it again. Nothing. Nothing. Envelope. Out of nowhere. It didn't move into position. It didn't fall. It merely appeared.

Jeff's eyes narrowed. "That's not possible. It can't happen."

Collin looked from the screen to Braydon. "How? How did it happen?"

Braydon nodded. "Exactly what I wanted to know. I looked at the time signatures. Twenty minutes are missing. Time enough for someone to come in, place it, and disappear." He looked from Collin to Jeff. "What I need to know is how they managed it. From what I can tell, there was no power outage. The cameras were never off. All the monitors show green."

Collin stared at the floor, then at Braydon. "How?"

Jeff said it. "Someone tampered with the video itself."

"Bingo." Braydon nodded. "I hate to think any of my people are involved in this, but there it is." He tapped the screen of his laptop. "Proof. I will go through the rosters and find out who had access to this footage and the name of the person on duty at the time."

Collin shook her head. "Unless they confess, you can't prove they tampered with it. Videos fail all the time. And it won't tell us who's responsible on this end."

"No. But it might be enough to get the police to help me set up a sting operation and catch them both."

"And in the meantime?"

"Gretchen can be your backup. And a great deterrent."

Collin looked at Jeff. "She would be good to have until the police can be brought up to speed. And agree to help."

Jeff sighed. "If this wasn't so serious, I'd accuse the two of you of plotting this to get a dog in the household."

Collin started to protest. Jeff waved her off. "I didn't say you did. I know better." He paused, looked from the dog to the sleeping babies. Then nodded. "We'll do it."

Collin felt the first surge of happiness she'd felt in a long time. "Thank you."

Jeff looked at Braydon. "Tell me how to take care of her. And not ruin her for future work."

Braydon smiled. "I wouldn't worry about it. I brought her kibble. A cup in the morning around six. Another cup in the evening around the same time. Lots of fresh water. And she'll need to be walked daily. At least five miles. She's excellent on a leash and will run alongside a jogger or a bike, whichever is easier."

Jeff's jaw dropped. "Five miles? Every day? Do you know how much time that will take?"

Collin nodded. "I do. And we can split it between us. I need the exercise. And the motivation."

Jeff groused and grumbled. Looked at the baby pile. Looked at Gretchen lying beside them. Sighed. "Okay. I yield. Gretchen can stay."

Collin kissed him. "Thank you."

"What else do we need to know about her?"

"She's house-trained. She'll let you know when she needs to go out. But you need to show her where 'out' is and how to get there. She'll sleep on the floor." Brandon nailed Gretchen with a stern look. "No matter what she tells you. Do not let her on the couch. And no feeding her from the table."

Jeff's eyes widened. "What? What kind of dog sleeps on the floor? Can we at least get a dog bed for her? And not eating from the table?"

Braydon chuckled. "I'm certain your littles will have a vacuum following behind them at all times. She won't need the extra pounds from the table."

Collin smiled. "We will make it clear Gretchen is not to be fed people food. Unless it drops on the floor. But nothing on purpose."

Braydon smiled. "I can live with that. I'm sure Gretchen will as well." He looked at the floor. "She's had all her shots. I can't think of anything else right this minute. I'll write down the number for the vet in case you need it."

Jeff slipped into the family room and petted Gretchen's head. "You win, girl. We'll let you protect the babies. I don't know who's going to protect you from them, but we'll work it out."

Braydon closed his laptop. "Okay, I'm going to take this to the police on Monday and see what we can arrange. If they'll listen to me."

Jeff's eyes darkened. "Between the monkey, the envelopes, the break-ins, and the stalker, they should have plenty of incentive."

Braydon turned to Jeff. "Stalker? I haven't heard about a stalker. Who? When?"

Jeff pointed to Collin. She shrugged. "I'm pretty much the only one who's seen him. Guy in a three-piece business suit. Always the same suit. He's been outside the house, at church twice, outside Harmon and Lacey's house… He smiles and salutes me, then either drives away or melts into the crowd."

She looked at Jeff, then back to Braydon. "Today at church, there were three men in the same suit. Same exact suit. We're not a 'suit wearing' kinda place, you know? But Jeff didn't see him. Hasn't seen him. I'm the only one who has." She lowered her head. "I'm afraid the police will think I'm losing the few marbles I've got left. Hysterical female. You know."

Braydon hugged her before Jeff could. "I know you. You are the farthest thing from a hysterical female I know. If you say you saw a man, then there is a guy out there."

Jeff added his vote. "Agreed. And I've known you longer. Rob can vouch for you before I knew you. Zena, the Warrior Princess, does not imagine stalkers."

Collin held up her hand. "Um…let's keep the title a family secret, okay? I don't want it getting spread around."

Braydon laughed. "I can understand." He kissed Collin again on the cheek, hugged Jeff, patted Gretchen's head, then turned and left.

Jeff put his arm around Collin. "We got us a dog."

"A very good dog. I feel better with her here."

"Yeah, I suppose I do, too. But five miles..." He snorted.
"Well, you said we needed exercise. Guess I'm going to get it."

"We both are."

The baby pile began to stir. Caleb woke first, crawled out
from under his brother. He rubbed his eyes then saw Gretchen. He
squealed. "Puppy! Puppy back!"

His shrill woke Talitha and Joshua. They both rolled over, saw
Gretchen, and scrambled to their feet to hug the dog. Collin let
them adore her for a few moments, then said, "Okay, everybody
listen. Sit down." Three bottoms hit the floor. Three heads turned
to look at Collin with wide-eyed attention. Collin smiled.
"Gretchen is going to stay with us for a little while. She's not ours
to keep. She belongs to Uncle Braydon. But she's going to live
with us for a few days. She's going to help watch over all of us."

Bodies bounced in excitement but didn't leave their place.
Collin continued, "You three are going to help take care of her,
too. You will feed her and give her water when she needs it. But
she only eats puppy food, got it?"

Three heads nodded in solemn agreement. "Yes, Mommy."

"Okay. Let's take the blankets and pillows back to your room,
put them on the bed, and then let's go outside with Gretchen. She
needs to stretch her legs."

*She needs to do more than stretch. Better find a shovel and a
rake for cleaning up after her. And a designated trashcan for her
deposits.*

Whatever work it takes, she'll be worth it.

Agreed.

SUNDAY NIGHT

Jeff and Collin dropped the trio off at Erin and Vy's house before going to the prayer meeting. The debate about whether to bring them or not had been brief. They'd already spent two hours in the church nursery for the day. Asking them to spend even more time in the evening went beyond what Collin wanted for them. And "Unka Ewon and Auntie Vy" were happy to keep them for the evening.

The parking lot looked half-full when they pulled in. Jeff surveyed the cars. "I hoped more people would come."

Collin shrugged. "It's still early. Maybe some will come for the gripe session."

"Then they're missing the point of the whole evening." Jeff's frustration could be seen in the tension in his face.

Collin laid her hand on his arm. "It's okay, Jeff. I'm not afraid of anything anyone might say. Or think. I'm satisfied the Lord has this."

Jeff laid his head on hers. "I love you, milady."

"I love you, kind sir. Now, let's get inside. I want a good seat."

Jeff chuckled. "Down front, I know."

"Fewer distractions down there. And I can see better."

"Truth."

They entered the auditorium and found it half full. Collin craned to look in the balcony to see how many seats were occupied there. None. No one sat there. Collin turned to check and saw the doors to the balcony had been shut. *Okay, he wants everyone down here. Makes sense. I guess.*

Music played over the speakers. Gentle instrumental praise

tunes. *Not sure what mood Pastor wants to create. Solemn? Prayerful? We'll know soon enough.*

Pastor Thomas started the gathering promptly at six. "Welcome. Thank you for taking time to make this a priority in your day. We honor the Lord when we make room for Him to work in our lives."

He glanced over at the congregation. "We have a grave problem in our 'family.' Too many whispers and rumors and accusations and backstabbing. We—those of us who love the Lord and are surrendered to Him—make up the Body of Christ. We represent Him to the world. When we bite and tear and eat our own, we are not ambassadors. When those outside see us, they point their fingers, and rightfully so. 'Hypocrites.' 'They're no better than we are.' And they're correct."

Thomas bowed his head. "We are no better. We're forgiven. We belong to Jesus. We need to live like it. Only when those outside see the reality of Christ in us will they want to know the Lord we serve.

"Tonight, I'm asking you to search your hearts. Search your minds. With the Psalmist David, ask the Lord to search you and show you yourself. Where are we failing our brothers and sisters? Where have we listened to rumors and not sought the truth? Where have we gossiped? Where did we spread an untruth, half-truth, or a 'fact' we didn't know for a fact."

He walked the length of the platform. "I'm asking you to let the Lord reveal those areas to you. And I'm asking Him to clean us. We'll spend half an hour in prayer. Longer, if anyone feels they need. After we're done praying, we will clear the air about these rumors. I'm going to ask people to come forward with what they've heard, and we'll get the truth."

He stared into the auditorium. "This is not a time for debate. Not a time for who started it, where did it come from. This is a time for honesty in our own lives. But we need to start in prayer."

Pastor Thomas closed his eyes, raised his hands, and prayed, "Lord God, we belong to You. We are Your children. We need You to search our hearts, our minds. We need You to show us our own selves. The good, the bad, the ugly. Clean us. Wash us white as snow. Then help us make amends to our brothers and sisters. Heal this body, Father. In Jesus's Name, I ask it. Amen."

Pastor Thomas stepped down from the platform and kneeled on the floor. Moments later, people began to join him. A row filled beside him. Another formed behind the first. Then a second. A third. Collin saw people kneeling at their seats. She held Jeff's hand as they both kneeled where they were. Time to let God take inventory. *Search me, Father. You know me. You know every thought, every word. Clean me. Make me over in Your Image. It's all I want. To be more like You. Mold me, Lord.*

Half an hour passed. Collin got off the floor and sat down. Jeff remained on his knees. Several people from the front returned to their seats. Others stayed on their knees.

Fifteen more minutes passed. Pastor Thomas rose and resumed his place on the platform. A handful remained at the front. Jeff twisted around and sat down, brushing his face with his sleeve. Collin leaned in and kissed his damp cheek. He nodded, kissed her in return.

Five more minutes and the assembly faced the platform. Pastor Thomas picked up the microphone again. "Thank you for being willing to look at yourself first. Now comes the hard part." His voice hardened. A little. "These rumors must stop. The gossip must stop. Scripture is clear. If you have something against your brother, go to him. Not anyone else. Not me, not the Elders, not your neighbor, or your prayer partners. Go to the person."

He looked around the auditorium. "I'm going to go out on a limb here and do something I've never done before. And hope never to have to do again." He looked at Collin. "Mrs. Farrell, will you come up beside me, please? Mr. Farrell, you, too."

Collin gave Jeff a surprised look. His face wore the same expression of not knowing. Together they climbed the stairs to stand beside Pastor Thomas.

He hugged them both. "Collin. Jeff. You've been at the center of this firestorm of rumors for way too long. It's time you were able to face your accusers."

Thomas surveyed the assembly. "Anyone who has shared a piece of information about the Farrells to someone else in the past month, I'd like you to come forward and share it here. Now. In front of them. There is a microphone set up down front for you to use. Use it."

A murmur ran through the seats. When it died down, Thomas

nodded. "You got it. I'm going to give you the chance to accuse them directly." His eyes moved from one side of the room to the other. "I'm not concerned about who started it or who you heard it from. I want it out there, and I want it answered. We're family. Let's have a family meeting and clear the air."

Several breaths went by. Kells moved to the microphone. She locked eyes with Collin. "I heard Collin had abused her children." She lowered her eyes. "She told us what happened. She had a flashback and bruised the children's arms." Kells turned to face the assembly. "I believed her. And I used the rumor against her anyway." She faced Collin again. "I am sorry. Will you forgive me?"

Kells wiped water from her face. Collin did the same. Collin whispered, "Forgiven. I love you, Kells."

Kells smiled, tight-lipped. She returned to her seat.

A woman Collin knew only from passing in the hallway came next. "I heard the story about Mrs. Farrell hurting her children. I heard CPS had been called." She, too, looked at the assembly. "I told my prayer circle. I was too ashamed to put my name on the paper. But I put her name." She lifted her hands to Collin. "I'm sorry."

Collin nodded. The tightness in her throat wouldn't allow her to do more.

Greg stepped forward. "I heard CPS had been called. I called Samuel. We..." He hesitated. "We went to the Farrells. They told us what had happened. We asked Collin to step down from serving. We... I thought someone might get the wrong idea about the church. I didn't care about the truth. Only what it looked like." He faced Collin. "I apologize. Will you forgive me?"

Collin and Jeff both nodded. Greg climbed the platform and hugged Jeff. Then Collin. Greg whispered, "I'm sorry."

Collin whispered back, "I love you, brother."

And so it went. Until an hour or more had passed. And no one else queued up to the microphone. Pastor Thomas waited, then addressed the assembly. "Thank you all for allowing the Lord to move. Thank you for being broken and honest. There are two takeaways from this meeting I want everyone to remember. One: the Farrells are innocent of any wrongdoing. Next time someone comes to you with a rumor or half-truth or story, spit in their eye and tell them 'bug off.'"

General laughter. Thomas smiled. "Okay, so the 'bug off' may be a step too far. But tell them what the truth is. And if they persist, tell them, 'Let's go ask the Farrells. And I'll go with you.' That should stop them from coming to you, anyhow.

"The second takeaway is: remember to ask your brother first. Go to him. Or her. Or them. But address it between yourselves. First. There are procedures in Scripture for church discipline. Talking behind someone's back isn't part of it." He looked around again. "Thank you." He looked at Collin and Jeff. "Thank you for not hitting me for surprising you with this. I didn't know I would do it, either, until we were done praying. And then it seemed like the most appropriate thing to do." He smiled. Faced the assembly. "One last request. If anyone who didn't come to this meeting asks you about it, tell them what happened. All of it. Maybe we can avoid any repeats. You are dismissed."

He hugged Collin and Jeff, smiled, stepped down from the platform. Collin and Jeff followed. A crowd of people waited to greet the three of them. Hugs and words of encouragement and pats on the backs. And half an hour later, Collin and Jeff got to leave the building.

Jeff stopped before the double doors. "Wait. I forgot. I need to tell Wayne something."

"Meet you in the car."

Collin started out the door. She looked up. The man in the three-piece suit held the door for her. *The* man. He smiled at her. "Very nice evening, don't you think?"

Collin felt ice moving its way from her brain to her limbs. Freezing her one inch at a time, one muscle at a time. Her eyes lost focus.

A voice inside commanded, *Move. Walk forward. One foot. Two feet. Move. Step. Forward. Move. One inch. Go. Do it.*

Her brain obeyed. One inch. Another inch. Her foot moved. Her leg moved. Her knee bent. She walked. The man held the door until she passed him. Then he let go, saluted her, and walked out of the light. Into the shadow. Back into the dark.

Collin stared where he'd been. She closed her eyes. *Help me. Help me. If I'm losing my mind, tell me. If he's not real, tell me. If he is, tell me. But don't leave me like this. I can't. I can't.*

Answered warmth seeped through her. Gave her comfort. Assurance. He loved her. It's all she needed. For now.

Collin walked to the car, unlocked it, strapped herself in, locked the doors again. She focused on the warmth. She repeated, "I'm not losing it. I'm not. I will not go back to the hospital. I will not break. I will not break."

Jeff knocked on the window. Collin unlocked the doors. He slid in, looked at her face. "What happened? What's wrong?"

Collin shook her head. "Nothing. Let's go get our tribe."

Jeff eyed her sideways. "Are you okay?"

"I'm fine. Let's get the kids and go home." Home to a guard dog who would keep burglars at bay. Maybe even shadows. Maybe especially shadows. *Yeah. Those.*

Jeff pointed the car toward Erin and Vy's.

MONDAY

Collin ran alongside Gretchen, trying to clear her head. The early morning run would be a great time to plan her day, get her blood moving, maybe vanquish the last of the 'baby fat' she carried. Gretchen ran with ease, barely breaking a sweat. *Show off.*

Jeff ran the dog first, leaving Collin to finish Gretchen's daily five miles. After that, it would be all rough and tumble and tug with the trio. Which ought to give Gretchen plenty of exercise. But the prolonged cardio came first.

Collin kept an easy pace. Not because Gretchen needed it. No, Collin needed it. Gretchen could probably run all day. *Dogs. Oh, well. This will improve my game. And my ability to keep up with the littles. If possible.*

As she rounded the corner leading to home, she saw a lone figure leaning against the back fender of a car. She would pass him on the opposite side of the street.

Not this time. Collin slowed her pace to a walk. She stopped in front of the man. Maybe having Gretchen by her side gave her courage. Maybe she'd had enough. Either way, she faced the man.

His vibe sent warning sirens up her spine. His eyes chilled her soul.

He smiled at her. "Good morning, Mrs. Farrell."

Collin nodded. "Morning. May I ask why are you shadowing me? Why do I see you everywhere I go?" *No challenge. Inquiry. Mild inquiry.*

He shrugged. "Streets are public passages. I can travel wherever I want."

"And my church?"

"You invite all to come. I come."

Collin nodded. "Yes, you do. Do you stay for the service, or show up so I can see you and then leave?" *Watch it there. Careful. No sarcasm.*

He shrugged again. "It varies."

"Neat trick last weekend with the three men in your suit. Must have cost some money to hire them. And outfit them. That's not a cheap suit." *Okay, a little sarcasm. But keep it under control.*

He held out his hands. "This? It's something I threw together."

Collin returned to her question. "Why are you shadowing me?" She put some heat behind the question.

"No reason. We happen to end up in the same places."

"I see. You have a name?"

"It's not important. And I must be going. Have a good day, Mrs. Farrell."

He saluted her, got in his car, and drove away.

Collin watched him until he turned the corner. "GFL440." She patted Gretchen on the head. "Can you remember GFL440? We're going to check it out when we get home, right, girl?"

Gretchen panted. Collin chuckled. "I'll take that as assent. Come on. We have a run to finish." She resumed her run, rehearsing all the details of the car, the man, the conversation in her mind. So she could tell the police. If they ever came out.

She arrived home. Jeff had the trio up, dressed, and eating breakfast as she turned Gretchen out into the backyard for a break. Collin kissed him as she passed him. "I'm going to shower. Don't leave until I get out."

He kissed her back. "Never."

Collin did a "splash and dash" and returned to the kitchen. The littles were dutifully sitting at the table, one by one telling Daddy all about what they did at "Unka Ewon and Auntie Vy's house" last night. Collin listened. Tall tales, all of it. She laughed and let Gretchen in the door. Gretchen made her way under the table. Picking up scraps, no doubt. Oh, well. One less floor to worry about.

Jeff packed his lunch. "How'd the run go?"

"Probably the same as yours. Any cars along the way?"

"You mean besides the usual? I don't remember any." He cocked his head. "Why? Did you see something?"

"Four-door luxury sedan. Latest model. License GFL440. Deep, metallic blue. Over on Crenshaw."

Jeff rolled his eyes up, thought a moment. "No. Can't say I remember seeing it."

Collin shrugged. "Thought I'd ask."

Jeff's eyes narrowed. "Did you see someone? Your stalker? Is that what he drives?"

Collin nodded. "Yeah. We talked this time."

"You talked to him?"

"Yeah. He said it was a free country, and we happened to be in the same places at the same time. And our church invites all comers."

Jeff hesitated. Seemed to think deep. Looked up at her. "What impression did you get from him?"

"Bad. Evil bad."

Jeff pulled out his phone. "I know who he is."

"He's not my imagination?"

"No, and I'm sorry. This is my fault." He waited. "Erin. Remember I told you about the guy coming in the office wanting the bribe? And he called you Erol? Yeah. Him. You haven't run into him, have you? He hasn't come by your place?"

From the depths, a memory slammed into Collin's consciousness. She covered her mouth with her hand. The world around her receded. *Erin talking. 'A pedestrian crossed the street...he saluted her...'*

Collin grabbed Jeff's arm. "Vy's accident. The pedestrian. Ask Vy what he wore."

The puzzlement on his face made her grab his phone and demand, "Ask Vy what the pedestrian wore. It's important. If she remembers."

Erin sounded as confused as Jeff looked. "Okay. Hang on. I'll see if she's still here."

Collin muttered, "Be there, Vy. Be there."

Erin came back on the phone. "She said he looked like a businessman. Wearing a suit."

"Three-piece? It matters. She works for the DEA. She notices details."

"You talk to her. Here."

Vy came on the line. "What's this about, Collin? The man

stayed to help. He gave the police the license number of the car which hit me."

"Which the police never found. Vy, what kind of suit did he wear? It's important. Please."

Vy paused. "I think it might have deep blue. Light blue shirt. Had a vest to match the suit. I know because he took his jacket off to cover me with."

Collin felt her soul drop. "Vy. Give me a minute. Hang on. Just a minute. This is important."

Vy's voice mirrored the confusion of the two men. "Sure, Collin. Sure."

Collin grabbed a sheet of paper and began writing as detailed a description as she could remember of the man she'd seen. And seen. And seen. Five-ten. One-eighty. Chestnut hair.

He's not a horse. No one calls hair chestnut.

Shut up. Watch.

Collin closed her eyes to better remember the encounters. Late twenties. Salutes with his hand straight, as having been in the military. Watch or band on his right hand. Which would actually make him left-handed, but you only salute with your right....

She handed the paper with the description to Jeff then put the phone on speaker. "Okay, Vy. Everything you can remember. Every detail."

Vy hesitated only a moment. "Maybe five-ten. Five-eleven at most. One-seventy, maybe one-eighty. Chestnut hair." *See? Now leave me alone.*

Vy picked up steam. "He had a watch on his right wrist, so he must have been left-handed. That's all I can tell you."

"You say he saluted you. What did it look like?"

"You mean like a real salute? Or a mock one?"

"Whichever you saw him do. Describe it."

"I'd say he might be former military. And not too far removed from it. Very sharp, professional salute. Fingers straight. Hard snap. What's all this about, Collin? He stayed to help."

"Right." Collin looked at Jeff.

Jeff's face paled. He nodded to Collin. "It's the same man."

Collin bit her lip. "Vy, we need to get a sketch artist out to compare faces."

Now Erin's demanding voice sounded. "Not until you tell us

what this is about."

Collin drew in a deep breath. "The man who's been shadowing me. That's his description. And it's the description of the man who came in Jeff's office looking for the bribe."

Silence. Silence. "Are you saying it wasn't an accident? He set it up? To what, kill Vy?"

"Maybe. Maybe to hurt her. I don't know. I don't know what he wants. But I think we need to be sure we're talking about the same person. And we need the police to start looking for him. And maybe then we can get our answers."

She heard some quiet murmurers. Vy came back. "I'll have a sketch artist meet me at the office. Then I'll send someone to your house." Vy managed a small chuckle. "I'm sure they'll get a better description from you if the babies are occupied."

Jeff leaned into the phone. "What about me?"

"Give yours to the police artist. If we have three different artists, we can't say they were prejudiced or had preconceived notions of who the guy is."

Collin nodded. "Smart thinking. I'm so sorry, Vy. I hate bringing this back up. And I know the implications of what I'm suggesting."

Vy's voice sounded firm. "I'd rather know the truth. We'll get it figured out. Love you, Collin. You too, Jeff."

Jeff's phone went silent. Collin wrapped herself into Jeff's arms. "I'm sorry. I am."

Anger laced his voice. "I'm the one who's sorry. If I had known he would cause all this trouble, I'd have reported him to the police in the first place. It's my fault."

Collin touched his cheek. "No, it's his fault. Let's leave it there."

"Right." Jeff kissed the top of her head. "Guess I'll work from home today."

"You don't have to do that."

"I know. But I'd rather be here. I'll make an appointment to go to the police station and have the artist draw who I saw. But other than going there, I'm staying here."

Jeff called the complaint about the stalker in again. With the addition of the information about Vy's accident, the complaint moved up on the priority list. They would send someone out to take Collin's statement within the hour.

Collin leaned her head back against the top of the couch. "Do you think it's over, now? I mean, no more envelopes? No more threats?"

Jeff raised his eyebrow. "I'd like to think it. I'd like to think a lot of things, but I don't know milady. If Ryan Woolfort and your stalker are the same, it should be over. But is he the one who put the monkey in the house? Who gave the monkey the envelopes? And who put the envelope in the house after the monkey had been captured? I don't have answers to all those questions."

Collin thought a moment. "You think I could interview the monkey?"

"If you thought it would help, go for it."

Collin shook her head. "No, I'll let it pass. Not sure I could make a lot of sense of the answers."

"Good point."

Collin stared off over the heads of her children. "But if it wasn't Woolfort, who could it have been?"

"Who hates you?"

"No one I know of. No one who isn't still in prison."

"Okay, who likes you but has a grudge?"

"I still don't know. I try to keep short lists. Talk to people directly if I think I've upset someone, or I have something against them."

"Makes life easier. I agree."

Collin thought it over again. "The only people who have even been to the house are the mom's group. And they're all friends. Or I think they are."

Jeff turned to face her. "How long have you known each of them?"

Collin had to think. "Kells, I've known for years. We worked in the same building. We were friends before we ever got the group together."

"Who else?"

"Bri and Nonnie have been there from the beginning. Macie and Oscar are about the same age. Grace and Julie came about the same time, then Tia. And now Eliza."

Jeff broke up a potential fight between Caleb and Talitha over a truck they were using to drive over the "Mount Gretchen." "I'd say you can eliminate Eliza. She hadn't started coming when the envelopes started."

"I'm not sure sitting here playing 'who dun it' is going to get us far. I'd like to try something more productive."

"Like what?"

Collin reached across the table for her phone...

...only to find it not in its place. She surveyed the room. Joshua seemed mighty content sitting by himself in the corner, his back to the room. "Joshua?"

He hastily put something under his legs and turned to face her. "Mommy?"

Collin swallowed her smile. "Joshua, have you seen Mommy's phone?"

His face reddened. His lip puckered. His eyes dropped to his lap. "No, Mommy."

"Joshua...bring me my phone, please."

He held up both hands. "No has it."

"No, you're sitting on it. Bring it to me."

Joshua stood up. He picked up the phone and carried it to Collin. "I find it, Mommy."

"I'm sure you did." She waited until he handed it to her. "We have rules about Mommy and Daddy's phones, don't we?"

He nodded. His siblings stopped their play to see what was going on with their brother. Collin asked him, "What are the rules?"

Joshua didn't answer. He looked at his toes.

"Joshua. Answer Mommy. What are the rules?"

He looked up quickly, then looked down again. "I not know."

"You do know. We all know. Mommy and Daddy's phones are not toys. You do not play with them. Right?"

Look at toes. Look at Mommy. Look at toes. "Yes, Mommy."

"Go to the time-out corner, buddy."

Tears and wails burst from the boy. He ran to the far corner of the room and sat in the appointed chair.

Caleb looked from his brother to his mother. "Jo-u-a in time out?"

"Yes, buddy. He's in time out. He had Mommy's phone. We don't play with Mommy or Daddy's phone. He knows, but he did it anyhow. So he has to be in time out."

Caleb nodded. His lower lip quivered. "Cayeb be in time out?"

"No, Caleb doesn't have to be in time out. He didn't play with the phones. Only Joshua did."

Caleb nodded again. He looked at his brother, still wailing. He walked over and sat on the floor beside him. "It okay, Jo-u-a. I sit, too." Tears ran down his chubby cheeks.

Not to be left out, Talitha ran to join her brothers. She sat on the other side of Joshua and repeated between sobs, "It okay, bubby. It okay. We okay. We okay."

Collin pointed to Jeff, then to the children, "They're yours. You do something with them. I'm going to call Bri and Nonnie. After I make sure no one placed any orders on Amazon. Or made any calls to Taiwan." She shook her head and walked from the family room to the kitchen.

She hesitated about who to call first. She stared at her phone for inspiration. Failing any, she prayed, *Lord, a direct answer would be wonderful. A hint would be nice, too. Anything? Anything?*

Nothing. She sighed and dialed Brianna.

The woman answered on the third ring. "Collin. What's up, girlfriend?"

"Wanted to let you know we're back at my house this week."

"Did they catch whoever broke into your place?" Brianna laughed. "Or will this be another one of your 'you have to come to find out' ploys?"

Collin heard a belligerent tone in her friend's voice. She paused. "I'm sorry. I don't mean to. Or do I do it too often?"

Bri stopped her. "No, no. I didn't mean it that way. You've had some interrupted weeks, I know. Like a continuing drama. It's understandable."

Collin wasn't sure she bought the reversal. She went with it, anyhow. "Well, it has been a lot of drama. I think we're about to the end of it, anyhow. But I called to see if you were free this week. Like, Tuesday? Coffee?"

"I can't Tuesday. Can we make it Wednesday?"

"No problem. Wednesday works."

"Where?"

"Your place? My place? Downtown?"

"Downtown is nice. The Blue Cup?"

"Time?"

"Nine works for my schedule."

"I'll make it work for mine. Now, the real question: accompanied or un?"

Brianna laughed. "Oh, let's pretend we're single again. Unaccompanied. If you can swing it. Mom's always telling me she'd love to watch Oscar for a few hours. I'll take her up on it."

"Great. Jeff is working from home this week. He'll take care of the littles while I act like the adult."

"Why's he at home?"

Collin thought fast. "He says he gets more work done here. I don't see how, but I don't argue with him."

"I certainly wouldn't. Okay, it's a date. I'm excited."

"Me, too. Coffee with a friend. How civilized!" Bri ended the call. Collin sighed. One down. One more to go. This next call would not be as brief.

"Nonnie? How are you doing?"

Her friend's voice came through guarded. "I'm fine. We're fine."

Collin stepped lightly. "How is Macie's hip doing? Is she recovering well?"

"They say she's doing great. I don't know. I haven't...been able to see her."

Even more lightly. "Where is she, Nonnie?"

"She's with my sister now. Leonard and I aren't allowed to see her except with supervision." Nonnie's voice broke into sobs. "He hurt her, and I can't see her. It's not fair. It's not. It wasn't my fault. He's the one who broke her leg. Why are they punishing me?"

Collin chose her words carefully. "I'm sure the authorities want to do what's best for Macie. Until they can prove how she got hurt, they want to protect her."

"But I told them what happened. Leonard hurt her. He broke her leg." Anger radiated through the airwaves.

"Did you see him break it, Nonnie?"

"Yes! I told them exactly how it happened. He picked her up by her leg and shook her hard. Then he threw her down, and she screamed and cried. That's what I told the police. Why don't they believe me?"

"It's hard, Nonnie."

"They didn't take your children away. You told them what happened, and they didn't take yours. Why did they take my Macie and not your children?"

Collin stiffened. She breathed slowly. "Those are different situations, Nonnie. My children..."

Nonnie cut her off. "...were hurt like Macie. But they didn't take yours away. They believed you, didn't they?" The woman swung her sarcasm like a knife.

Collin ducked the blow. But refused to turn the blade on its owner. "They saw the bruises for themselves, Nonnie. They could see there had been no abuse."

Again, the knife slashed. "I heard a different story. I heard you knew one of the CPS agents, so they didn't take the children."

Collin stepped back. "I knew one of the agents, yes. She wasn't the only one who came. The other agent saw everything for himself and determined there was nothing to the complaint. They didn't take the babies because there was nothing to find."

She decided to deescalate the fight. "Can you meet me for coffee this week? Tomorrow, maybe?"

"I don't know. It will depend on when I can see Macie. I suppose I'll have to come to your house, won't I? Since you have your children with you and I don't."

"No, I'll meet you wherever you want to meet. Jeff will stay with the children while I go out."

"You always say the same thing. I can't believe your husband gets it so easy. He must not work hard. Or he doesn't have a job where he has to work all the time."

Collin started to respond, then stopped. "He has an understanding boss."

"I've never met one."

"What time, Nonnie?"

"I'll have to call you. I won't know until I find out if I can see Macie or not and what time. I have to make sure I don't go the same time Leonard does."

"I'll wait to hear from you, then."

"Bye."

Collin set her phone down. She shook her head. *Whew. Brutal.*

She's not helping herself stay off the naughty list.

Collin went back into the family room. Joshua's sentence in timeout had ended, and he and the other littles were all playing together. Gretchen had moved away to a more sheltered and isolated spot, under the coffee table. Jeff had stretched out on the couch but had his eyes on the children. Collin sat beside him. "I thought you were working from home."

"I am working. I'm working at keeping my eyes open and the babies entertained." He motioned to her phone. "You get hold of anyone?"

"Coffee with Nonnie possibly tomorrow and Bri on Wednesday." She shook her head. "Nonnie is a basket case. I can only pray CPS will determine which parent actually hurt Macie. And then get help for all three of them."

Jeff sat up. "Right. Bad situation all around. Wish I knew Leonard better. He might need a friend about now."

Gretchen met the knock at the door with a low "woof" but nothing more. Collin looked out then opened the door. Two men stood on the porch, holding police IDs up. "Come in, gentlemen. Thank you for coming."

Detective Gentry and sketch artist Landon Halcion entered the room. The babies immediately stopped their play and ran to sit by Daddy. Collin smiled. "They run in packs, but they're harmless."

Gentry nodded. "I see. We received a call about a stalker and possible involvement with a hit and run?"

"Yes. Jeff..." Collin turned.

Jeff met the two men and shook hands. "I made the call. I'd like to talk to you in my office if you don't mind." He motioned to the three littles. "Less confusion."

Collin motioned to Landon Halcion. "And I want to put a face to the stalker. We can go in the kitchen." She smiled at the trio. "Everyone in the playroom for a little while. Gretchen will watch you play while Mommy talks to our guest. Okay?"

Three heads bobbed. "Yes, Mommy." Ten legs ran down the hall. Collin let them into the playroom, then closed the half door.

Landon chuckled. "You've trained them well."

"They really are good babies. Um, toddlers." Collin offered, "Coffee? Anything?"

"Coffee is fine."

Collin made a fresh pot. Landon spread out his portfolio of facial types, eyes, lips, ears… Collin motioned to the layout. "You have quite the collection. How long have you been drawing?"

"For the police? Five years. But drawing itself? All my life."

Collin sat and looked at the layout. She closed her eyes, tried to remember the best look she had of the man in the suit. She looked at the outlines and pointed to the one closest to the same contours. "The one there. That's his outline."

"How well did you see him?"

"Face to face? On multiple occasions."

"I'd say close. Okay, so this outline. Eyes?"

"Besides cold and evil? Um…" Collin studied the offerings, then picked out the closest one. "This. Except one eye seemed more closed than the other."

"Okay." Landon sketched over the eyes. "Like this?"

"Better. Yeah."

So it went for a good hour. Collin broke long enough to check on Gretchen, let her out, let her in, take the children to potty, then back to finish with Landon. "I apologize for the interruption. Where were we?"

At last, Collin had a face she believed represented her stalker. As close as if he sat before her, in black and white. She nodded. "It's him. It's the man."

Landon ducked his head. "You've got a real eye for detail."

"Thank you." She didn't bother to explain it had been drummed into her from birth. "What happens now?"

"We'll compare this to anything we've got. Computers can do facial recognition faster than we can. If we get a hit, we'll let you know."

"Thank you for coming. I hope we can catch this guy. And find out what he wants." *Before he gets it.*

Good point.

Landon walked to the living room, where Jeff and Detective Gentry were standing. Gentry nodded to Landon. "You get what you came for?"

"Yes. Good sketch. Want to see it?"

Jeff held up his hand. "I'm not supposed to see the sketch. I need to make an appointment to have someone sketch the man I saw, so we can compare the three."

"Three?"

"My sister-in-law was in a hit-and-run accident. The same man may have been involved. We're doing our sketches separately so we can be certain it is the same man, and we're not simply feeding off each other's memories."

Gentry nodded. "I'm impressed. Very smart on your part."

Landon held up a hand. "I can send out my partner. He'll be happy to get out of the office for a while. I won't show him what I drew. Then we can compare sketches." His eyes smiled. "And see who has the better recollection."

Jeff and Collin shook hands all around then the men left. Collin leaned against the door. "That was informative. And exhausting. What did you and Detective Gentry discuss?"

"The bribe attempt. And you being stalked. He doesn't know the name Ryan Woolfort. He'll cross-check it back at the office. And he'll talk to Lyon Ebertson. He's also going to touch base with Vy and Erin. We'll get this figured out, and then we'll get it stopped."

Collin kissed him on the cheek. "I love you. Thank you."

"I love you. And I'm sorry we didn't do this sooner."

She shrugged. "It's fine. It is. We're on it now, and that's what matters."

"Mommy!" Shrill cry from the playroom. Angry cry from angry female child.

Collin and Jeff hurried to the room. Both boys had their cheeks puffed out as if holding something in their mouths. Talitha pointed. "Bubbies fin' canny, but Yitha not got any."

Collin approached Caleb. Jeff took Joshua. Same command in stereo, "Spit it out." Both boys obliged, spitting a mouthful of watery something into Collin and Jeff's hands. Both boys immediately started gagging and crying. Collin sent Caleb to the water fountain for a drink; Joshua followed. They both continued to gag and cry. Collin shook her head. She studied the 'canny' in her hand. Jeff did the same. The candy looked like a jelly cube. Both boys had bitten into them, but only just. Collin squeezed the cube. Clear liquid came out. Jeff mirrored her actions. Collin studied the unknown substance for several moments. "I have no clue. We'll take it to the police lab later."

He nodded. "Works for me."

Collin brushed her hands together to rid herself of the offensive material. Then rinsed them under the water. Jeff followed. They both turned to face their sons. Both boys sat on the floor, sup-supping at the end of a good cry. Collin and Jeff sat down in front of their sons. "Caleb, where did you find the candy?"

He pointed to the play kitchen. "Ina can'net. Wit the turkey an' hot dogs."

Jeff went to the play kitchen and looked in the single cabinet. There on the shelves were a miniature turkey, hot dog, mac 'n cheese, and other pretend items. Jeff held up two square jellied cubes. "Was this what you found?"

Caleb nodded. "Jo-u-a eat it. I eat it. I not let Yitha eat it. She too yittle."

Talitha begged to differ. "I not yittle. I big girl. I eat cannies too."

Collin shushed her. "Enough. No one should have eaten the candies. We don't put things in our mouths Mommy and Daddy haven't given you. Right?"

Accusations slammed into her brain. *Another rule? Another way to control every move they make? Afraid God might do something you don't like? When do you give Him room to work, hmm? Never.*

Collin's eyes lost focus. She stared at the floor. *I'm being a good mom. I'm protecting my children. These are rules they need to live.*

Rules, rules, rules. All you do is give them rules. No faith. No trust. Dr. Bliss had it right. You have no faith. You're a fraud. A fake. A hypocrite.

Collin battled back. *I'm not. I love my children. I want to keep them safe.*

Safe from who? God? Yeah, let's see how that works.

Jeff touched her arm. "You okay, lady?"

She looked up at him. "What?"

"You zoned out. Are you okay?"

She stared off, then came back to herself. "Yeah." She looked at the boys. "No putting things in your mouth. Those were yukky, weren't they? They could have made you very sick."

The boys nodded. "Sowwy, Mommy. Daddy."

"Okay. I think it's time for lunch. Let's clean up in here, then go to the table."

Toys flew into boxes, feet pounded down the hall to the kitchen. Collin cocked her head. "You look pale. Are you okay?"

Jeff snorted. "You should talk. Are you okay?"

Collin shrugged. "Eh. I think I could use a nap once the babies are down."

"Let's make it a double."

"Sounds good."

Collin fixed peanut butter sandwiches and poured milk for the littles. Swallowing became hard. *What is the problem here?*

The littles went to their room to nap; Gretchen joined them. Collin left the door open in case Gretchen needed to make an exit. Eyes closed, stuffies cuddled, and babies slept.

Collin pointed. "Couch or bedroom?"

"Couch. You take the bed."

"Good." Collin walked to the bedroom, lay down, and felt strength seeping from her. She felt heavy, her limbs unable to move. *What is this?*

Fear coursed through her. She tried to call out to Jeff, but nothing came out. She moaned. *The candy. Poison? Lord, help me.* Her fingertips reached out. Hit 9-1-1.

"9-1-1. What is your emergency?"

She whispered the only thing she could. "Help."

MONDAY AFTERNOON

Paramedics from Station Five took the call. "Unknown emergency. Police are en route. 112 Harper Court."

Vin entered the address in the GPS. He studied it a moment. "I know that address. Why?"

Samons checked it. "Farrell. Jeff Farrell. We've been out there for barbeques."

Vin's eyes narrowed. "Let's move."

No one answered the door when they knocked. The police unit arrived at the same time. A dog barked at the door. Not a "go away" bark. A "hurry up and get in here bark." Vin could see the Shepherd jumping on the door. He looked at the officer with the sledge. "Break it in."

They slammed the device against the door, and it smashed open. The dog barked and ran in circles, running out of sight, then returning. Vin motioned with his head. "Follow him."

The dog led them to the family room, and the man flat on the floor. His limbs were rigid. Samons kneeled beside him. "He's got a heartbeat. But barely." He opened one eyelid. The victim's eyes moved frantically side to side, attempting to focus on something. Anything. But no emotion reached his face. Vin dropped the medical kit beside his partner and prepared to give aid.

The Shepherd wasn't satisfied with the progress, however. She barked and ran down the hall, then ran back, barked, ran down the hall, ran back...

One of the police officers followed the dog. Vin heard a shout from the back. "I've got a female victim in trouble back here." A pause. "And three toddlers in panic mode. Call CPS. Get someone out here."

Samons motioned with his head. "Go check out Mrs. Farrell."

Vin hustled to the back and found the woman lying rigid on the bed. Her heartbeat sounded slow. Dangerously slow. Vin checked her eyes. Same response as her husband. Frantic movement. But no expression on her face. Vin yelled, "We need more help. Have dispatch get a second unit out here. And two ambulances. They need transport now." He cursed, not for the first time, the squad's inability to transport people. Oh, he could render all the immediate aid, but getting them to the hospital was the job of the ambulance. Which would only be sent out after the paramedics determined one was needed. "Proper utilization of resources," management said. "Waste of precious time," said those on the front line. And on and on the battle went.

The second police officer reported to his partner. "There are emergency numbers on the fridge. I'm going to call those."

"Fine. But get someone here, now."

The toddlers lay on the bed by their mother, crying, curled up next to her, on her. The dog nosed the babies, maybe trying to comfort them? The toddlers: two boys and a girl. One of the boys sat up and pointed to Vin. The desperation in his tone broke Vin's heart. "You hep Mommy?"

He nodded. "I'm going to help your mommy. My friend is helping your daddy."

Vin motioned to the policeman. "Stay here with them. I've got to get some supplies." He ran back to the family room.

Samons had started an IV and pumped oxygen. He met his partner's eyes. "He's bad."

"Yeah, so is she. I've got to get the other tank."

Officer Cantley got off his phone. "I'll get it. The kid's grandparents will be here in fifteen minutes." He smiled grimly. "Unless they get stopped for speeding. I told them I'd try to get an escort for them."

"Thanks." Cantley disappeared out the front door. Vin grabbed supplies and raced back to the bedroom. He started the IV, all the while talking to the toddlers. "Grandma and Grandpa are on their way over here. They're going to take care of you while we take care of Mommy and Daddy."

Cantley brought in the oxygen tank. Vin attached the mask to the woman's face, turned the volume up full. "Breathe, Mama. Breathe."

Merritt came into the bedroom. "Base says it's probably poison of some kind. They said give atropine." The officer handed Vin the medication. "I'll be runner."

"Thanks. Let me know when the ambulance gets here."

Vin pushed the medication into the vein. He listened to the heartbeat. It sounded stronger. Maybe. Maybe he wanted to believe it. He muttered, "Come on, woman. You've got babies to take care of. You need to fight this thing."

Cantley picked up the little girl. "It's going to be okay, honey. Grandma and Grandpa are coming."

Merritt reappeared. "Base says push another ampule of atropine."

Vin nodded. "Got it." He administered the second vial of medication. He rechecked her heart rate. Definitely stronger this time. "Ask Samons how his patient is responding."

Merritt kneeled down. "What are your names?"

The little girl pointed to her brothers. "He Cayeb. He Jo-u-a. I Tay-Yitha."

"It's nice to meet you all. Do you know what happened to Mommy and Daddy?"

Three faces gave solemn and sad no's. The boy Tay-Yitha named Cayeb sobbed. "We eat cannies. Mommy Daddy say spit out. We spit out. Nassy. Yuk. Mommy Daddy hab cannies. Daddy see cannies in can'net. We eat lunch. Take nap. Puppy wake us up. Mommy here. Daddy in famy room. We no wake 'em." His lower lip trembled. "We scare."

Vin looked over at the boy. "You did a good job staying with your mommy. She needed you to be with her. You are all very brave."

He motioned to Merritt. "Find out what the ETA is on the ambulances and the second squad."

Merritt rose and left the room. Vin continued to monitor his patient. "How old are you?"

"We two." Cayeb...(Caleb, maybe?) held up two fingers. Jo-u-a (no guesses on that one) did the same. The little girl made it a threesome.

"You're all two. So you all have the same birthday?"

Three nods. "Mommy says we get cake. Cayeb get cake, Jo-u-a get cake, Ta-Yitha get cake. She get yittle cake. She yittle one."

Talitha (if his guess was right) put her fists on her hip. "I not get yittle cake. I get big cake. Cayeb get big cake. Jo-u-a get big cake. Tayitha get big cake."

Vin hid his smile. "I see. When is your birthday?"

Cayeb answered. "A morrow."

"Tomorrow?"

He nodded. "A morrow. And a morrow."

"I see."

Merritt returned. "Base says five minutes out. I think the grandparents pulled up. The garage opened anyhow."

The dog picked up its head and woofed. Caleb put his arms around the dog. "Getchen goo puppy. She stay wis us."

An older woman came up to the door but stopped out of view of the children. Her eyes were grim, her lips pulled into a straight line. She stared at the figure on the bed, then shifted her gaze to Vin. The question in her eyes needed to be answered.

Vin nodded. "Alive. It's all I can say."

The woman nodded, then fixed a smile on her face. She came into the room and immediately dropped to the floor to hug the toddlers. "Hello, bubbies. Grandma and Grandpa are here."

The toddlers swarmed her. Caleb pointed. "We has puppy!"

"I see your puppy. What is the puppy's name?"

"Getchen. Unka Baydon say name is Getchen."

"Oh, you got her from Uncle Braydon? I see." Vin watched the woman's eyes flare ever so slightly. She patted the dog's head. "I bet you've been a very good dog, haven't you, Gretchen?" Gretchen answered with a tongue hanging out, panting.

The woman held her hand out to Vin. "Lacey Farrell. Jeff's mother. This is Collin Farrell, his wife."

Vin shook her hand. "Nice to meet you, ma'am. Sorry about this."

"Thank you for being here for them." As together as she appeared, Vin could still hear the catch in her voice and see the pain in her eyes. She gathered the toddlers in her arms. "Why don't you get your stuffies and your jammies? You can come stay with Grandma and Grandpa tonight." The boys jumped up and down in excitement and ran for the nursery.

The little girl stared at her grandmother with wide eyes. "Mommy, Daddy not come?"

Lacey Farrell kissed the child. "Not right now, honey. Mommy and Daddy are sick and need to go to the hospital. While they are there, you'll stay with Grandma and Grandpa. Okay?"

"Mommy Daddy sick?"

"Yes, little one. But Jesus will look after them. I promise."

"Mommy Daddy go hos-pi-ya?"

"For a little while. Just for a little while. Until Jesus makes them better."

The girl stared at her grandmother. "Jesus make Mommy Daddy better?"

"Yes, He will. Jesus will take care of Mommy and Daddy."

"I gib Mommy kiss?"

"Of course, baby." Vin picked the child up and set her beside her mother. The little girl stroked her mother's hair, then kissed her. "Luv oo, Mommy."

Lacey's voice cracked. "She loves you too, little one."

"I kiss Daddy?"

"Yes. We'll go kiss Daddy, too. Then we'll get your pajamas and your penguin. Okay?"

"Okay."

Vin shook his head. He held Mrs. Farrell's eyes. "Good job."

She smiled grimly. Then she carried the little girl out.

Vin turned back to monitoring his patient. And muttering, "Get here. Come on, guys. We need the help."

* * *

Harmon Farrell sat beside his son on the floor in the family room. He held Jeff's hand. His voice broke. "Lord, please. You know what it is to lose a Son. If there is any way for this trial to pass from us, please." He paused. "But Your will, not mine, be done. In all things, Your will."

Tears filled the man's eyes. Samons nodded his head. "It's all we can say, right? In the end, it comes down to that."

The older man looked off to pull himself together. He ducked his head in agreement but didn't speak. Footsteps from the back of the house brought both Samons and Harmon's heads up.

Lacey Farrell and the children walked into the family room. Each child held a stuffed animal and a small suitcase. Big enough for a pair of pajamas, a change of clothes, and maybe some socks. All three children kissed their father.

One of the boys tucked his stuffed bear under his daddy's arm. "Bear stay wis Daddy. Bear keep Daddy safe."

The little girl whispered something in her grandmother's ear. Grandma nodded, the two disappeared to the back, then reappeared. The little girl's penguin was missing. She kissed her daddy again. "Pen-gin stay wis Mommy."

The third child's lip stuck out and quivered. "Yion want stay, too."

Lacey smiled. "We'll let Mommy and Daddy share lion. Okay?"

The boy nodded. "S'okay."

Lacey tucked the lion up under her son's arm, next to the bear. She instructed the two animals, "Now, you watch over Daddy and keep him safe. Make sure he doesn't get lonely. And penguin will do the same with Mommy."

She kissed her son. "I'll see you soon, Jeffrey." Her voice cracked. She swallowed, then shepherded the children and the dog to the backdoor. Harmon followed her. Samons heard the door open, then close. The van started, pulled away. Drove down the street.

Sirens sounded. The ambulances came. Help had arrived. The attendants came in with the gurneys. Jeff and Collin were moved, strapped, loaded, and taken away. Vin and Samons cleaned up the supplies they had used. Merritt and Cantley waited for the forensic team to come out and search the house for the poison which might have been used. If they didn't find it in the 'can'net' in the playroom. They could always hope it would be simple. For once.

It took hours, but eventually, the forensic team left, the police boarded up the front door, locked the backdoor, and everyone departed. Leaving the home empty and silent. And the deep metallic blue car pulled away from the curb and drove into the glooming twilight.

TUESDAY

Collin screamed silently. *Father, please. Please. I'm terrified. I can't live like this. I can't. Please. Please.* She wanted to thrash and kick and writhe and scream and cry and shriek. And move even her pinky. Wiggle a toe. Feel anything. Something. But the suit of iron she was encased in brooked no such movement.

A voice sounded in Collin's ear. "We know you can hear us. You're on a ventilator until you can breathe on your own. We're doing everything we can to flush the poison out of your system. We're pumping in fluids as fast as your body can expel them. You were lucky the paramedics arrived when they did and got you here so quickly."

The speaker paused then assured her, "Your children are safe. They're with your in-laws. We won't have them visit until they can see Mommy and Daddy sitting up and breathing on their own."

Collin wanted to say "thank you." Or anything. But she had no control of her vocal cords. Or any other muscle in her body. Her brain locked in a stone prison that did not respond to her commands. *How long? How long will I be like this?*

She tried desperately to convey her question to the speaker. *ESP? God? Please? Have him tell me.*

God moved. The voice continued, "Both you and your husband have been here twenty-four hours. Those who make it that long usually make a full recovery. So rest and think positive."

"Think positive?" "Think positive?" Of all the lame platitudes...

Collin jumped off the train. *I'm alive. I'm in a hospital where they know I'm alive. They're keeping me alive. Jeff is alive. My babies are safe with Gramma and Grampa. This will pass. I will be grateful.*

She shuddered mentally. *Someone nearly poisoned my children. Someone tried to kill my babies. Who? Who would do it? Why? Why is this happening?*

Lord, I don't care what happens to me. Protect my babies! They don't deserve...

She stopped. Refocused. Cried out. *Lord, please. We deserve nothing. You are God. You are Good. You are Love. Jesus asked His disciples once if they wanted to leave Him. Peter told Him no, because who else could they go to? It's all You, Lord. Take it. Take me. Take them. Be Lord and God and Savior and King.*

Collin's mind went from high alert to calm. God had her. She would rest in Him. Because He loved her. And it was enough.

WEDNESDAY

Nine a.m. Kells knocked on Bri's door. And knocked. And knocked.

Bri looked out. "What are you doing here?"

Kells rubbed the moisture off her face. "I need coffee and a friend."

Bri opened the door. "Come on in. I'll fix you some."

"I don't care if it's yesterday's. I need a caffeine fix." Kells's voice broke as she stepped into the kitchen and sat at the table.

Bri used her instant coffee maker to brew a fresh cup, then handed it to Kells. "Here."

Kells picked the mug up by the handle. "Thank you." She stared off into space. "I can't believe it. I cannot believe Collin and Jeff are in the hospital, and they might not..." She trailed off, closed her eyes, turned her head to the floor.

Bri touched her arm. "It's going to be okay, Kells. They're both strong. They'll beat this thing."

Kells stared at Bri. "Who does this? Who poisons babies? Why?"

Bri cocked her head. "Poisons babies? What do you mean?"

"You didn't hear? Collin found the poison in the babies' playroom. In the little kitchen playset. Four pieces of it. The boys had it in their mouths. Collin told them to spit it out, and the poison came out on her hand. If she hadn't, the boys would have been killed. And such horrible deaths. Who poisons babies?"

Bri looked at the floor. "I don't know. It's awful. Do the police know what kind of poison they ingested?"

"I heard Tetradoyoxin. The kind you find in Pufferfish?"

"Who has that kind of poison lying around or can get ahold of

216

it?" Bri's face radiated disbelief.

Kells shrugged. "I don't know. What's truly awful is there were four pieces of candy in there. Four. Which means they intended it for all three of the Farrell children and Macie or Oscar. Except everyone knew Macie couldn't be there. So it had to be for Oscar."

Bri's eyes widened. "For Oscar?"

"Yeah. It only makes sense. You know how the babies love to share. The candies were placed there before the group would meet. The scumbag wanted all four children to die, not only the trio." Kells shook her head, her tears falling again. "How can someone be so cruel? So heartless?" She held Bri's eyes. "Your Oscar. I don't know how'd I live if it happened to Allison."

Bri dropped her gaze. "I don't know how, either." She raised her head. "Where is Allison?"

Kells gave Bri her prearranged lie. "Her father had the day off. I asked him to watch her while I came over. He said no problem. He loves spending time with her. They have such a good time." *Lord, forgive me for lying. That worthless excuse for a man is nowhere near to loving Allison. Or me or anyone except himself. He....*

Kells pulled out of her harangue over her departed spouse and gazed around the kitchen. "Where is Oscar? I know he's quiet, but I don't see him."

Bri hesitated. "He's at my mom's. She tells me how much she enjoys watching him, so I took him over to her."

Kells laughed. "Must have been early, then. You're still in your slippers."

Bri shrugged. "Yeah, well, sometimes it happens."

Kells drank some of the brew. "It's so hard to believe. Everything that happened to Collin and Jeff. Almost losing Talitha the first time and now being poisoned like this?" Kells stared off into space. "But I'm sure Collin would rather die herself than let her children die. Wouldn't we all?"

Bri nodded but said nothing. She patted Kells's hand. "It's terrible, I know."

"And I've been so rotten to her. I kept telling her she needed to get her life right. And here...here she gives it for her children." Kells let the tears fall. "How could I be such a horrible friend?"

"Don't beat yourself up, Kells. You had her best interest at heart, I'm sure."

"Did I? Or did I want to see her brought down? You and I've talked about her before. How she has the beautiful house, the great marriage, all the money they could ever want. We wanted her to bleed like we do, right? To see her break. Well, we got our wish."

Bri gazed out the sliding glass door. "Yeah, well, you know. We talked about it, but we never really wanted anything to happen to her. And I never knew about Talitha being kidnapped."

Kells shrugged. "I knew about it. I know it almost killed Collin for her baby to be missing those two weeks. I saw her faith tested, and she still didn't break."

Bri shifted in her chair. "Do the police have any suspects at all?"

"I don't know. Not for certain. I think they're looking at Rob as the guilty party. But there's no way. No way Rob would ever harm Collin or those babies."

Bri's eyes widened. "They think it's Rob? Why?"

"Because he's the adopted kid. If the babies and Collin and Jeff are gone, he gets the estate. Who else had access to the house to leave all those letters? Especially when no one ever saw anyone coming or going. Rob is the perfect fall guy."

Bri's face lost all emotion. She turned her head to the side to look out the window. "Yeah. He would be."

"I'm sure they'll ask you about him. They haven't been out yet, have they?"

Bri looked back at Kells. "No, no they haven't. When they do, I'll be sure to tell them it can't possibly be Rob. He adored those children."

"Right. I'm going to tell them no way Rob could do any of that."

Bri nodded. "Right. But I could see how they could get the idea."

"And they'd be wrong. But he's got no way to prove he didn't do it. I mean, yeah, he has access to the house. And no one ever saw who put the letters in. With all the security they had, you'd have thought someone would have seen something. But no one ever did. Not once."

She sipped at her mug. "I worry he's going to take the fall, though. The police will want to wrap this up quickly, and Rob is the easy target."

Bri's eyes turned thoughtful. "I suppose he's got an alibi if he was in school though, right?"

"Not one to stand up in court. Professors don't take class attendance. I doubt if people will remember whether he was in class or not. So many people, so many classes…no one will swear to him being anywhere. And with his background from the streets, he's going to look even more guilty." She bit her lip. "I love Rob. I hate they will railroad him for this."

Bri nodded. "I know. It is terrible."

Kells finished her cup, held it out. "Can I have another one, please? It's going to be one of those days where there's not enough coffee in the world, but I have to keep trying."

Bri squeezed her shoulder. "Sure, friend." She fixed another cup and handed it to her. Again, Kells carefully took it by the handle. Bri studied Kells a moment. "How do you know what's going on with the investigation?"

"I'm friends with Collin's brother, too. Erin? He's telling me about it. His wife has some law enforcement connections. She tells him, he tells me. He's totally broken up over this, believe me."

Bri nodded. "I can see why. Does he think Rob is involved?"

"I don't know. Not for sure. I know they've questioned him several times. They keep going back to how did someone get inside without being seen. Especially with all the cameras. I don't think Rob stands a chance of beating this. And I frankly don't think the police will look hard for anyone else. Rob is too convenient."

Bri lowered her head. "Yeah, I see what you mean."

Kell's tears fell again. "That poor young man. I feel so sorry for him."

Bri squeezed her shoulder. "I know, I know. I do, too. But the police will be thorough. They won't convict an innocent person."

"Yeah? As popular as Jeff and Collin are, you don't think they're going to be under pressure to solve this? To find someone guilty? They'll pin it on Rob, I know they will."

"But what solid proof have they got? I mean, they can't convict him just because he looks like the only one to fit the bill. They have to have proof."

Kells leaned in. "I know. But they found out he has an apartment over on Delaware. Close to the campus. They're working on getting a warrant to search it. Supposed to have it by this afternoon. They won't find anything. But I wouldn't put it past them to plant evidence." She scowled. "I hate this." She held up the mug. "I have to get moving. Can I take this with me?"

Bri laughed. "My cup is your cup."

Kells stood up and hugged Bri. "Thanks, Bri. I knew you'd listen. I'll see you for group at my house next week. I don't think I could handle us all getting together yet. I want to see if Collin makes it."

Bri hugged her again. "She'll be fine. I'm sure she will."

Kells teared up. "There's no antidote. They have to pull through on their own."

Bri nodded. "I'll be praying for them, Kells. Are you okay to drive home?"

Kells wiped her face on her sleeve. "Yeah, I'll be fine. I will. Thanks for the coffee and the friendship, Bri. It means a lot to me."

Bri stood at the door until Kells climbed into her car. Kells held up the coffee cup in salute. Bri disappeared back into the house. Kells dumped the coffee out into the container on the floor. Set the cup carefully in the box she'd been given. Closed the lid. Muttered, "Last one." Drove off.

Past the metallic blue sedan parked on the side of the street.

* * *

Bri's phone rang. She picked it up. "What?"

"What did she want?"

"A cup of coffee and to talk."

"And she told you what?"

"The police are looking at Rob, the adopted kid, as the suspect."

"Really. Now, why would they think it would be him?" Woolfort's voice reflected curiosity.

"Motive and opportunity. Why else?"

"And what can we do to help the investigation along?"

"He's got an apartment. The police are waiting for a warrant to search it."

Woolfort's smile came through the airwaves. "I think our little friend should supply them with all the proof they need."

"Great." Bri didn't bother to cover her sarcasm. "But our little friend is still at the Farrell's. I wanted to go get him yesterday, but you jumped the gun and put the poison out where the babies could find it. Now no one will get in there. And he's liable to tear the place up. They'll find him and trace the radio collar back to me. Won't take them long to figure out we were giving him the instructions when and where to put the notes. And you better believe I'm not taking the fall for this."

Woolfort lost his humor. "Do not threaten me, Brianna."

"It's not a threat, Ryan. It's a fact."

"I'll take care of getting the monkey. I'll take care of planting the evidence on Rob. We're going to be fine. Trust me. Give me the kid's address."

"I don't have it. Kells only said he lived over on Delaware, by the campus."

"I can do some research. I'll find it."

Bri debated. Her eyes narrowed. "Tell me this. Why were there four pieces of candy? For only three children."

Long silence. "We discussed this in the beginning. You wanted out. Start a new life, unencumbered by anything. Or anyone. This conveniently took care of the problem."

Bri stared at the phone. "I didn't... I mean... I don't..." She stopped. Pulled herself together. "This whole affair started because you wanted money. Big man, big promises. You could walk in, ask for bribe money, and poof. Contractors would happily hand you money."

"You mishandled the whole matter of the psychiatrist."

"I handled it perfectly."

"You bungled it. Badly. You were to forge a signature from the church office, not create one no one recognized."

Bri snarled, "Get back to the money. How are you going to get it now with both Farrells nearly dead?"

"You lack imagination. A creature which can leave envelopes can also collect them. I have blank checks I can write for any amount."

"And get who to sign them? Let alone cash them? The police will monitor all the accounts."

Pause. "Well, then, I believe a young man being wrongfully accused of attempted murder would be happy to pay for a defense lawyer. With an upfront fee."

"You're going to plant evidence to convict him, then be his lawyer to get him off?"

"Of course not. Once I get the retainer, we're out of here."

Bri could see the plan working. Maybe. But, "So we're talking another week? Two weeks? How long?"

"We've been patient this long. We can be patient a little longer."

"Easy for you to say. I'm the one stuck with the husband and the kid. He wants to adopt another child. I'm so tired of smiling and saying, 'yes, dear' every time he suggests it. Dutiful wife my…"

Bri stopped short. "When I hear the police have found hard, physical evidence of Rob's guilt, then I'll be patient. Right now, all I hear is talk. And I'm getting tired of it. I'm taking all the risks."

"We are inches away from the prize. I've got to go get our little friend and have him leave evidence for the police to find. You'll have your announcement this afternoon."

"I better." Bri disconnected the phone. "Lousy dog." It wasn't what she wanted to say, but it worked for the moment.

WEDNESDAY NOON

Erin sat in the family room, waiting. Waiting. Waiting. He muttered, "Come on, Woolfort. Make your move. I want to see your face."

The face of the man who killed our child. Tried to kill my wife. Almost killed my sister and Jeff. Meant to kill my niece and nephews. I want to throttle the smile off your face. See you gasping for air...

A knock sounded at the recently replaced front door. Erin called, "Hold on a minute." He pulled himself to his feet, used his arm crutches to move to the door and open it. "Can I help you?"

A youngish man in jeans and a rumpled khaki shirt stood on the porch. He shifted from foot to foot, head down, eyes flitting from side to side. Over one shoulder, he wore a satchel of leather. He looked up at Erin. "I'm sorry, sir. I hate to be a bother. But I really, really need to come inside for a moment."

Erin cocked his head. "Why?"

"Uh..." The man looked embarrassed as well as uncomfortable. "Um...I live over on the next block. We moved in recently. And uh, well, um...I lost my monkey."

"You what?"

The man nodded. "Lost my monkey." He held out his hand to Erin. "I'm Terrance Loper. I train Capuchin monkeys to be service animals. They are highly intelligent and can be very useful to those who need an extra set of hands...if you will."

Erin motioned for Terrance to come in. "Okay, but what makes you think he's here?"

"I don't know if he is. But I've been knocking on doors all morning looking for him. He got out last night. I'm afraid he's holed up in someone's crawl space or attic and might frighten a family with the noises. I thought I would ask homeowners if I could set out some food for him and see if he shows up. If you don't mind."

Erin smiled. "No, I don't mind. Where do you want to put the food?"

Terrance looked around the entrance. "Do you have an attic? He'll most likely go somewhere high."

Erin motioned to his crutches. "I wouldn't know about an attic. I do know we have an access panel in the bedroom ceiling."

Terrance shrugged. "I'm not sure. It won't hurt to look."

Erin led the man to the nursery and opened the closet door. "Up there. Maybe?"

Terrance looked at the paneled opening. "It could work for him." He gazed at Erin, dropping his eyes. "Do you mind if I put some food up on the top shelf and see if he comes down to get it?"

"Knock yourself out. What do you feed a monkey?"

Terrance smiled. Small smile. "Bananas. They really do like bananas. And apples. Most fruit."

Erin stepped back and watched Terrance pull some baby bananas and apple slices from his satchel. He placed them on the shelf, then stood back. He looked around. "Um…is there a way I could open the panel so he could get down easier? If he's even up there."

Erin nodded. "We've got a step ladder in the pantry closet. You can use it." He motioned to his crutches. "Kinda hard to wrangle it on my own, you know?"

Terrance nodded. "I understand. Thanks." He followed Erin's directions to the pantry, opened the door, retrieved the ladder, and set it underneath the panel. "I appreciate this. I really do. You can't imagine how frightened the little guy must be."

Erin chuckled. "I know how frightened I would be if he came down in the middle of the night and I saw him in the kitchen in the dark."

Terrance laughed but nervously. "Yeah, I can see it happening." He climbed the ladder, pushed the panel open. He called out in a high, shrill voice, "Pasha! Paaasha!" Then he dropped down. "Thanks. I really appreciate this."

"How long will it take to know if he's up there?"

"He's got to be hungry, so I'm sure it will only be a few minutes. If he doesn't come out of hiding in, say, fifteen minutes, it probably means he's not up there. I'll have to go bother the rest of the neighbors."

"Should we wait here or give him some privacy?"

Terrance shook his head. "I'll leave my satchel on the shelf. He knows it's a safe, secure place and means he's supposed to go in it."

Erin ducked his head. "Smart monkey."

Terrance grumbled, "If he does it. He's supposed to be better trained than to go running off, too. We may need some more work on recall."

Erin grinned. "Maybe a touch."

The two men sat in the rocking chairs. Terrance looked around the room. "I like the way this is decorated. How many children do you have?"

"None. My wife and I were expecting, but someone hit her, then took off. She lost the baby."

Terrance looked up. Erin studied his eyes. The face showed compassion and caring. The eyes...the eyes were empty of any concern. "I'm so sorry. It must have been terrible."

Erin nodded. "It is. I'm still working on forgiving the driver. And his accomplice."

Terrance looked up in surprise. "Accomplice?"

"Yeah. My wife had to stop for a pedestrian who crossed against the light. He made sure she stopped in the middle of the intersection, so the other car slammed into her broadside." Anger crept into Erin's voice. He swallowed it. "Forgiveness is a work in progress. I'll know I've done it when I can see the dude and not want to wring his neck."

"Hmm. Must be really hard. How is your wife taking it?"

"Like any woman who loses a child. She's grieving. We both are. My grief comes out in anger and a desire for revenge. Hers comes out in sadness. We're both trying to commit our feelings to the Lord."

Terrance nodded large. "Oh, you're those kinds of people. Everything is okay if God does it."

"God didn't kill our child. But He'll make use of the circumstances."

The man's eyes narrowed. "Yeah, right."

Erin held up his hand. "Don't criticize what you don't understand. We could have a long talk about how God works and what our responses to Him can be. But I don't think you want to be here that long."

Terrance shrugged. "Probably not."

Silence filled the room again. After five minutes, the satchel hit the floor. A capuchin monkey leaped down and stood on the flap, banana in its mouth, apple in its hand. Terrance stood. "Pasha! There you are. You're a bad monkey, you know?"

Pasha jumped up on the man's arm. Terrance caught hold of him by his collar. "I apologize for disturbing you. I do. And I promise Pasha won't be any more trouble to you."

Erin eyed the monkey. The monkey eyed him back. Erin decided to retain possession of all of his fingers and did not reach out to pet the monkey. He watched as Terrance carefully returned Pasha to the satchel, then closed the flap and secured it.

Terrance reached out to shake Erin's hand. "Again, thanks. I appreciate you letting me come in looking for him."

Erin smiled. "I appreciate him coming down when he did. Better for both of us."

Terrance smiled. "Yeah, I can see how it would be. Thanks again." Erin and the man walked to the front. Erin watched him go down the walk and climb into a tan jeep. Terrance put the satchel in, then climbed in, closed the door, and drove off.

Erin lifted his voice loud enough to be heard on the microphone. "Monkey is away." He muttered, "Good thing. I'm one hundred percent positive Cane would ring my neck for the police bringing it back here." He leaned against the wall. "It's up to You, Lord. We make plans, but You make them work. Catch these people, Lord. Whoever they are. And whatever they wanted. Make me willing to forgive." He looked down, looked at his heart. "Which will be Your toughest job, Lord. But You can. And I will."

He pushed off the wall and headed to the kitchen, where Braydon had his cameras set up. "You get it all?"

"Yep. And yep, same man. Or so the sketches would lead a jury to believe."

"Then let's pray the police finish the job."

"Amen." The two brothers lowered their heads to storm the

gates of Heaven.

WEDNESDAY AFTERNOON

Ryan Woolfort paced outside the offices of Delaware Park Rentals. The sign said the manager would be back at one p.m. It was already one-thirty. "No wonder nothing ever gets done in this town. No one shows up on time. Or at all."

Ryan kept his grumbles to himself. He wore, after all, the guise of an underclassman, waiting to return remedial classwork to a student-teacher working on his Master's. The lowliest of the low begging a favor of the exalted upper class. *Please, sir. A little more time?*

Office management walked past him and unlocked the door. Ryan waited until the woman came in and settled before interrupting her with his inquiry. "Hi. I'm really sorry to bother you. I'm looking for my teacher…well, he's student teaching, and I know he's got a room at this building."

The woman smiled. "Gotta name?"

"I'm Bob Stanwich."

"I meant your teacher's name."

"Oh, right." He blushed. "I'm a freshman. It's so confusing around here."

She smiled at him. "You'll get used to it in the next four years."

Bob shook his head. "I don't know. This city…it's so big. We haven't got anything this large anywhere close where I come from."

"Which is?"

"Little place. Outside of Carlisle, Iowa. Doesn't even have streets. We only have rural routes and boxes."

"Sounds nice."

"Oh, it is, in its way. I thought I couldn't wait to get to the city and hit the college. I wanted to tear up the world."

She raised her eyebrows. "And?"

"Guess the world doesn't tear up easy. It's been way harder than I thought. I wrote a letter to Mr. Farrell telling him I quit and would be going home. Gonna turn in my books with my report and call it quits. I can't do it."

"Now hold on, there. Are you talking about Mr. Rob Farrell?"

"I think Farrell's his name. Didn't know his first one."

"Rob's a good man. He wouldn't want you to quit. Not without talking to him first."

"You think so? I mean, he's got to have plenty of other students to worry about other than a quitter like me."

She smiled. "Give him a chance. He's good about listening. And I think he relates to being nervous and scared about being in a big place. Why don't you wait and talk to him first?"

"You know when he'll be back?"

"He's got class this afternoon. But he's usually free in the evenings. You might try back later, say after five."

Bob shook his head. "I've got basketball at five." He looked at his feet. "You think I could leave him a message in his room? I don't want to leave it out where other students can find it. Don't want anyone thinking I'm a quitter."

The woman closed one eye and studied him. "Well...I suppose I could let you in and keep an eye on you, so you don't try anything funny like stealing answer keys from the tests."

"I'd never do that."

"You'd be surprised how many enterprising students say the same thing." She pulled out a set of keys. "He's on the third floor. You can follow me."

Bob made sure to keep his satchel carefully at his side as they climbed the stairs of the old dormitory. Students passed them coming and going, usually in a hurry, usually accompanied. Everyone going somewhere.

Bob and his escort reached the third floor. She walked to the fifth door down, knocked, called, "Rob? You in there?"

Silence greeted her. She put the key in the lock, turned it, then backed out of the room. She smiled at Bob. "No funny business."

"No, ma'am. I'm only going to take my bookbag and the

books in the room. I put a note in it earlier, for in case I changed my mind." He pulled out an envelope. "See? This is the one where I would quit school and go back to Iowa." He pulled out a second envelope. "This is the one where I ask him to help me make the decision to stay. And it's the one I'm going to leave here."

The office manager smiled. "You've got the spirit. Good decision. Now get out of here and go to class. And don't let them scare you. You deserve to be here, same as all the other students."

"Thank you, ma'am. You made my day. You really have."

The two turned and walked back out the door, the bookbag dropped on his way out. The office manager locked up; Bob bounced down the stairs two at a time, hoping she wouldn't notice his lack of bag. He waited until the crowd thinned out, when no one would be watching, climbed into the deep metallic blue sedan.

He punched the phone number on his dash. "Done. Completed."

"What is?"

"Our little friend is placing the letter of confession in Rob Farrell's notebook. The monkey is also placing the vial of Tetrodotoxin in Mr. Farrell's bathroom cabinet. Hiding it behind some bottles to make it look less incriminating."

"And...."

"And to seal the deal, our little friend will hide between the sheets and the pillow, make himself as inconspicuous as possible. Until after the police search the room. And find the evidence. Then he'll slip out without being noticed and return to his owner. If he's lucky."

"If who's lucky? The monkey or me?"

"Either. After it's done, I don't care." Ryan pulled the shirt off and slipped into his own silk button-up shirt. He'd change the jeans later. How people lived in them....

"And we get the check how and when?"

"You know how these cases go. There'll be lots of motions and hearings and arraignments and bail... my guess is it'll be another week."

"Unless the Farrells pull through and forgive him."

"I'm counting on them pulling through. And forgiving him. In fact, this whole thing only works if they do."

"Are you out of your mind?" Brianna's voice rose an octave,

"No. Think. If the Farrells think he's guilty, they aren't going to fork over money to get him acquitted. And he's certainly not going to have the money himself. We need the Farrells to do what they do: be loving and forgiving and want to defend their son as a good Christian does. It will make the end all the sweeter."

Brianna's voice sneered. "You do hate them, don't you?"

"I don't hate. I know how to play the game. And they're so easily played. Watch. Watch and listen for the police reports this afternoon."

Someone tapped on the glass window. A uniformed police officer stood alongside the car. He motioned for Ryan to roll the window down.

Ryan complied. "Is there a problem, Officer?"

"I need you to step out of the vehicle, please."

Ryan looked around. No sense causing a scene and being caught at the scene. He stepped out. "What's this about?"

"Ryan Woolfort?"

"Yes."

"You're under arrest for the attempted murder of Collin and Jeffrey Farrell." The officer whirled Ryan around, grabbed his arms, and handcuffed him. None too gently, either.

"What are you talking about?"

"You have the right to remain silent. You have the right to an attorney…"

Ryan looked over at the apartment building and saw the manager standing outside, a police lanyard around her neck. Beside her, Erin Winger. And a couple men Ryan could bet were detectives.

One sauntered over to the car. "Would you like to give up your right to remain silent?"

Ryan sneered at the man. "What do you think? I want my lawyer."

The detective smiled. "I bet you do. Brianna lawyered up as well. But that's okay. We have plenty of evidence, including fingerprints on the application to purchase the capuchin monkey. DNA to match him to the Farrell's house. I won't bore you with all the details. You're going away for a long time."

Ryan shrugged. "Give it your best shot, then. I've got nothing to say."

The detective took his arm and walked him to a black and white cruiser waiting at the curb. Ryan watched the detective nod to Rob and Erin. Erin's eyes narrowed as the cruiser moved past them. The man's eyes held Ryan's. Erin saluted. Then turned away.

Ryan shook his head and sat back in the seat.

THURSDAY

Collin and Jeff listened to the wrap-up of the case as detailed by Kells, Erin, Rob, and Vy. The group held court in the family room of the Farrell home, where Collin and Jeff were recovering. Chairs had been pulled in from the kitchen to ensure everyone had a seat. (Everyone included Harmon and Lacey, Gretchen, and the littles, who moved from seat to seat with frightening regularity.)

Kells beamed. "I did good. I deserve an Oscar." She stopped. "Okay, an Emmy, anyhow. Met with everyone, got their prints on the coffee mugs, and took them to the police like they wanted." She stopped. "But now I have to give them all back, and I don't remember whose is whose."

Collin laughed. It felt good to breathe on her own. Being able to laugh made it even better. "You can set them out at group, and everyone can claim their own."

Kells shrugged. "Whatever. The police compared the prints on the mugs to the adoption application for the monkey. And then they nailed Bri."

Erin took over. "Then Terrance—Woolfort—left his prints on the pantry door and on the panel to the attic. Conveniently."

Collin eyed her brother. "So you had the police bring the monkey back to the house...back to my house and put it in my attic...after all the trouble they went through to catch it the first time?"

Erin chuckled. "I knew you would have a problem with the idea." He grinned at her. "How else were we going to catch Woolfort? And tie him to the monkey?"

"I don't care. No more monkeys in my house!"

The littles all bounced and cheered. "Monkey in house! Monkey in house!"

Collin shook her head. "No monkeys in the house!"

Rob waved them off. "Don't worry. Woolfort got his monkey and brought him to 'my apartment' over on Delaware."

Jeff shook his head. "You don't have an apartment."

Rob grinned, pure evil. "Woolfort didn't know it. Kells told Bri I did. So he went there. And met up with an undercover officer posing as the rental manager. She let him into the apartment. He dropped the bag with the monkey and the poison in the room. Police busted him in his car. And that, as they say, is all she wrote."

Jeff smiled and caught Collin's hand. "And we appreciate all of it."

Kells held up a hand. "Motive?"

"Revenge. Malice. Spite." Collin shrugged. "From Woolfort. Bri, I'm less sure of. I guess the chance to get out of her marriage and away from Oscar." Collin shook her head. "The poor baby."

Rob gave Collin the side-eye. "We could always adopt one more."

Collin shook her head. Slowly. "I'll say it's a hard no from me."

Kells chuckled. "Crandall, Bri's husband, will give Oscar a good home. He hasn't given up on him."

Collin nodded. "I'm glad. He's a great kid."

Rob wasn't giving up. "Can we still see him? Have him come over when I'm here? I got attached to the little guy."

Collin beamed at their son. "I'm sure Crandall will be happy to let Oscar come over on playdates. You can be his big brother. But he lives with his father. Understood?"

Rob crossed the room and kissed Collin. "Yes, Mom. I hear you."

Kells raised her hand again. "Do we know anything more about who hurt Macie?"

Collin shook her head. Her heart ached. "No. The police can't figure out who actually abused her. So neither parent is allowed unsupervised visits. They'll both have to go through counseling and complete parenting classes. It's going to be a long process. Main thing is Macie is safe and loved and protected."

Kells shook her head. "It's tough."

"Yeah. Sometimes there aren't any easy answers."

"Tell me about it." Kells picked up Allison from the floor, where she endured tummy time. "No matter how much we want to pretend otherwise."

Collin motioned for Kells to come over to her. "I love you, Kells. You'll work it out. I know you. Allison will have a great life."

Kells bent down and kissed Collin. She held the baby out so Collin could kiss the chubby cheeks. "We've got to head home. I've got an appointment with a lawyer at noon."

"You want us to watch Allison?"

"No. She's going to be Exhibit A." Kells lifted her eyebrows, then dropped them again.

Collin nodded. "You go, woman."

Kells grabbed the baby carrier and headed out the door. Erin and Vy excused themselves as well, leaving Collin, Jeff, and the family alone. Collin closed her eyes and sighed. "This. This is what it's about. Peace. Family. Life."

Talitha screamed, "Mine!"

Joshua screamed back. "No! Mine!"

Caleb yelled, "Mommy, bubbies fighting!"

Collin dropped her head. Jeff chuckled. "Life. We have it."

And on it went.

If you enjoyed Deception, sign up for Colleen Snyder's Newsletter to stay up with new books and new projects. It will also give you a place to talk to the author directly. And she loves to talk to her readers. Trust me!
Emails will NOT be sold, shared, or used for any other purpose. Promise.
Go to: colleensnyderauthor.com and leave your email to sign up.
Read on to learn more about Colleen's other books in the series.

Did you miss the first book in the Collin Walker series?

VERDICT AT THE RIVER'S EDGE

What terrifies you?

In the dark recesses of your soul, what is it that you've managed to avoid, to hide, to bury deep, never to be faced? And what if the Lord asked you to face that fear for no other reason than, "Because I'm asking?" What would you do?

Welcome to Collin Walker's world.

Collin Walker, a social worker from the inner city of Oakton, Ohio, comes to Camp Grace for what is billed as "an extreme sports camp." Her single purpose: to show her ward, Rob Sider, that there is more to life than the streets "...show you can be strong and still love, win without cheating, and succeed in life without all the bells and whistles...." Collin has no way of knowing that God has other plans for her week: facing a lifelong terror of rushing rivers, and perhaps her greatest fear of all, the possibility of real love.

Available now on Amazon: Verdict at the River's Edge

Also available: Book Two in the Collin Walker Series:

INHERITANCE

Three hundred MILLION dollars. Your inheritance. Buy anything you want, go anywhere you want, do anything you want. All yours. Except...

You're a social worker. How do you maintain "street cred" with the kids you've devoted your life to?

How will that kind of money affect the man you love?

And then there's your birth family. The ones that abandoned you to die at fourteen. The ones you suspect even now are trying to have you killed over the money. How do you share with them? Or do you?

What would Jesus do? What would He want you to do? Would you do it?

Welcome back to Collin Walker's world

Collin's life has been both turned upside down and inside out. With her grandfather's passing, Collin has been forced into a position she never wanted. Her inheritance of millions comes with baggage. Her father and his brothers have been fighting for it since before she was born. It is the very heart of the reason she's been estranged from her family the past twelve years.

But now, with the will coming into effect, Collin must revisit all the old relationships and all the old traumas. She thought she had made peace with her past through the Lord. But when the past becomes the present, will she still forgive? Even if it's her family that wants her dead?

Join her and find out.

Available now on Amazon: Inheritance

Also available: Book Three in the Collin Walker/Farrell Series

ACCUSATIONS

When was the last time you lied? Do you lie to keep a secret? Or do you keep a secret to hide a lie?

Collin Farrell has a secret, and she can't wait to tell her husband.

Jeff Farrell has a secret, too, one he's been hiding from Collin since before they married.

Collin's brother, Erin, has a girlfriend with a secret she won't tell.

Vy Johnson is a DEA agent who knows all about lies and secrets.

What happens when Secrets and Lies collide?

Cars get crushed (with the drivers inside.)

Homes explode.

Marriages implode.

Careers—and lives—are jeopardized.

Can God work even this together for the good of all involved and still get the glory from it?

Available Now on Amazon: Accusations

Also available: Book Four in the Collin Walker/Farrell Series

DESPAIR

"Choose. One lives. One dies."
What do you do when hope is all you have?
Is it really all you need?
Where is God when every choice looks dark?
Erin Winger's fiancée and his infant niece have been violently kidnapped. . The kidnappers don't want money. They want revenge. And not against Erin or the baby's mother. No, the kidnappers want revenge against Erin's father. The father Erin and his sister put in prison three years ago. A cold-hearted man who has no interest in saving anyone.

Bound, gagged, and imprisoned in an abandoned shack in the deep of winter, can Erin's fiancée and the baby survive? In the race between hypothermia and life, can they both endure the sub-freezing temperatures long enough for help to reach them?

Available now on Amazon: Despair

Look for Book Six in June:
(I'm a bit of an optimist.)

Drake stared at the bright red paint on the coal-black bumper of his truck. The dent in the front fender. The push-bar smashed into his grill. The shattered headlight. His head pounded. He rubbed his hand over his face. It hadn't been a dream. If it had been, now it became a nightmare. A waking nightmare.

"Nice wreck. Who'd you hit?"

Drake stared at the front end of his truck but growled, "Who says I hit anyone? Maybe someone hit me."

Perry stepped out of the kitchen, two mugs of coffee in his hands. He gave one to Drake. "Drink. Get sober. Then tell me about it."

Drake swallowed some of the still-warm brew. "Someone ran the light and hit me."

Perry leaned against the fender. "Yeah, you want to try that one again? This isn't the damage from someone hitting you." He finished his coffee and set the cup down on the workbench.

Drake glared at his roommate. "What do you know? You playing Crime Scene Investigator now?"

"Nope. Body damage inspector. My job. Six days a week. You hit someone. Who and where?"

Drake guessed the when was obvious. Last night. Sometime in the latest drunken stupor that led to the blackouts. That he suffered with increasing regularity. He started to shake his head, thought better of it. "I don't know. I don't know where I was. I went to Neil's to help him with the a/c on his truck. Got late, so I went...went...to... to get freon from...um...Pap's. That's it. I went to Pap's. Picked up the freon and the charging unit."

"Then where?"

Drake focused his eyes on the garage floor, hoping the concrete would give him inspiration. "I don't know." He swallowed the last dregs of the coffee and set his mug on the hood of the truck.

Perry opened the side door, looked in the cab. "Freon cans are in here." He picked one up, held it for Drake to see. "Still full. You never left Pap's, did you?"

Drake stared into the older man's eyes. "Maybe. Maybe not. I don't remember. What's it matter? There's not much damage. I can buff that out with no problem."

Perry swung on him. He grabbed Drake by the shirt and slammed him into the fender. "Because you might have killed someone. You might have run someone off the road and killed them. Or worse. They could be upside down in a wreck off the side of the road, waiting for the police to come. Thinking, of course, the driver who caused the wreck would go get help. Someone would call 911. Right?"

Perry dropped his hold. His face curled into a mask of anger, bordering on hate. "But no. You have no idea who you hit, when, or where. Do you?"

Perry grabbed the mug off the hood, stalked into the kitchen, and came out with his keys. He motioned to Drake. "Get in."

"Where we going?"

"To find your victim."

Drake complied but kept his eyes on Perry as the man slid behind the steering wheel, cranked all four-hundred horses into life, and jammed the truck into reverse. He spun the tires, slung gravel across the yard, then pointed the vehicle down the dirt path leading away from the house.

They drove in silence for several minutes. Drake reached for the radio. Perry backhanded Drake's fingers. "Forget it. This isn't a joy ride. You sit there in silence, and you pray. You pray for whoever you hit that they're alive and not hurt too bad. Then you pray something gets ahold of you, and you quit drinking. Because God's the only way you'll get out of this one."

Drake snapped back. "You don't even know if I hit anyone. I could've hit a pole."

"Not with that color paint. That's an SUV. Compact. Newer model. And yes, I know these things. So will the police."

Drake looked at the mud on his boots. "You gonna turn me in?"

"No. You're gonna turn yourself in."

"What if we don't find anyone? Or anything? You still gonna turn me in?"

"Nope. You're gonna. I've had enough, Drake. You promised. Swore. Gave me your word. No more drinking. Drinking is poison, you said. And one week…" Perry smashed the steering wheel in his anger. "…one week later, you're out doing the same thing. Only this time, you took someone down with you."

Perry glanced at him. "But you still can't bring yourself to care about them, can you? You're worried about you. What if there are kids in that car? What if you killed their mom, and they're trapped inside staring at her dead body?"

Drake snarled. "Go ahead. Make it as graphic as you can. Like it's gonna make it any worse. I'm a walking dead man, Perry. I haven't felt anything inside in months. Why should I care now?"

"You shouldn't. Because it's all about you, dude. It's always all about you. You don't care, so why should anyone else? Yeah, well, other people want to live, you know?"

"Why should I care about them?"

"You don't. I do. That's why we're gonna go find your victim. So I can save them from you." He motioned to the road ahead. "Pretend like you care. Watch the side of the road."

"Why should I?"

Tires screeched. Perry locked up the brakes and grabbed Drake by the shirt again. His fist came around and connected with Drake's jaw in an agonizing whack. "Because I said so. Or I take you to the end of the line, drop you off, and you can walk back. Or walk off. I don't care anymore. Brother or not, I don't care."

Perry spun around and put the truck in motion again. Drake's eyes widened in shock. And awe. And maybe fear. He settled back in the seat and scanned the shoulder for tire marks. The trees for recent gashes. Bushes crushed or broken. Paint on the guard rail. Anything.

Fifty minutes in, and nothing. Drake eased back in the seat further. Maybe there wasn't a crash. Maybe he had driven home...

He saw it. In his mind. The headlights. The curve. Heard nothing. Radio too loud, loud enough to wake the dead. Except it hadn't. Felt the thump. The steering wheel jerk sideways. The shudder in the engine. Then everything righted itself, and he was cruising again.

Drake turned his head to the side window. Perry couldn't see his face. Not until he got himself under control. Where was I? What turn? Five mile? Ten mile? Which embankment? He searched the chasms below the ridge. Where? Where?

Perry's tone indicated his growing frustration as well. "Sure help if you knew which way you went from Pap's place. You didn't go the backway, did you?"

Drake hardened his voice. "This is your fiction, man. You're the one that insisted I drove back and hit someone on the way."

"You drove back, Drake. You hit someone. How bad is what we're trying to find."

Drake looked at his knees. "The back way. I came home the back way."

"You sure?"

"Of course not. If I was, I'd have told you to start with. Cut across Five Meadows, and then you can drive that much of the way out to Pap's place. I'll drive back, and you can search the other side."

Perry risked a look at him. "Yeah? You starting to take this serious?"

Drake nodded with as much sincerity as he could fake. "Yeah. I'm not a monster. I care. And I have been praying. I hope God takes care of whoever it is. Maybe someone will have already found them, and they're safe."

"That's what I've been praying ever since you didn't come home last night." Perry sagged. "You're my only family, Drake. You're all I got. I'm sorry I hit you. I just get so frustrated."

Drake nodded. "Yeah, I know. I know, big brother. I probably deserved it. But it'll be okay. You'll see. God will take care of them. He will." If he existed. *Which he doesn't.*

The two men drove on.

Made in the USA
Las Vegas, NV
20 March 2023

69365016R00138